Also by Talia Hibbert

THE
ROOMMATE
RISK

TALIA HIBBERT

Cover and Jacket Art © Erin O'Neill Jones
Developmental Edit by Zahra Butt
Proofread by Jennifer Scarberry

Published by Nixon House
Print ISBN: 978-1-913651-04-6

www.nixonhouse.co.uk

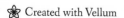 Created with Vellum

This one is for my readers.

Content Note

The Roommate Risk is a super-spicy friends-to-lovers romance with a healthy dollop of angst and a guaranteed happy ending.

However, this story contains elements that could trigger certain audiences, including:

- Parental neglect and abandonment
- Parental death
- Accidental bloody injury
- Alcohol abuse and dependence.

Please take care of yourself when reading.

Chapter 1

Now

"We should get back to work. We've been gone well past lunch." Usually, Asmita said that sort of thing with firm authority—the kind that might convince Jasmine to listen.

But today, Asmita didn't *say* it at all; she mumbled it tearily into a McDonald's napkin. So Jasmine felt well within her rights to ignore the suggestion. Instead, she rubbed a hand over her friend's narrow back in slow, soothing circles and murmured, "Not yet, love. Not until you tell me what's wrong."

Asmita hiccuped.

A nearby staff member looked up from his sweeping brush to glower at them. "Are you ladies buying anything today, or...?"

Jasmine stifled a sigh and dredged up a smile. "So sorry. We will, eventually. Only, we're having a crisis." She nodded towards her dour friend, whose perfectly kohl-lined eyes were looking dangerously red and runny. "You understand, don't you?"

The employee pressed his lips together, then huffed out a breath. "Suppose."

"Oh, thank you!"

He moved on with a dark glare.

Asmita tutted between sniffles. "We're not buying anything. You can't stand McDonald's."

True. Dad had made Jasmine work at the nearest restaurant for a year when she turned sixteen, to teach her the value of money or some such fatherly nonsense. Just the scent of those crispy golden fries was making her feel slightly sick.

But they had been walking past this McDonald's when Asmita had started almost, sort of, *maybe*, crying. Jasmine had bundled her into the cursed establishment before anyone important could see the indomitable Asmita Shah in tears.

Mita would've done the same for her, after all.

So Jasmine gave her friend a quelling look and got right to the point. "Is it something to do with that woman?"

Asmita glared. The usual effect of her flinty gaze was marred by a sheen of unshed tears. Rather than vaguely terrifying, she looked... woeful? Wretched? Something along those lines.

"It *is*," Jasmine nodded sagely. "I can tell."

"Piss off," Asmita muttered. Then she gave a sudden sob, and real, actual tears spilled from her eyes. She blinked in obvious shock. It wasn't often that Asmita's body disobeyed her commands, and Jasmine knew very well that she'd been commanding it *not* to cry.

Christ, this whole thing was unsettling. Jasmine had watched in alarm for months as Asmita was slowly infected by humanity's greatest curse: *love*. Now her friend's infamous self-control was shattering beneath Cupid's heel.

It was enough to give a girl nightmares, really.

But what Asmita needed right now was support, not further doom and gloom. So Jasmine filed away her own horror at the situation and tried to think like a normal human being.

"Darling," she murmured. "Just spill. You'll feel so much better." At least, that was what the magazines always said.

The words seemed to work. Or maybe it was the tone, or the back-rubbing, or the vibe—Jasmine had been trying to project comfort. Whatever it was, something made Asmita talk. Or rather, word-vomit.

"IjustlovehersomuchandshesjustperfectandI'msoohmygodI-don'tdeserveherbutIcan'tletgo—"

"Asmita!"

The rampaging jaw snapped shut. Embarrassed eyes met Jasmine's. Asmita's olive cheeks darkened as she cleared her throat. "Sorry."

"Don't be sorry, love, just—slower, perhaps. Take a breath."

"Right. Um..."

Jasmine waited patiently as her friend corralled obviously messy thoughts.

"Well... We've been dating for a while."

Yes. I'm aware. By Jasmine's count it had been over three months since Asmita first showed signs of losing her fucking mind.

"And she wants to take things to... the next level."

Jasmine stared. Was that some kind of euphemism for public group sex? Because Asmita hated exhibitionism.

"I mean, she wants to be..." Asmita lowered her voice, eyes wide. "*Girlfriends.*"

Jasmine's brows flew up. "*That's* why you're upset?"

Asmita nodded solemnly, her lips pressed together so tight, they were almost white.

"But I thought you liked her? A lot?"

"I do!"

"So isn't that what you want?" Jasmine wasn't an expert on romantic relationships, since she'd never actually had one, but the love songs and the rom-coms and the dirty romance novels were all pretty clear. Asmita should be happy about this development. Shouldn't she?

Apparently not. "I can't, Jas! I'm not—I'm not good enough for her!"

Jasmine stiffened. "Asmita. I hope you, my intelligent, hard-working, gorgeous, funny friend, are not putting yourself down over some girl."

"She's not *some girl!* She's special. And I..." Asmita looked down, her jaw shifting, her long, silky hair falling over her eyes. When she spoke again, her voice was soft and hopeless. "Ah, Jas. You know what I'm like. I'll ruin it. I ruin everything."

For a moment, Jasmine couldn't speak. She'd said those same words so often, in the middle of the night, in the safety and threat and possibility of darkness—to herself.

Hearing them come from a woman she respected so much felt like a slap.

Determination steeled her spine. She caught Asmita's face in her hands, forcing her friend to look up and meet her eyes. "Now you listen to me, you absolute mango. You are currently afflicted with a grievous illness known as feeling, emotion, sentiment—the virus's names are numerous. But no matter what you call it, the result is the same: you can't see things clearly. You can't trust your own judgement right now. So trust mine. No-one—no-one on *earth*, Asmita—is too good for you."

Mita sniffed loudly and opened her mouth, as if to argue.

Jasmine narrowed her eyes. "Shut it. I'm talking."

Mita's mouth shut with a *click*.

"Thank you. Now; I'm sure your magical dream girl—"

"Pinal."

"Yes, yes, Pinal." Jasmine *did* know the woman's name. Had met her. Tentatively liked her. But that could change at any time, if she fucked with Asmita. "Pinal is delightful. Divine. But you're Asmita fucking Shah. You could shag the Queen herself, and she'd say thank you. So you've never done this sort of thing before—who gives a fuck? You've never tried. You've never *wanted* to try. But now you do. And, because you're an irritating bitch, you'll be brilliant at it first time, just like you are with everything else."

Asmita gave a wobbly, wet sort of smile. "Do you think?"

"I said it, didn't I? Stop fishing for compliments, you cow."

Asmita's smile widened. "But I like compliments. And you were really on a roll."

With a grin of her own, Jasmine released Asmita's face and sat back. "I was, wasn't I? But that's quite enough fluffy shit for one day. For one decade, even."

"You're right, I'm sure." Everything about Asmita was slightly brighter now, in a hopeful sort of way—like a sun-starved flower turning to the light. She dabbed strategically at her eyes with a napkin, raising her phone to use as a mirror. "Christ, I've fucked my makeup right up."

"That's what you get for wearing a bloody smoky eye to work, you drama queen. Who do you think you are?"

Asmita snorted and elbowed Jasmine in the ribs. Jasmine kicked her gently beneath the table. A minor fight broke out, and then the man sweeping the floor returned, and somehow they ended up buying a strawberry milkshake to share.

Teenaged McDonald's trauma aside, the milkshake was pretty good.

"Oooooh, *my God! Jasmine!* You won't *believe* what's happened!"

Knowing Tilly Potter-Baird, Jasmine probably wouldn't.

What with Asmita's minor breakdown at lunch, and general office fuckery—working for a housing charity was no joke—it had been a long day. Still, Jasmine kept her expression pleasant as she stepped into the flat and shut the front door.

"What, poppet? Did you blow something up in the microwave again?"

Jasmine's roommate, landlady, and old school... *acquaintance,* stood in the hallway, wringing her filthy hands. They weren't filthy for any reason other than aesthetic. Tilly was living in the city, in this crappy flat that her father owned, for the *experience.* The experience of slumming it.

And she left no sartorial stone unturned when it came to authenticity. The artful dirt beneath her fingernails was accessorised by lank, matted hair that supposedly imitated dreadlocks, and a stained old denim jacket that, aside from anything else, was highly inappropriate for the sweltering weather.

But it was not Jasmine's place to judge. At least, not if her broke self wanted to keep this God-send of a flat-share.

"There's been a *flood!*" Tilly wailed.

Jasmine raised her brows. "Did you leave the bath running again, Matilda?"

"Don't call me that," Tilly snapped. "It's Mattie!"

Oh, yes. After all their years as classmates at Evelyn Jameson's School For Girls, Jasmine did struggle to adjust to Tilly's new 'street' name.

"Mattie, then," she acquiesced. "Have you put some towels down?"

"Umm..." Mattie/Tilly/Who-Gave-A-Fuck? continued to wring her hands, face twisting into a hesitant sort of grimace. "I mean, no, but—"

"Oh, for heaven's sake." Jasmine hung up her bag and kicked off her heels, striding into the flat. "You have to soak up the water or the floors will lift, you widgeon. We've talked about this. Do you want your father to fork out for new laminate unnecessarily?"

A silly question, really. Tilly didn't think about trivialities like money; she hadn't been raised that way. But Jasmine had.

No matter how wealthy they became, Dad would never let her forget where they'd come from. And now, looking at Tilly, she was quietly grateful for that.

"I think Daddy will be paying for more than laminate," Tilly said, tone hesitant.

Jasmine opened the bathroom door and stopped short. She stared down at the bone-dry floor. "Darling," she said, very slowly and with admirable calm. "Where is the flood?"

"The spare room," Tilly said promptly.

Jasmine gritted her teeth. "Do you mean *my* room?"

"Ah, yes." Tilly nodded like a bobblehead. Perhaps she was nervous. At school, Jasmine had developed a reputation for being awfully terrifying and possibly violent, because her father was from *Bulwell* and he had a *gold tooth,* and all he did was sell paper!

It was a generally undeserved reputation, and yet Jasmine felt herself suddenly ready to live up to it.

"Why would there possibly be a *flood* in my bedroom?" she asked, with a patience that she personally thought was rather impressive.

"Well, it's something to do with the flat upstairs," Tilly said. "And the pipes."

Ah, yes. The building's faulty pipes. But... "Upstairs?" Jasmine asked faintly.

"Rather funny, really." Tilly gave a nervous laugh. "A sound like a waterfall woke me up, a little past lunchtime. So I got up, and I ran into your bedroom, and Lord, you should've seen it! Water was absolutely *pissing* from the light fitting!"

"The... the light fitting?" Jasmine echoed.

So this was how it felt to be utterly without one's wits. *Fascinating.*

"Yes! Rather exciting, actually. I think I swooned. I—"

Jasmine's brain chose that moment to reboot. Her body,

which had felt as though it were floating through a haze of worst nightmares, became hers to command once more. She pushed past Tilly, ignored the woman's outraged, "*Oh!*" and ran to her bedroom.

It was a fucking disaster.

Jasmine stared, mouth shamelessly agape, at the sodden mess that was—well, everything she bloody owned.

The light fitting had been removed and now sat on the floor, a twist of chrome and frosted glass, in the vast puddle of water that gleamed on top of the carpet.

Water.

On top of the fucking carpet.

She turned to Tilly, who was hovering nervously a good metre away. Smart girl. "How long was this water... running?"

"Oh, hours," Tilly said. "It took me a while to figure out that it was coming from the flat upstairs, you know. Who'd have thought? And then I had to decide what to do. Actually, I didn't really figure that out; I called Daddy, got his secretary of course, she passed on the message, he called me back about an hour later—"

Jasmine held up a silencing hand. Tilly's mouth snapped shut with an audible *click*.

"Why," Jasmine said, "didn't you move any of my things?"

Tilly blinked. "Pardon?"

"My *things*," Jasmine roared. Then she cleared her throat, pressed her lips together, and clawed back her placid facade. Tilly looked terrified. And Jasmine did *not* need Tilly to feel 'intimidated', or she'd lose out on the cheapest and safest flat in the city. So she stretched her mouth into a smile and tried to remember how to charm someone who didn't want to sleep with her.

After a few seconds, her mind remained blank. Bloody impossible.

She abandoned the charm idea and focused on trying to stay calm. "My things," she said, at a normal volume this time, "are still in my room. The clothes on my bed. The pictures. My ornaments and my fairy lights and my—" She took a deep, soothing breath. "My Vivienne Westwood Pimlico. It's *calfskin*, Tilly. Why didn't you save the Westwood?"

She could see the gorgeous handbag on her dresser, taupe and sad and sodden. The first designer item she'd ever bought with her own fucking money—and she might be a lawyer, but since she worked in the charitable sector, money wasn't something she had much of.

She'd have to hold a funeral.

Jesus Christ, everything in the room was soaked through. Jasmine thanked God that all her skin and hair products were in the bathroom, and that she'd shut her underwear drawer that morning. At least her knickers would be dry.

She hoped.

"Oh, sorry," Tilly said. "I was petrified where I stood. Like Mrs. Haversham! I thought I might be electrocuted!"

Jasmine had to admit—Haversham reference aside—that Tilly made a fair point with regard to electrocution. "Right," she said. "And what *is* the verdict, so far as that... issue goes? What did your father do in terms of safety? I assume he sent someone?"

"Oh, yes." Tilly nodded. "He's ever so sorry. He's going to sue the building!"

Jasmine squeezed her eyes shut and pinched the bridge of her nose. "Matilda. Listen to me very carefully." She paused. "Are you listening?"

"Yes?" Tilly squeaked.

"Tell your father that he absolutely must *not* sue the building. Tell him to employ a secretary in resolving the matter of the pipes, and of the wiring. Tell him to have this room restored and to compensate me for my damaged items."

"Um... Can I write this down?" Tilly asked.

"If you must."

Jasmine heard the pat-pat of Tilly searching through her myriad pockets, and then the tap of nails against glass. "Go on," Tilly said brightly.

"Tell him I need my room back within a reasonable time period, to be decided upon by an impartial third party, and that I want that time period established within seven days."

"Right..." Tilly said slowly as she typed. "Gosh, you are clever, Jasmine."

"Send it to him via email. CC both secretaries. Alright?"

Tilly nodded dutifully. "I'll do it now!"

"Thank you, poppet. Oh, and I'm in dire need of alcohol, if you wouldn't mind."

"What a good idea!" Tilly skipped off to the kitchen.

Jasmine waited until she heard the bang of a cupboard door opening. Then she slapped herself.

It was one of her many bad habits, but it worked.

Her sluggish mind zinged to full productivity, and she felt the last of her childish desire to scream fade away. Gasping at the sharp pain in her cheek, she blinked rapidly. Then she pulled out her phone.

She couldn't stay here. God only knew how long Tilly's darling dad would take to fix this problem. He was notoriously disinterested in anything related to his daughter, and usually coked up. It would be fucking ages, regardless of the email she'd just dictated.

Of course, she could take the easy way out. Could call Dad, tell him what had happened, and he'd send her all the money she needed to fix the room herself as soon as possible.

But she couldn't do that. For one thing, Dad was on a

Caribbean cruise with Marianne, and she didn't want to worry him during their... 'romantic getaway'.

Blech.

And for another, she was twenty-eight years old. A grown woman. She had her own horribly-paying job, her own pitiful amount of money, and... well, her pride. She wouldn't rely on the Bank of Daddy.

But looking at this ruined room—all the little decorations, the careful touches, destroyed—was making Jasmine feel slightly violent. She couldn't stay here and sleep on the fucking sofa while her bedding rotted away down the hall.

She could call Asmita—except the idea of reaching out for something so awkward and painful and embarrassing as *help* made her feel... edgy. Anxious. Skin-crawlingly disgusted.

Jasmine didn't pretend it was a reasonable reaction. But it was real, and it was one she didn't enjoy.

If she was honest with herself, there was only one person— aside from her father—that she'd ever trust enough to ask for help. There was only one person she could call without that vile, creeping discomfort.

Although it still wouldn't be easy.

"Here you are!" Tilly said brightly. "It's new. And it's Parma Violet flavoured, can you believe?"

Jasmine turned to find her flatmate holding out a shot glass of lavender liquid. Pushing away her knotty thoughts, she took it and swallowed gratefully.

The sweet flavour did little to hide the raw bite of alcohol, which was good. She resisted the urge to smash the glass against the wall and settled for a fortifying gasp. "Wonderful, Tilly. You're a darling."

Tilly winked, downed her own shot, and took both glasses. As she toddled off, Jasmine found the right contact in her phone and hit *Call*.

11

He answered almost immediately, his voice clipped and smoky. "Jas."

"Rahul. I need you to pick me up."

There was a slight pause. It was barely six o'clock, so he might be at work. He was always at work. Still, after a moment, he said, "Where are you?"

"Tilly's. Home, I mean."

He didn't ask any more questions. Maybe he could hear the fact that she was, despite her best efforts, on the edge of panic. Maybe he knew something must be wrong for her to summon him like this, without a smile in her voice. Maybe it was blatantly obvious, even through the phone, that calling had made her feel like she was going to vomit.

Whatever the reason, all he said was, "Be there in ten."

Chapter 2

Seven Years Ago

H e saw her on a Monday.

He'd gone home for the weekend, to reassure Mum that he was still alive and hadn't lost any weight, or contracted any life-threatening illnesses, since last month.

But on Monday, he returned to university and went to his usual spot in the library—second floor for accounts and finance, at the back, by the windows that wouldn't open, just to *feel* like he was getting fresh air.

And there she was. In his seat, actually.

But of course, no-one owned library seats. Rahul just liked to stick to his routine.

He sat a few rows away and wasted an hour staring at her. At first, he told himself he was actually staring in longing at his seat, which she'd stolen, but that was a terrible lie. He knew from the start that he was staring at her.

And she was staring out of the window, her hair a dark cloud around her face. It was a pretty face. That wasn't why he stared, though.

He stared because she was sexy. Sexy like Marilyn Monroe or Sridevi. When she raised her arms in a languid, lazy stretch, it was sexy. When she wrapped a springy curl around her finger, it was sexy. Fuck, when she stared blankly out of the damn window, it was sexy. He'd never seen raw sex appeal in person. He told himself that studying it closely was academic.

The rest of the accounting floor seemed to agree. They were staring, too. But she didn't notice, or if she did, she must not care. Because she kept shamelessly *not* studying, and kept being sexy. He suspected she couldn't help the last part.

"Jasmine Allen."

Rahul turned at the whisper, delivered with the kind of smug bite that suggested bad news was forthcoming. Luke Schnaigl, from his Financial Management seminar, had come to sit beside Rahul at some point in the last hour. He hadn't even bloody noticed.

Rahul raised his brows, leaned in close and whispered, "What?"

Whispering in a library was an Olympic sport. Trying to out-silence silence while *not* being silent took practice and dedication. Rahul was shit at it.

But Luke was okay. "The girl," he murmured. "That's Jasmine Allen."

Rahul's gaze slid back, inevitably, to her. *Jasmine.* Yes, he decided. It suited her. But Allen? He wasn't sure. Jasmine Khan would sound much better.

Not because Khan was his last name. He was just spit-balling.

Since Luke seemed to expect a response, Rahul whispered, "She's pretty."

Jasmine Allen looked away from the window. She looked right at him. She smirked.

Rahul felt his cheeks heat. He raised a hand self-consciously to his hair, stopped himself, and pulled off his glasses instead. Now she was just a blur, and he couldn't see the sharp amusement in those dark, dancing eyes. But he could still feel her gaze. Fuck.

Beside him, Luke released a little huff of laughter. "Careful, mate. If you give her a reason, she'll eat you alive."

Rahul snorted, cleaning his glasses needlessly on the hem of his T-shirt. "What are you, the student body's fucking tour guide?"

"Just looking out for you. Everyone knows Jasmine Allen. But I know you don't get out much. Thought I should warn you."

Rahul's lips compressed. "Warn me about what?"

"She's a look-but-don't-touch kind of girl. For guys like us, anyway."

"And what does that mean?" Rahul put his glasses on again and was relieved to find that Jasmine had returned to the window. Relieved, and yet a little deflated. In the instant he'd had her gaze, he'd been as alive as he was embarrassed.

There was something powerful in her attention. He supposed that was part of the sex appeal.

"It means she's out of our league," Luke said dryly. "She's a genius. Her family's loaded. You know she's secretary of the Law Committee? You know she's a *cheerleader?* And," he added darkly, "she looks like *that*. I don't know what she's doing here. I bet it's part of an elaborate plot to get one of us to make a fool of ourselves."

Rahul raised his brows. "Why would she do that?"

"It's what they do," Luke said. "Those kinds of girls."

Rahul stared at his friend—well, *acquaintance*—for a moment as he turned that logic over in his head. He made sure he was quite positive of his conclusion before he spoke. "You're a fucking twat."

Luke scowled, holding up his hands. "Piss off."

"Alright." Luke hadn't meant it literally, but Rahul gathered up his things. It wasn't hard; he'd barely unpacked anyway. Certainly hadn't got a head start on the term's assignments, as he'd intended. He shoved his stuff into his rucksack with no concern for order—for once—and made his way towards Jasmine Allen.

He had no idea what he was doing.

But she was looking at him again. Watching him. In fact, everyone in the vicinity was watching him, most with looks of dawning horror. He didn't care. He came to the table where she sat and took the end seat, leaving space between them. She studied him with a little smile.

"Hi," he said awkwardly.

She nodded. "Hello." She sounded like Joanna fucking Lumley. Posh, but like she'd just finished screaming someone's name.

What the fuck is wrong with you right now?

"I usually sit here," he said, words tripping over themselves. "And I... didn't like that table."

The tables were all identical.

But she murmured some sound of vague understanding and turned back to the window.

Rahul pulled out his work and tried to focus on his research assignment. For almost another hour, he failed. Then she left. It should've been a blessed occurrence, should've improved his concentration at least—but of course, it didn't.

He was surrounded by the ghost of some tropical scent that might belong to her. Why had she been on this floor, if she was a law student? And why had she stayed so long and only looked out of the window? And why the hell had he come to sit next to her?

He left the library woefully early. When he came back the next day, she was in his fucking seat.

———

On Tuesday, he sat beside her like a fool, imagining a taut string stretched between them. A thread of glittering tension that connected his furtive gaze and his pounding heart to her raw beauty. He knew he was the only one who felt it.

On Wednesday, he finally got some work done. Not as much as he'd like, but more than he'd managed over the past few days. He must be getting used to her. Growing immune to her magnetic pull. He'd just started on the second part of his assignment when the rain began.

"Ah, fuck," she said. "I didn't bring a jacket."

She was still staring out of the window, but she didn't sound as if she was talking to herself. So Rahul looked out of the window with her, at the insistent drizzle, and said, "You can have mine."

She looked at him, finally, a little smile teasing her lips. "You'd give me your coat?"

Rahul shrugged. He couldn't speak. Turned out, he wasn't used to her at all.

"What a gentleman," she murmured, her smile growing into a full-blown grin. Her cheeks plumped up and little lines fanned from her almond-shaped eyes. She had an adorable smile. That was unexpected.

Rahul smiled back. "I don't mind a bit of rain."

"That's good to know, but I can't take your coat." She said it with authority, in a tone that brooked no argument.

Still, Rahul hesitated to give in. His father had raised him to be a gentleman, whatever the hell that meant. So he said, "Look, I really don't mind—"

"But I can win it."

He blinked at the interruption. "Win it?"

"Yes." She turned back to the window and said, "Choose a raindrop."

"A raindrop?"

He watched as Jasmine leant forward. She put her finger over a fat drop dribbling on the outside of the glass. As it moved, her finger followed it. She had a dark, raised scar on the inside of her forearm, long and narrow. "Go on," she said. "Choose."

Feeling self-conscious, Rahul ignored the stares from the people around them. He got up to stand beside her and chose a drop at random.

She clucked her tongue. "That's higher than mine. Choose one about the same."

"For what purpose?"

She smiled up at him. "I like the way you talk. You should talk more."

He didn't point out that he'd had no reason or opportunity to talk to her before now. He didn't point out that they didn't know each other, so for all she knew, he might be the most talk-ative person in the world.

Instead, he repeated, "For what purpose?"

"Your raindrop is your horse. The windowsill is the finish line. I bet your coat on my raindrop."

Gambling. Dad would smack him upside the head for even considering it. But it wasn't *really* gambling, because he intended to give her his coat no matter what. It was a game, a game that brought a smile to a pretty girl's face. He wanted that smile to stay. He wanted a reason to stand beside her. He chose a raindrop.

"So we start like this?" he asked, frowning slightly.

"Yes," she said. "This is how we begin."

———

Rahul's raindrop won, and she refused to take a rematch. Refused to accept his coat, either. So he put it over the back of her chair, packed up his things, and left her laughing protests behind. She'd have to take the coat now.

He remembered belatedly that his iPod was in the inside pocket, and prayed she wouldn't be stubborn enough to leave the coat behind.

She didn't. The next day, she was there, coat and all. She'd found his iPod and listened to every song. She had very strong opinions on *Songs About Jane*.

As she spoke, animated and carefree, he realised that she was the most compelling person he'd ever met. He was so sure of that fact, it almost disturbed him. Rahul didn't count himself certain of many things. There was his life plan, which could be summed up as *study and succeed*; his beloved family; his numbers, which would never deceive him. And now, apparently, he was also certain of Jasmine Allen's brilliance.

His attraction to her was unsettling—but not unsettling enough to make him stay away. It didn't stop him talking to her for hours, far too loud and enthusiastic for the library. It didn't stop him taking her to lunch in the cafe downstairs and buying her a small mountain of sweets, even though he disapproved of refined sugar. It didn't stop him saying her name as often as he could, loving the way it rushed from his lips like a waterfall, loving the way it tasted like connection.

When she'd asked his name, he wondered if she'd pronounce it right, or if she'd ignore the *h* and lengthen the *u*, and he'd have to teach her, have to press his lips against her skin as he sounded it out.

She'd pronounced it perfectly, of course.

Their library meetings became something of a habit. He'd study; she'd stare out of the window. She'd interrupt to make him laugh, or to draw him into some ridiculous bet. He'd bore

19

her with his thoughts on the accrual principle, and laugh when she said she was allergic to spreadsheets, and then a library assistant would come over to shush them, and they'd both apologise and laugh harder.

And whenever they parted, she'd hug him.

The first time, she did it so easily. So casually. She slid her arms around his neck and pressed her body against his, and her hair brushed his cheek, and at every single point of contact he felt a surge of skin-prickling heat, like the air before a summer storm. And then he felt her breath catch in her chest, and she pulled back and looked up at him with wide eyes, and he thought...

He didn't know what he thought. In an instant, her face cleared, and she smiled, and she left.

But after that, every hug seemed fraught with tension, heavy with a delicious sort of pressure. Every accidental touch of their hands felt like a secret held close to the chest. Sometimes, when they laughed, he'd catch her eye, or she'd catch his, and shared humour would turn into something slower and thicker and sweeter, like dripping honey. Something he wanted to taste.

He wasn't surprised that Jasmine made the first move. Wasn't surprised when, two weeks after they met, she invited him back to her flat.

She shut her front door behind them. He looked around at the real wood floor and the art on her hallway wall, and remembered that Luke Schnaigl had said her family was loaded.

Then she caught him by the shoulders. He expected her to kiss him. He *wanted* her to kiss him. But she didn't. Instead, she pushed him down, down, down, until he sat on the cool wood. He wondered what she was doing, then decided he didn't care. Wondered if he should mention the fact that he'd never done this before. She looked at him with every inch of her champagne sparkle, and he thought that this must be drunkenness.

Then she reached beneath her skirt and pulled down her knickers, and everything came into sharp focus. When she began to touch herself under the skirt, he almost died. It was a bad idea, but still he gritted out, "Let me see.'"

Her confident smile softened into something breathless and wide-eyed. Slowly, she raised her skirt, and showed him.

She was one of those women who seemed petite above the waist, but below it, things got deliciously heavy. He had seen and salivated over her muscular calves before, but now he saw her heavy thighs, her wide hips, the softness of her belly and the dark curls between her legs. She slid a finger through those curls, spreading her delicate folds for him. He saw the stiff nub of her clit and the deep pink of her inner flesh, stark against her brown skin.

He knew in that instant that he wouldn't last.

Rahul undid his jeans with frantic hands, as if she'd change her mind if he was too slow. Hell, she just might. Still, it took him longer than it should've because he couldn't take his eyes off her. When he finally freed his cock, he gripped the base of his shaft so tight his knuckles hurt.

"Come here," he ordered.

She smiled slightly as she knelt. "You're bossy."

Apparently, yes. "Touch yourself." Because there was no way he could make her orgasm. He'd never touched a woman in his life. But he wanted her to come—and fast, because there was so much slickness gleaming on the head of his cock, he wondered if *he* wasn't coming already, slow and stealthy.

She rubbed her clit in tight little circles, and his mouth went dry. With her free hand, she pushed her purse over to him, a little thing she carried everywhere. He opened it, glad to have something to focus on that wasn't her, because she was driving him out of his fucking mind. In the purse he found her student ID, countless hair slides, money, and a condom. Huh.

He hoped he could get the condom on without coming, or fucking it up. He gritted his teeth, thought of statement analysis, and rolled on the latex without disaster. One hurdle dealt with.

Jasmine crawled towards him, her skirt falling, which was both good and terrible. She pushed him back until he laid on the floor, his erection jutting up from his body, almost painfully hard. She straddled his thighs, and he must enjoy torture, because when she grasped his cock he gathered up her skirt with one hand so that he could see.

Rahul watched as her pussy swallowed his length. Felt power surge at the base of his spine, felt an insistent ache in his balls and pure desperation zipping through his nerve endings. Saw her stretch around his cock and felt her velvet heat choke him, burning and wet even through the condom. She moaned as she settled against him, and he swore not to disgrace himself completely. He would last minutes rather than seconds.

She started to ride him, slow and easy and impossibly perfect. Rahul reached forward and circled the pad of his thumb around her clit, the way he'd seen her do it.

"God, yes," she whispered. "Touch me like that."

Had he ever heard anything so arousing in his life? *Would* he ever? No. He was ruined. Absolutely ruined, from this moment on.

He reached up and tugged down the neckline of her T-shirt, exposing her sweet little tits—no bra. Barely any flesh for a bra to hold. Her nipples were dark and thick and hard because she wanted him. He could feel her wetness slicking his thighs because she wanted him. She arched against him, rode him hard, because she wanted him.

He shouldn't have thought about that. Now he was going to come.

But he would have every inch of her while he could. Rahul rubbed her clit a little faster, and almost shouted when he felt her tighten around him. God, it was so good. So fucking good. How could anything on earth feel like this? How could people do anything other than fuck?

She put her hand to his face, caught his jaw, forced him to look her in the eyes. Her voice was low and shaking as she whispered, "Say my name."

"*Jasmine.*" The word was harsh, strangled as release tore through him. His vision blurred. She threw her head back, and her lips parted, and she let out a choked, keening cry—and then her pussy was clenching his cock impossibly, beautifully, and it was just too fucking perfect.

He might've passed out for a second. He wasn't sure. One minute, she was milking the come from him and he was dying happily beneath her, and the next she was sprawled against his chest, her hair in his face.

Oh; that was something he'd forgotten to have. He hadn't touched her hair.

And she hadn't kissed him. He was greedy, because even after all that, he wished she would kiss him.

She pushed herself up all at once, with a little huff. She was smiling, of course. That smile would haunt his dreams, even when he was in his fucking grave. She patted him on the shoulder in a friendly sort of manner, as if they'd just finished a football match.

"Christ," she panted. "Aren't you a surprise?"

He decided to ignore that. As she clambered off of him, her heat releasing his softening cock, Rahul fumbled in his jeans pocket and produced a handkerchief.

"Do you—?"

"Don't worry," she smirked. "I'm good. Is that a hankie?"

He ignored that too. He sat up, panting, and looked around her hallway. Fuck. He'd barely even gotten in the door. He wondered what the etiquette was now. "What are you doing tonight?"

She shrugged, but her smile turned sharp. "Not much. I'm open to a repeat."

He dealt with the condom—for now—and scrambled to his feet, her words shooting through his veins. She was already standing, straightening her clothes.

"Come out with me later," he blurted, before he lost his courage.

Her smile faded. She didn't speak.

That was bad; that was very, very bad.

"I..." For a moment, the confidence she wore like a second skin seemed to fade. But then, all at once, it returned. "I don't really do that," she said, looking away, fiddling briskly with her skirt's waistband. "The dating thing, I mean."

His heart leapt from his ribcage and landed on the floor with a splat. Of course she didn't.

Look but don't touch.

Well, he'd touched. And now she was looking at him with something like pity, and he couldn't bear that.

Fix it.

"I didn't mean it that way," he said quickly.

She paused. Her expression cleared slightly. "You didn't?"

Keep going.

"No. I meant like... like before. Like friends."

Her look was assessing. After a long, painful pause she said, "Thing is, I don't shag my friends."

It took him a minute to grasp the implications of that statement. Rahul was smart, but around her, everything had to sink through a layer of mindless desire to reach his brain.

So that was his choice? Friendship or fucking?

The first thing that struck him was the thought that they

might do this again. He should take that option. It would be glorious.

But then what? She'd get bored, probably. Move on to someone else. Which would be fine—it *would*, he told himself firmly—only he'd probably never see her again. He'd just be some notch in her bedpost. How... undignified.

He wanted to see her again. Always. He tried not to think about why.

"Okay," he said, steeling his spine. Making his choice. "I get that."

She arched a brow. "Still want to be friends?"

"Yes." It wasn't a lie. He *did* want to be friends. He also wanted to knock her up and tattoo her name on his forehead, but she hadn't asked about that. And it was just a twisted, juvenile urge, the sort of infatuation that would fade soon enough.

"Alright," she said finally, carefully. "Friends." And then she smiled.

Rahul smiled back.

He liked her. He *really* liked her. Friendship would be... fine.

Wouldn't it?

Chapter 3

Now

Rahul pulled up in front of Jasmine's building eleven minutes after receiving her call. He focused on that extra minute, and on berating himself for it, because it was easier than wondering what the fuck was going on.

She was waiting outside, a lonely figure on the narrow pavement, that monstrosity of a building she lived in looming behind her. He hated the fact that she lived there, in the roughest part of the city—the sort of place her dad had worked hard to leave behind. In fact, her dad, Eugene, had said the same thing. She'd told both of them to piss off and mind their own.

But her usual spark seemed absent now. He rolled down the window, and she sauntered towards him with a smirk on her face, only it was counterfeit. He knew every inch of her, every quirk. He knew when she was happy, and he knew when she was not.

She dumped a huge bag on the pavement, then leant down and rested her arms against his window.

"Evening, sugar," she murmured. In concession to the summer heat, she was wearing some floaty vest thing that barely covered her chest. With a strength born of many years practice, Rahul absolutely did not look down.

"Hey," he said. "Everything okay?"

"Peachy." She patted his cheek. That, he knew, was her way of saying *Thank you*. Then she straightened up and heaved the bag into her arms. He didn't bother offering to help. They didn't need a ten minute argument in the middle of the street right now, especially not an argument he'd lose.

Instead, he waited as she came round to the passenger side and got in. He watched as she shoved the massive holdall between their two chairs and onto the backseat. It was covered in patches: red fists and anarchy signs.

"What the hell is that?" he asked, when she finished the manoeuvre.

"It's Tilly's."

"Tilly's an anarchist?"

"Publicly, yes. Let's *go*."

"Right." He started the engine, checked his mirrors. "Seatbelt."

"Yes, Daddy."

Rahul gritted his teeth and had a mental word with his libido. *No, she didn't mean it like that. Trust me, mate. Go back to sleep.*

It didn't do much good. So he focused on filtering into the side street's slow traffic and said, "Where are we going?"

Somehow, she managed to slouch gracefully in a bucket seat. "Yours."

That gave him pause. "Okay. And we're doing that because...?"

She burst into tears.

Shit. Rahul's worry blossomed into full-blown concern. He cut across a lane, receiving at least one middle finger for his trouble, and pulled over. They were barely twenty metres from her bloody flat. But he ignored that, ignored the rightfully angry drivers, undid his seatbelt and reached for her.

She leant over the centre console and into his arms. Her hands went to his hair, like always, then found it carefully styled for work—which she hated—and moved to his shoulders instead. When she didn't even make a snarky comment about the product taming his thick curls, he knew she was really upset.

She clutched at him and pressed her face against his chest, just for a moment. This wouldn't last long; he knew that. So he held her tight and felt the soft cloud of her hair against his cheek, and waited for her to calm down.

When she pulled back, looking predictably mortified, he began his inquisition.

"Jasmine," he said calmly—because if he showed any emotion, if he seemed too worried, she'd clam right up. "Why are you crying?"

She sniffed loudly, clearing her throat, avoiding his gaze. "I'm not."

"While I hate to contradict Her Royal Highness—"

She let out a choked little burble that might've been a laugh.

"—You definitely *are* crying. I'd like to know why."

She sniffed loudly, then wiped at her cheeks with the heels of her hands. Rahul pulled a handkerchief from his pocket and handed it over.

She snorted as she dabbed her eyes. "You're such a fucking nerd."

"Careful. I'll take the hankie back."

This time, she definitely laughed. "Jesus, I'm sorry. I'm so embarrassed."

"Don't be. It's just me."

She gave her cheeks a final pat with the handkerchief and pulled down the visor mirror. If she'd asked, he would've told her she looked beautiful. But she wouldn't ask, because she didn't care what anyone else thought.

"My room has been, ah... damaged."

He raised a brow. "Damaged?"

"Extensively. Plumbing issue."

"You mean—"

"I mean unless I sleep on Tilly's sofa while her dad gets around to fixing things, I... well, I don't have anywhere to go." She fluffed her hair in the mirror, then flipped it shut. "I was going to ask—" She broke off, hesitating. "I was going to ask if I could stay at yours tonight."

"Tonight?" He frowned. "How long will it take to fix?"

She looked away. "I don't know. I mean, I'm not sure—a while, probably, but—"

"So where are you going to stay while you wait?"

She shrugged jerkily. "I hadn't figured that out yet."

Rahul swallowed his sigh of exasperation. He wanted to shake her sometimes. "Okay, well, I've figured it out. Stay with me."

The look she gave him was so fucking sad, he felt like he'd been punched in the gut. "That's sweet of you. But I can't, um... I can't impose on you for that long."

"You've never minded *imposing* on me before."

"Not the same," she said tightly.

Right. And he realised all at once why it wasn't.

When she crashed at his flat after a night out because it was closer than hers, or came over to drag him along on some scheme, she didn't *need* him. She didn't *need* his space.

But now she did. And Jasmine did not like to need.

Rahul tapped his fingers against the steering wheel and searched for a strategy. Found one pretty quickly, actually.

"Your dad's still on his cruise, right?"

"Yep," she said.

"You don't think he'd be pissed at me if I let you run off and stay with someone he doesn't know?"

She gave him a dark look. "Goodness, you're right. My dearest father, masculine protector of my person, has officially appointed you his second-in-command, until such a time as I might gain a husband to contain me." The words dripped with derision.

Rahul gave her a cheerful smile. "Glad you understand." He started the car again.

"You're a fuckface," she mumbled. Which sounded like an agreement to him.

———

Two hours later, Jasmine was sitting on the plush bed in Rahul's spare room, trying her best not to scream.

She had to do *something* to get rid of all this... this nervous energy crawling around inside her, and screaming felt like a solid option. But if she screamed, Rahul would come barrelling in, demanding to know what was wrong. And then she'd have to say something like, *Oh, well, I know you're the best friend a girl could have, and it's totally amazing of you to put me up, but relying on your charity makes me feel like I'm coming apart at the seams. Like, this is physically painful for me. Not to sound ungrateful, or anything.*

Yes, she had issues. Blah blah blah, move on.

Jasmine got off the bed and wandered the room, her eyes running over the familiar decor as she paced. Cool blues and chrome, spotlessly clean like everything Rahul owned. She remembered visiting his accommodation back in their uni days. His shared house had been the typical student pigsty—except for the bathroom he used, his part of the fridge, and his bedroom. Those had been fucking spotless.

Ah, Rahul. If she had to rely on someone, she was glad it was him.

Jasmine returned to the bed and rifled through Tilly's awful holdall. The things she'd been able to rescue from her room were an... eclectic mix, that was for sure. But she pushed past the mini skirts and granny knickers and worn-out Converse to hunt down the stuff she really wanted right now: brand new stationery, fancy shit she'd been saving in its plastic bag, until some arbitrary point in her life when she might feel fresh and earnest enough to open a new notebook.

Now seemed like a good time. Jasmine unwrapped the stationary from the plastic that had saved it. The notebook was thick and pink, a soft moleskin decorated with gold lettering that read, *Fuck It.*

She was definitely in a *Fuck It* sort of mood.

For one treacherous moment, her mind flew to Rahul. Rahul, whose room was just across the hall, who'd made this bed up with fresh sheets for her, who claimed to be making them dinner. Rahul, her best friend since forever.

She put the notebook down on the bed and pulled out the pens she'd bought with it. Ridiculous, glittery things with fluffy feathers at their tip. She had a vague idea that she'd rub those feathers against her chin or nose like Cher from *Clueless*. Why? No fucking clue.

Was it too pathetic to laugh at her own jokes? Jasmine decided she'd had a trying day and allowed herself a snicker.

She was saved from further internal ramblings by the chime of her phone. She had a text. A text that made her unreasonably happy.

Asmita: Talked to Pinal. We are officially totally together, LOL. Only feel mildly terrified. Aren't you proud of me?

Jasmine grinned as she typed out her reply.

Beyond proud, love. You don't even know.

"Jas." Rahul's voice came with a gentle knock at the door. It was open, but he was Rahul. She turned to find him carefully *not* looking through the gap.

So she took the opportunity to look at him.

He'd showered and washed that gel crap out of his hair. Now it sprung around his face in soft curls—though nowhere near as curly as hers—all glossy and shit. Sickening, really. Caramel highlights shone through the dark brown strands as if strategically placed, but that was just how his hair grew.

Yes; *sickening*.

His simple, wire-rimmed glasses were perched on what she liked to call a heroic nose. It was the evening, so he had his version of a 5 o'clock shadow, which was more like an ebony bloody carpet covering his sharp jaw. He stood there, all lean muscle and broad shoulders and cinnamon brown skin, and she thought what she always thought when she saw him.

Fuck, yes.

Then she cleared her throat and said, "What's up?"

He finally looked at her, meeting her eyes with a smile. "Dinner."

She snorted. "Are you sure it's dinner? You sure it's not braised carrot sticks and chopped cucumber?"

His face blank, he deadpanned, "That's not dinner?"

Jasmine rolled her eyes. "There better be some carbs on my plate, cupcake." But she followed him out with a smile on her face.

Rahul was all about clean eating. Jasmine was all about eating in general—but so many healthy foods tasted like absolute crap. And they didn't have nearly enough calories to make cooking worth her while. Why waste seven minutes of her life slicing and chewing celery when it would hit her stomach and break down into thin fucking air?

There were more enjoyable ways to waste her own time.

Rahul knew all about her culinary attitudes, so she wasn't surprised to find that he'd made what could only be described as a fuck-ton of pasta. He plated up at the kitchen counter while she hovered on its other side, where the open-plan space became a living room.

"Pasta looks funny," she sniffed, just to piss him off.

He gave her a look. "It's whole wheat."

"Gross."

His movements slow and patient, his hands big and steady, he picked up a second plate. "It's good for you."

"Are there vegetables in there?" she demanded, catching a flash of green amongst the sauce.

"Yep. And you will eat every last one, brat."

She stuck her tongue out at him and accepted the plate.

He had a narrow kitchen table, but they headed to the sofa to eat. It was a habit he scolded her for, yet continued to participate in. Rahul couldn't do anything even vaguely naughty unless, A: she forced him to, and, B: he got to complain the whole time. She was okay with that.

They settled down, and her eyes bypassed the turned-off TV, focusing on the window behind it. Outside, the sun hung low over the cityscape. Traffic passed in a snatch of engine revs and blaring radio stations. Rahul lived in one of those fancy high-rise blocks in the good part of town, and the view was a city sort of beautiful.

She scooped up some pasta and murmured, "Thanks, love."

He didn't ask what for, exactly, and she was glad. The answer was a bit too long and complicated, and uncomfortably emotional besides.

His hand came to rest on her shoulder, just for a second, and she felt a spark of electricity surge between his skin and hers. He gave no indication that he'd felt Jack-shit. Just said in that deep, smoky voice, "You know I've got you."

The words wrapped around her like goose down. She should probably doubt him, like she would anyone else.

Dangerously, she didn't.

Chapter 4

Now

He was *not* avoiding Jasmine.

That's what Rahul told himself, every night that week.

He always left early in the mornings to go to the gym—so it wasn't his fault that he was out of the house before Jasmine even opened her bedroom door.

And if he'd stayed at the office later than usual, studying spreadsheets and reports with a fine-tooth comb—well, what could he say? He loved his job. He loved the soothing satisfaction of it all. He wasn't necessarily staying out of the house to minimise time spent with Jas.

Of course, the fact that he'd called Mitch every night after work and insisted they go for a beer—even though Rahul didn't drink beer and hated pubs—*might* seem suspicious. Maybe. Perhaps.

Mitch clearly thought so. When Rahul had left work today and stepped into the warm evening air, the first thing he'd done was call his friend. And the little ginger fuck had answered with a bored, "I'm not going out again."

Rahul had been perplexed. "Why?"

"It's Friday night, mate. Whatever you're running from, find someone else to do it with. I've got a standing date with my lady in leather."

So here Rahul was, on a Friday night, working out his frustration at the same gym he'd been to just that fucking morning.

No, he wasn't avoiding Jasmine. Why on earth would anyone think that?

Since he'd finished leg day earlier, and he'd rather die than mess with his carefully curated routine, Rahul attacked the gym's punching bags. For a while, he managed to lose himself in the rhythm of pounding fists, the ache at his shoulders, the bite of his laboured breaths and the sting of sweat dripping into unseeing eyes.

But it didn't take long for him to think of her. It never did.

He hadn't intended to start avoiding his own bloody flat like the plague. He hadn't intended to avoid his best friend, either. But here he was.

It had started on the second night. The second night, when he'd bumped into her while she was leaving the bathroom, wrapped in a towel.

He'd seen her in a towel before. Plenty of times. He'd seen her in less, for fuck's sake, in the barely-there bikinis she loved so damned much.

But seeing Jasmine in a towel was one thing; seeing Jasmine in one of *his* towels, in *his* flat, knowing that she'd be changing just across the hall every damn night for God knew how long... all at once, the reality of what he'd done sucked him under like a typhoon. Even the sight of Jasmine's smile hadn't lightened his mood. *She was living with him.*

There'd be so many opportunities for him to fuck up. To show her somehow, through word or deed, that all this fucking time he'd wanted her. And if she ever found out...

Okay, yeah; he'd been avoiding Jasmine.

As soon as he admitted that to himself, guilt became as suffocating as the anxiety. He stilled the swinging punching bag, his chest heaving, and thought about going back to the seated leg press he'd worked on that morning. A treacherous voice in his head whispered that tearing himself apart would help; that he'd meet his goals faster, feel the knife-sharp satisfaction of his numbers improving, the weight he could bear increasing, and he'd feel better.

He nipped that idea in the bud because avoidance was cowardice. He'd fucked around long enough. He was going home.

—————

Thirty minutes later, Rahul kicked off his shoes in the hallway and called, "Jas. I'm back."

Silence.

It was a little past eight—much earlier than he'd been coming home, true, but Jasmine should definitely be back from work. She was one of the in-house solicitors for a local housing charity. Pay was shit; job satisfaction and hours were good. It was basically shift work, and she always got the best shifts.

How? He'd never asked. The answer was almost certainly sheer charm.

Rahul wandered through the flat. She might not be home now, but she had been at some point. The shower glass was still wet, and the bathroom counter was littered with tubes of makeup he vaguely recognised. Tubes like mascara and lipstick, and foundation, or something like that.

Jasmine had what he privately called her *every day makeup*. It was the kind of makeup that had taken him two years to even notice, and she wore it... well, every day.

And then there was the makeup she wore at night. He held up a scarlet tube of lipstick and sighed.

She'd gone out.

Of course she had. It was Friday night. She was Jasmine.

He took a long, hot shower and tried not to think of her as he scrubbed the last of the pomade from his hair. Then he got out, threw on a pair of pyjama bottoms, and made himself something to eat. The stream of action was intended to scour unwelcome thoughts from his mind. Unwelcome thoughts like what Jasmine was doing right now and who she was with.

He hoped she was with Asmita and the rest of her *platonic* girlfriends, but he knew Jas well. She hadn't really been out all week. Which meant she hadn't slept with anyone.

Maybe if you'd spent some time with her instead of being a dick, she'd be home with you instead of out shagging her latest admirer.

Maybe. Probably not.

Reeling in his thoughts, which were becoming pointlessly possessive, Rahul decided to make use of his wasted Netflix subscription. When in doubt, find something shitty to watch.

Only, the first show he stumbled upon turned out to be kind of... great. And then all of a sudden he was five episodes in and his eyes were burning.

And *then* he heard the tell-tale sound of Jasmine's key scratching at the door.

A slight frown on his face, Rahul paused the TV and strode into the hall. He unlocked the door, opened it, and found Jasmine on the doorstep, key in hand.

She was wearing that fucking red lipstick, and a little black dress that he hoped she hadn't paid too much for, because there was barely a metre of fabric involved. Rahul dragged his gaze firmly away from her mostly-exposed lower half and said, "You're back early."

She smiled, and it gutted him. She was so fucking beautiful, effortlessly. Sometimes he wondered how it was possible.

She stepped through the door, her body brushing close to his, her gaze flicking over his bare chest. Rahul shut the door and turned to face her.

She cocked her head and said, "Hello, buttercup. Don't you look delicious?"

He frowned. "I do?"

She leaned in and put her hands on his shoulders, her eyes boring into his. "Rahul," she whispered. "Your eyebrows are very intimidating."

Ah. She was drunk. Sometimes it was hard to tell.

"Come here," he said. He grabbed her forearm and steered her towards the living room.

"Get off," she snorted, batting uselessly at him. He ignored her.

When he pushed her onto the sofa, she collapsed as if he'd shoved her off a cliff.

"I'm going to the kitchen," he said slowly. "Don't stand up." He didn't trust her in those shoes.

While she arranged herself comfortably, resting her heels against the cushions—the little brat—Rahul busied himself pouring two glasses of water.

He returned, sat at the very end of the sofa—nudging her feet out of the way—and held out a glass. "Drink."

She took it and gulped down the lot. Then she put her feet in his lap and said, "More."

He gave her the second glass and thanked his lucky stars that neither of her stiletto heels had stabbed him in the dick.

"Ta." She downed the second pint and put both glasses on the floor. He winced as they clinked hard against the wood.

Then he looked down at her shoes. They were black, like her dress, with high heels and pointed toes and straps that made his eyes feel slightly blurry. They criss-crossed over each other again and again, wrapping around her ankles and then her calves, ending just below her dimpled knees in little bows.

He was grateful they didn't go higher. Looking at Jasmine's thighs was always a struggle.

He took the end of one bow between finger and thumb and tugged. It didn't budge. A double knot. There was no way she'd get them off.

"So," he said, as he began to work the bow. "You're very drunk."

"And you're highly observant," she drawled. Or slurred. One of those.

"Remember how we talked about safe ways to drink? And unsafe ways?" *And the fact that you shouldn't get like this if you're coming home alone?*

That brought her up short. She sniffed, sounding almost like her sober self. Then she muttered, "Why do I even like you?"

"Because, despite your many flaws, you have excellent taste."

"I have no flaws." She gathered her mass of hair up with both hands, piled it on top of her head. Despite himself, Rahul watched the show. Took in all that bare, brown skin, the red lips, slightly parted, the glitter in her eyes. She said, "Show me a flaw, kitten."

He shook his head. "What did you do tonight?" *Who sent you home alone like this?*

She let her hair fall back around her face in a soft, dark cloud. "I got dumped."

He froze. "I beg your pardon?"

"You heard me, darling."

"I wasn't aware you were in a relationship."

She leaned forward until her chest was practically flat against her thighs. She'd always been flexible. Her tone conspiratorial, she whispered, "Me neither. And isn't that a bitch?"

Rahul frowned and decided to focus on her shoes. It was far simpler than this conversation.

But his silence didn't stop her from talking. Nothing stopped Jas from talking, actually, not when she was on a roll. "Paul told all his mates that I was his bloody bird! Can you believe it? Cheeky fucker!"

Oh, she was so very drunk. Her dad's city accent wormed its way through the plummy tones she'd learned to survive. Rahul rather enjoyed it when she got like this.

"So I told *him*—not in public, mind, but I told him anyroad —don't run about chatting shit like that." Jasmine rolled her eyes. "Oh, he got proper shirty, he did. And he said he's *ending* it. I said, ending *what*? You daft twat." She snorted.

Rahul felt slightly sorry for this mysterious Paul, who must be her latest fuck. If Jas were a goddess, she'd look down from the clouds, see supplicants kneeling at her altar and think, *Who are they waiting for?*

He carefully unwound the straps of her right shoe, lifting her leg a bit as he went. There were criss-cross impressions in the soft flesh of her calves. He frowned. "These are too tight. They'll cut off your circulation."

"Oh, you're so dramatic. There's nowt wrong with them."

He ran his fingers over her calf, felt the little indentations. "They left marks."

She shrugged. "My feet are small and my legs are not. Beauty is pain, my darling potato."

Rahul bit back a laugh.

"Do you know what Paul said to me?" she asked. And then, without pausing for an answer: "He said I was going to die alone!"

Any sympathy Rahul had had for Paul evaporated.

"He said I wouldn't even have cats because I'd never come home to feed them. Which is bullshit, because cats know how to feed themselves. They're very resourceful creatures. In fact..." Jasmine paused, then said with an air of triumph, "Paul could learn a thing or two from cats! Fuck, I wish I'd thought of that at the time. Don't you hate that? When you think of things to say after the argument?"

"Yes," he murmured. He wanted to say, *Paul is a piece of shit, and you couldn't die alone if you tried.* But he limited himself to *Yes.* Then he pulled off her second shoe.

"Well, I've learned my lesson," she mumbled. "No more gingers. Emotional fuckers. Don't tell Mitch I said that. But it's true, though!"

He pushed down his laughter and managed a soothing hum instead.

"I'm bored," she said, stretching languidly. Her feet were bare now. He still hoped they wouldn't find his dick. "Want to play a game?"

This was the point where he refused and sent her to bed. Only she was looking at him with such hopeful eyes, and he was clearly fucking weak, because he couldn't shut her down.

So Rahul sighed and said, "Ah, why not?"

She grinned. Looked a little too devious for his liking.

He clarified hurriedly. "One game, yeah? Then bed."

"Alright." Her grin didn't falter. She reached for the drawer built into the coffee table beside them, pulling it open to reveal his not-so-secret shame. Jas had made a gambler out of him, and she hadn't even tried.

She chose a set of dice and shut the drawer. "Call it."

He arched a brow. "What are we playing for?"

"Time," she said.

"Time?"

Jasmine set the dice aside and scrambled to her knees. He

averted his eyes as her dress rode up. Next thing he knew, she was right beside him: her arm around his shoulder, her chest brushing his biceps, her lips against his ear. A shiver danced along his spine at the ghost of her cool breath over his skin. He willed his cock to behave, because he wasn't wearing any underwear and his pyjama bottoms were way too thin.

Then she whispered, her voice solemn, "You've been avoiding me."

Ah. Nothing like guilt to suffocate an inappropriate hard-on.

He turned to face her, then flinched as he found her lips even closer than he'd thought. Close enough to kiss.

Dangerous idea. Move on.

"I'm sorry," he said, leaning back slightly.

She grinned. It was slightly wild, thanks to the alcohol, but he caught a flash of something that worried him much more. Sadness.

He'd upset her. And now he felt like tearing his own heart out of his chest and offering it in apology—but, realistically, all that blood would upset her even more.

Was second-hand drunkenness a thing? He might be experiencing it right now.

"If I win," she said, "I get an hour with you tomorrow."

The words filled him with shame. "You don't have to win time with me, Jas."

"Well, I'm not gonna fucking ask for it." Her voice, so light and teasing, was suddenly harsh. He was struck by the instinctive certainty that, beneath her liquid courage, she was hating every second of this. And that trying to deny her, to placate her, would make things even worse.

So he nodded, swallowed hard, and said, "Alright."

She sat back, a look of satisfaction on her face, and picked up the dice again. "Call it."

"Seven."

"Nine," she said, and threw.

Snake eyes.

She fell back against the arm of the sofa, releasing a huff. She looked like a petulant teenager, her brow creased in a sad little frown. "You win," she mumbled.

"Great," he said. "I win an hour with you."

She looked up at him. "What?"

"You never asked me what I wanted." He caught her hand, laced their fingers together. "That's what I want. You and me, tomorrow. One hour."

For a moment, she eyed him darkly, scepticism all over her face. He wondered if she'd push him away like she did sometimes, when she thought he was getting too close.

Not physically; never physically. Other things bothered Jas much more.

But then she smiled slowly, and said, "Okay. What are we doing?"

"It's a surprise."

Her smile widened. Sometimes she got so excited over little things, so genuinely happy about life, that he wanted to give her the world on a plate.

But then, as if remembering herself, she cleared her throat and pulled away. Her smile was hidden. Clapping her hands with all the regality of a queen, she announced, "Time for bed!"

"Oh, is it?" he murmured dryly. "I hadn't noticed."

She scrambled off the sofa. His thighs felt cold without her feet taking up space there. "Look at you," she said as she wobbled to her feet. "Half-naked. You slut."

"You know me." He stood and guided her towards the bedrooms, a hand hovering near the small of her back. There were several moments when he thought she might fall, when he thought he might have to catch her—but she always righted herself. And then they reached the pair of doors that marked their respective bedrooms, separated only by a narrow hallway.

"I haven't done my twelve-step," she whispered. "Scandalous."

"I think your skincare can wait until the morning," he said.

"Skincare waits for no bitch, sugar-tits."

"Good God, Jasmine, go to bed."

She leant against the door frame and bit her lip. White teeth sank into crimson gloss. Enunciating every letter in the word, she said, "*Bossy*."

"Brat."

"You say that a lot." She grinned. "Type it into Pornhub."

Before he could digest that baffling statement, she slipped into her room and shut the door.

Chapter 5

Six Years Ago

"S o... you're not her feller?"

Rahul shook his head firmly. "No, Sir."

"You're just her... *friend?*"

"Yes, Sir. And that is not a euphemism."

There was a tense pause.

Rahul didn't know what he'd expected of the father his friend loved so dearly—but it certainly hadn't been this hulking, tattooed skinhead with a face that spoke of violence. The silence between Rahul and Jasmine's dad stretched out, taut and stringy.

Then Eugene Allen burst into booming laughter.

Rahul laughed along, mostly because he didn't want to be gutted like a fish. His gaze strayed to the window of Eugene's study, which had been pushed wide—but that didn't do much good when the air outside was swollen and heavy with heat.

He wasn't searching for a breeze, but for a familiar figure. *My garden is behind Dad's study*—that's what she'd said to him.

Yeah; that was another surprise about coming home with Jasmine for part of the summer. Her house was absolutely huge, and the grounds were extensive. He'd gotten so used to her private school accent that he'd forgotten what it meant. He'd forgotten she must be loaded.

Apparently, her father worked in paper.

The man in question jabbed a meaty finger at Rahul and said, "I like you, son. Fancy a drink?"

Since it was hot as hell, he said, "Yes, please."

"You a lager man?"

"I don't drink alcohol," Rahul said. "I'm happy with water."

Eugene's grin widened, displaying a gold tooth. "I like you even more. Tell you what: my Marianne's brought some pink lemonade round. Don't know what she puts in it, but it's right nice. Fancy some?"

Ah. Now Rahul felt slightly cornered. He didn't know Marianne, and her lemonade sounded nice, but he *did* know that Jasmine was quietly and frantically freaking out about the fact that her dad had a girlfriend.

She certainly wouldn't admit to it, of course—but Rahul could tell.

Drinking Marianne's lemonade might be some sort of best friend betrayal. But then again, when he'd asked Jas how she felt about the relationship, she'd said, *"I really couldn't care less, poppet."* Plus, he was really fucking thirsty. So he smiled and said, "Sounds great."

"Nice one."

Eugene went to get the drinks himself. Judging by the vast slab of mahogany that served as his desk, the Bugatti and Porsche on his driveway, and the *fountain* in what Jasmine called the 'main' garden, he could probably afford servants. But he clearly wasn't that kind of guy.

While he waited for Eugene's return—the kitchen was half-way across the damned house—Rahul stood and wandered over to the windows. They were an outdated sort, so the thin panes only opened half-way. He rested a hand against the wall, leaning in to catch the whisper of a breeze. God, that felt good.

The garden outside was well-shaded by an oak tree and decorated with splashes of colourful flowers. His eyes scanned the lush foliage lazily—

And then, all at once, he found what he was looking for.

Jasmine.

She emerged from a cluster of pampas grass with a hose in her hand and an absent sort of smile on her face. She wore a blue bikini top and tiny denim shorts. She hadn't been wearing that when she'd left him with her dad twenty minutes ago, but he wasn't complaining.

She looked like something out of a painting. She looked like art. Her skin glistened with a thin veil of sweat, the kind he'd lick off if things were different.

Yep. He was officially fucking depraved.

When she caught sight of him, her smile widened. She walked towards him, the hose still in hand, its stream trailing over the grass as she moved. It struck him that he hadn't seen so much of her body since they'd first met, since the day he didn't think about. She was still unbelievable. She was better. Heavier, he thought. Her hips—

Inappropriate. Think of something else.

But her *hips*.

Rahul committed himself to mentally cataloguing the assets of the last company he'd used as a case study. He'd only just begun failing miserably when she came within speaking distance.

"Hey," she called.

He tried to come up with an interesting greeting and settled on, "Hi."

Inspired. Utterly inspired.

She came closer. Aimed the hose at the bed of begonias below the window, and said, "How's it going with Dad?"

"Okay, I think. Why is he interviewing me, again?"

"He's not *interviewing* you," she smirked. "He just thinks it's weird I brought someone home, so he wanted to talk."

That sparked Rahul's interest. "*Is* it weird you brought me home?" Jasmine knew a lot of people. She was well-liked. In fact, that was an understatement; she was almost universally adored.

But since they'd become friends last year, he couldn't help but notice that she spent more time with him than anyone else. Sometimes, that gave him a pathetic sort of hope. Then they'd go to a party and she'd disappear with some girl, or she'd introduce him to her current fuck buddy, and he'd remember that she'd never had a real relationship and that she didn't sleep with friends.

He was most assuredly her friend now. Her best friend. And she was definitely his. He hadn't exactly meant for that to happen, but here they were.

She shrugged her narrow shoulders and looked down at the water streaming from her hose. "I don't know if it's *weird*," she said, "but I suppose I've never brought friends home from uni."

Rahul's brows shot up. "You haven't?"

"That's what I said, darling. Pay attention."

Smiling slightly, Rahul rubbed a hand over the back of his neck. Then he stopped himself, because physical tics were unnecessary. "So this is your garden?"

"Yes. But you should see it at night."

He gave the plants a skeptical look. "Um... why?"

"You'll see." Her smile was familiar by now; it was the smile used when she was sure of herself, looking forward to charming the shit out of someone. Apparently, tonight, that someone would be him.

He liked when it was him.

"Where's Dad gone?" she asked, as if only just noticing that Rahul was in the office alone.

"Oh, he went to get me a drink."

She raised her brows. "A drink?"

"Yep."

"What kind of drink?"

Rahul felt a smile creep over his face. "I don't know... he said something about pink lemonade?"

Her lips compressed. "*Marianne's* pink lemonade?"

"Maybe. But you don't care about that, because you don't care about anything, and you certainly don't need to talk about 'emotional bullshit'—"

His sardonic quoting of her own earlier rant was rudely interrupted. Without warning, she flicked the hose at him, drenching both the window and most of his head.

Rahul swore, laughed, swore again. She was laughing too, the sound washing over him like the sunlight. He yanked off his glasses and blinked icy water out of his eyes.

"Yeah," he deadpanned. "You *so* don't care about Marianne."

"Oh, fuck off," she grinned. "I'm adjusting."

He used the dry edge of his shirt to clean off his glasses, trying not to smile. "Might adjust faster if you talked about it."

"Talking is for nerds."

"Says the future lawyer."

"Future *solicitor*. Talking is for nerds; litigation is for warriors." And then, after a pause, she said, "Your hair looks better now."

He stopped cleaning his glasses and brought a hand to his head. Most of the product he'd been using to tame his uncontrollable hair had apparently been rinsed away. He sighed. "Great."

"Don't be vain," she said lightly.

He didn't bother correcting her. Vanity wasn't exactly the issue.

Control.

"Sit down before Dad comes back," she ordered.

"Why? Am I not allowed to talk to you until I've been vetted?"

"Don't joke." Her voice became solemn, her face haunted. "My father's killed people for less."

He stared at her, horrified. "Are you serious?"

And she, of course, burst out laughing. "Certainly not! Good Lord. You utter ninny." She raised the hose again, and he shut the window. Water splashed harmlessly off the glass.

She stuck her tongue out at him. Then she winked, turned, and walked away.

Rahul sighed and turned away too, because it was better than watching her leave like some adoring sap. He pushed his now-dry glasses onto his face and returned to the chair he'd vacated.

Eugene came back moments later, carrying two glasses of pink, fizzy liquid. He took one look at Rahul, raised his brows, and said, "Bloody hell. What's happened to you?"

Rahul wondered how the man would react if he replied, *"Your daughter."*

———

He must be hallucinating.

The day had seemed to stretch on forever—but not in a bad way. He'd been with Jas, and her dad was actually alright, and she had a snooker room, so not in a bad way at all. But it had been so hot, and the sun had set so late... maybe he had heatstroke.

Yeah. He had heatstroke, and now he was hallucinating.

He thought he saw Jasmine standing over him, shaking him gently awake, in a paper-thin vest and tiny shorts that might as well have been underwear. The vest was red with a sunshine-yellow circle in the centre. The words *Hakuna Matata* were printed across the circle in bold black letters. That seemed an odd touch for a hallucination, but the mind was a wonderful thing.

"Rahul," she whispered. "Come on."

He blinked. "Come where?"

"Outside."

Ah. This probably wasn't a hallucination after all. If it were, she'd be crawling into bed with him, not yanking him out of it.

Reality rushed in like liquid concrete, solidifying in seconds and depressingly grey. He dragged himself up into a sitting position, and the thin sheet covering his chest fell into his lap. Then he remembered he was naked and pulled the sheet up. "Close your eyes."

She smirked, and he could've sworn she was about to say something. Something about the day they didn't talk about. Something about the fact that she'd seen it all before. But she didn't. She just gave him one of those impossible smiles and turned with over-dramatic flare.

Rahul snatched a pair of shorts from the end of the bed and put them on, because he knew she was impatient when she got an idea in her head. "Okay. Ready."

She faced him with a grin and took his hand. His heart stuttered.

Control.

As she pulled him through the maze-like marble hallways, he whispered, "Why are we doing this in the middle of the night?"

"For maximum adventure points," she whispered back.

Which made no sense, but he enjoyed the confidence with which she wielded her nonsense.

It was summer-cool outside, refreshing and mild with a begonia-scented breeze. They ran barefoot through the grass, even though they had no reason to be barefoot and no reason to run. He had no idea where they were or which way they were headed, but he trusted her.

When they turned into the corner of the mammoth garden that she called hers, he stopped in his tracks.

She hadn't been wrong. This place *was* something. It was more than something.

Tiny fairy-lights were wound through every tree branch, along every stalk and by every bloom. The flowers that closed under the moonlight were transformed, and those that remained open were enhanced. In the star-dusted shadows, the garden seemed like something better than reality.

He looked at Jasmine and found her watching him with a quiet smile.

"You were right," he said.

"I always am." She pulled him down onto the grass, and he shouldn't have allowed it—and he certainly shouldn't have thought about the last time she'd pushed him to the ground—but it was Jasmine, so he did, he did, he did.

They lay side by side, and he didn't even think about the fact that a thousand midnight bugs could be eating them both alive right now. When she pointed a finger at the deep velvet of the sky, he looked.

"Let's make constellations," she said.

"I don't really know any."

"Neither do I." There was laughter in her voice. "That's why we make them up. See that?" She lifted a hand. He squinted, tried to figure out exactly which of the stars she was pointing at, and failed.

But still, he said, "Yeah."

"And that one... and that one..." She pointed twice more.

He murmured agreeably.

"Take it back to the first one aaaand... It's a tea cup!"

Rahul stared. He stared some more. Then he said, "You're full of shit."

"Where's your imagination?" She propped herself up on one elbow and turned to grin at him. "You try."

So he did.

He wasn't sure how long they wasted pointing at patterns only they could see, or how they moved closer, or when she slid into his lap. It was easier to follow her line of sight if he pushed her hair out of the way and pressed his cheek to hers, so he did. And it was easier for her to show him exactly what she meant if she held his hand and used his finger to point, so she did.

In-between stargazing, they spoke about her house, about her dad, about the things they'd done that day. Rahul was leaving in a week, going to his own home. Jasmine lived on the outskirts of the county, and his family lived on the other side of the city, so this felt something like a holiday.

"You should come to mine," he said. "I mean, our house isn't big like yours. You'd have to share a room. I don't know if you'd want to do that."

She snorted. He felt the sound as much as he heard it, because her back was pressed against his chest. "You think I'm too good to share a room?"

"Not exactly what I meant." But he couldn't stop the humour from creeping into his voice. "You are kind of a princess, though."

"True," she quipped. Then her tone grew slightly more serious. "We weren't always rich, you know."

That was interesting—not in itself, but because Jasmine

didn't talk about the past. She didn't even hint about it. Ever. He tried to remain relaxed, tried not to push. "Oh?"

"Mmm. When I was little, my dad had already started his business, but it hadn't taken off. So we still lived in a council house in Bulwell."

He didn't react at the name of one of the city's rougher boroughs. But he did wonder about her accent. "Was it always just the two of you?"

She stilled for a moment. Everything about her seemed to hesitate. If he put a hand over her heart, would he feel it pause?

Then she shrugged. "No. I had, you know, a mother."

Had.

"Is she...?"

"She's not dead," Jasmine said bluntly, her tone somewhere between amusement and impatience. "She's in Malaga, I believe."

"Malaga?"

"Yes. With lots and lots of Dad's money, thanks to the magic of divorce and his soft and mushy heart."

"I see."

She turned to look at him, her hair brushing his face. "Do you? Do you see?"

Rahul shrugged. "I might see more, if you wanted to explain it."

She'd been ready to argue. He could see all the signs. Sometimes, she didn't want to tease and laugh and flirt with anything that moved; sometimes she wanted to lash out. He understood that. He didn't mind that. He'd try to give her that, when it seemed necessary. But not right now.

She sighed, and the tension drained out of her. She relaxed back into his arms and said, "I always thought, maybe my mum shouldn't have had me. Like, not that I shouldn't exist! Just that *she* shouldn't have had me. I don't think she wanted to. It was probably an accident. And then every time she saw me she just felt pissed off and fed up and trapped. I know she wanted to leave, but she liked Dad's money. In the end, he made her go anyway."

Rahul's throat felt tight. The matter-of-fact way in which she recited the words made him want to punch something. He tried to imagine feeling like his mother—his *mother*, who had always loved him and cleaned his scraped knees and read him bedtime stories—didn't want him. He failed. It was unimaginable.

"So then what?" he asked. "Your parents divorced, and she... went to live in Malaga?"

"Not exactly. They were separated for a while. She used to come and pick me up on weekends. But then she got this boyfriend..."

He did not like the sound of this.

Jasmine swallowed. He wanted to say something comforting, but he had a feeling she'd react badly. So he caught her hand and held it tight, and buried his face in her hair, and waited.

"She got this boyfriend, and she kind of just... lost interest. In me, I mean. She wasn't that interested to start with, but at least she pretended to be, sometimes. For a while. Then..." Her voice trailed off. She shrugged. "Nothing. She ended up telling Dad that she didn't want to see me anymore. But he didn't tell me that until...Well, until I was fifteen, and I asked him about it. I don't think he wanted to tell me at all, but he has this thing about lying."

This thing about lying—presumably, preferring to tell the truth. What an utterly Jasmine way of phrasing it.

Rahul looked down at the woman in his arms, barefoot and barely dressed and achingly vulnerable in a way he'd never seen before. He had no idea how to tell her that she was perfect.

How to tell her that just because some woman—admittedly, a woman who was 'supposed' to love her—hadn't, it didn't mean she had to be afraid all the time.

Because she was. He hadn't realised until this very moment, but now things were clicking into place. She was.

"Jas," he said softly.

She huffed. "Don't start feeling sorry for me. Maybe my mother didn't want me or whatever, but my dad's a doll, right?"

He couldn't help but laugh at that. "Succinct."

"I know." She looked up at him, and the sadness in her eyes was suffocating, but she was still smiling. Always, she was smiling. He liked that about her, but he didn't like it in this minute.

"You know it's okay sometimes, to..." He trailed off, searched for the right words, and came up with something woefully inaccurate. "It's okay not to be okay."

For a moment, he thought they might maintain this openness, this raw, electric connection. It felt slightly dangerous, but it also felt necessary. He wanted her to feel things, and he wanted her to tell him all about it.

But in the end, she didn't, and he wasn't surprised. She rolled her eyes and deadpanned, "Deep, man."

Well. He knew not to push. She didn't respond well to pushing. So he laughed and pinched her arm and said, "Shut up."

She laughed too, and he could almost believe in it.

Chapter 6

Now

"You," Jasmine declared, "will die of boredom—*or* accelerated old age."

Rahul didn't look up from his tub of protein powder. Infuriating man. He tossed a scoop of pink whey into his plastic shaker and murmured, "You have a crystal ball over there?"

She raised her almost-empty bowl of cereal. "Does this count?"

"How would that count?" He finally looked up. He was standing at the kitchen counter and she was lounging on the sofa. She could practically feel his exasperation.

"I'm reading the dregs of milk," she said, "like tea leaves."

He sighed and shook his head.

It was barely ten o'clock on a Saturday morning, and judging by the sweat gilding his biceps, he'd already been to the gym. All he fucking did was work and work out. Honestly, he was lucky to be friends with her. She appeared to be his only entertainment.

Well, except for his *other* friend, her secret rival. Mitch. But Mitch was a different sort of friend, she told herself. Totally didn't count. She was definitely the supreme.

Jasmine, childish? Never.

"You're always doing something," she said. Then, clarifying: "Something useful. The gym, the office, whatever."

"You know why I go to the gym," he said. Avoiding the question.

Wait—she hadn't actually asked a question. She wasn't sure how to phrase it. She wasn't sure what she was getting at.

"And I like work," he added, as if that was that.

She mumbled a vague reply and decided to return to the issue at a later date. Recently, she'd found herself accidentally stumbling into emotional conversations with her friends. Something about Rahul's stiffness told her this might turn out to be one of those conversations.

If her instincts were correct, she needed tea first.

He poured water into his little plastic shaker, then came into the living room as he screwed on the lid. He was wearing basketball shorts and one of those T-shirts with ripped off sleeves. He should've looked vaguely ridiculous, especially since he was also wearing his silver-framed glasses and had scraped his lovely hair back with that awful pomade.

But he was a painfully handsome man, the kind of handsome that pulled anything off. Thick, black brows that always slashed into a frown, a strong nose, a square jaw permanently shadowed by stubble—no matter how often he shaved. Plus, he was kind of ripped. Her gaze hovered over his broad shoulders, focused on the beads of sweat decorating his brown skin.

"By the way," he said, "don't forget about your surprise."

Jasmine blinked. Had she missed something? It was entirely possible that she had. Her brain felt slightly fuzzy. Too much gin last night. She frowned up at him. "Surprise?"

"Yeah." He shook his watery, pink concoction. "I won last night, remember?"

No, Jasmine didn't remember. She didn't remember

anything beyond going home after a rather boring argument with Paul—or possibly Peter. Something beginning with a *P*. Her brain hadn't seen fit to show her anything after that, and she hadn't bothered to go looking. Now she cast her mind back, and found...

Oh. Oh dear.

Jasmine's mouth felt oddly dry.

Rahul grinned. "Yeah, you remember." He took a sip of his protein shake.

She found herself staring at his biceps. Specifically, at the way the muscle shifted under his gleaming brown skin as he raised the protein shake to his lips. And then, like a humming-bird, her focus flitted from his biceps to the aforementioned lips —to the way they pursed around the plastic. They looked... soft.

Thinking about Rahul's lips was definitely preferable to thinking about how pathetic she'd been last night, right?

Actually, she wasn't sure. It was a very close call.

"You still up for it?" he said.

Up for it? She was still trying to process the fact that she'd practically begged him for attention. Like a *child*. Holy shit. Was it possible for embarrassment to cause vomiting? Because her cereal was sitting in her stomach like ashes right now. Not even good, crisp ashes, like the ones burnt paper made. More like the thick, white fluff in a chainsmoker's ashtray.

Her mother's ashtray used to look like that.

Yeah, she was definitely going to be sick.

"Jas. You okay?"

When she surged to her feet, Rahul reached for her. She jerked away.

That didn't appear to perturb him.

"Hey," he said, his voice firmer now. He came to stand in front of her, put his hands on her shoulders, and said, "Look at me."

She dragged her gaze from the floor up to his eyes, the living room light gleaming off the corner of his glasses.

"What the fuck?" he said, but while the words were harsh, his voice was achingly gentle. "What was that? You just went all... pale."

She managed to choke out a laugh. "Pale? Are you sure?"

"It's a relative term." He smiled slightly, and she could see relief on his face. "Seriously, Jas, are you okay?"

What was the appropriate answer? *I just had heart palpitations through sheer embarrassment, and my skin feels too tight for my body, but I'm better than I was thirty seconds ago?*

No, that wouldn't do.

She forced herself to shrug. "I'm fine. Hung over."

He looked skeptical, but he didn't push. Somehow, Rahul knew when he shouldn't push.

"Are you... busy today?" he asked carefully. Giving her an out.

But she set her shoulders and shook her head. "No. Of course not. Let the surprises commence."

"Don't get overexcited," he murmured dryly. "It's a surprise, singular."

"Oh, dear," she said. "I'm disappointed already."

He snorted and tweaked her nose. She flicked his ear. He pinched her cheek. And she turned her head and bit the heel of his hand, and then wondered what the fuck she was doing, and almost passed out in relief when he just laughed and pulled away.

She was going to have to watch herself. After all, Rahul was the only person who'd ever crossed over her carefully curated social categories. He'd gone from *I'd fuck you* to *Let's be friends*, completely bypassing *I hate your guts, you can choke.*

Those were all the categories she had. He'd exhausted her

options. But sometimes she thought that, if he asked, she'd build a whole new one, just for him.

———

Rahul bit back a smile as Jas breathed, "You can't be serious!"

She didn't say it as if she were pissed, or outraged, or even amused. No; she was happy. Really happy.

For all her airs and graces, Jasmine was pretty easy. All he had to do was take her to IKEA.

He parked up and gave her a smile. "Surprise."

"You're the worst." Still grinning. "I hate you."

"Mmhm. I thought you'd want to do that thing you do with your room."

She arched her brows, amusement dancing in her eyes. *That thing I do?*

"Yeah. Cover it in girly shit. Let's go." He grabbed his keys and got out before she could whack him.

Truthfully, Rahul was not an IKEA fan. In fact, he considered it the fourth circle of hell.

When he'd found out about Jasmine's weird love of the place, he'd been more than a little confused. But, for some reason, she liked wandering through the enormous building, looking at all the fake rooms. And she liked buying useless, pretty knick-knacks and covering her space in them.

The room he'd given her wasn't very *Jasmine*. She was only there temporarily, but something in him rebelled at the idea of Jas laying down to sleep in a room that was all dull and boring and him, instead of bright and vibrant and her.

He wasn't doing too much, he told himself. He was just trying to cheer her up. He was making up for his behaviour this week.

And not just because the fact that he'd upset her cut through his gut like a knife.

Anyway, she'd need new crap for her room at Tilly's. Apparently, they'd given her a solid four week return date. All was on track.

Rahul ignored the way that information squeezed at his heart.

"Look at this!" Jas appeared at his elbow with a gold table clock in her hand. She had a thing for clocks.

He nodded with what he hoped was enthusiasm. "That's nice."

"Right? Don't you think it goes with the dome?"

He looked dubiously at the little glass dome she'd already put in her basket. He had no idea what it could possibly be for, or how it went with the clock in any way. He looked back at her face, alive with excitement, and said, "Yeah. For sure."

She put the clock in the basket and disappeared again.

Rahul wandered around the general area, careful not to turn any corners without her or get otherwise lost in the IKEA maze. He had no idea where Jas was at any given time, until she reappeared beside him with an armful of lavender feathers or a glittery cushion, plopped them into the basket, and dragged him on.

She was definitely having fun, though.

Until they came to the kids' section.

Jasmine appeared by his side with more stuff to put in the basket. She looked up with a smile at the next step in their IKEA adventure... and faltered.

Rahul frowned, trying to see whatever it was that had made her face fall. There were two entrances into this part of the IKEA maze; one heavily decorated walkway, and one little slide that a ton of kids were lining up to use again and again. Beyond the walkway, he could see piles of colourful children's furniture, plus an army of actual children, supervised by a worryingly small number of adults.

It looked like the best part so far, to his eyes. Put him in mind of a holiday at home with all his sisters and their broods present. He looked at Jas and found her jaw set as if they were walking off the edge of a cliff.

Whenever he brought her home for dinner or various family celebrations, she'd stay in the kitchen with his mother to clean up. He assumed it was because the two of them got on so well. But now it occurred to him that he'd never seen Jas play with any of his nieces or nephews.

He put a hand on her shoulder and felt her jump.

"You okay?" He asked.

She laughed nervously. "Fine. Just thinking."

"About?"

"Nothing." She'd shoved her hair up into an enormous, puffy ponytail—to concentrate, she said. Now she tugged nervously at the strands. "Shall we go a different way round?"

He raised his brows. "What, just to avoid the kids?"

She snorted. "Not to avoid them. I just meant... you know, we don't want anything in there."

"I don't know. There's a lot of glitter. You like glitter."

"Piss off," she said, then slapped a hand over her mouth. "Oh, see? We shouldn't go in there."

"First of all," he said, wrapping a hand around her forearm, "it's the quickest way out of this hellhole."

She gasped. "Hellhole?"

He ignored her, tugging her forwards. "Second of all, I don't think anyone's going to hear you swear over all the damned noise." Because IKEA wasn't quiet at the best of times, but here? The din rose to unbelievable heights.

Jasmine grimaced as he pulled her past the slide. She eyed

the kids around her with something that looked almost like anxiety. Which couldn't possibly be right. Could it?

They made their way through in silence, despite the noise around them. When they finally stepped onto IKEA's usual grey path, Jas released an audible sigh of relief.

Rahul arched a brow as they walked. "I take it you don't want kids."

"I do," she said immediately. She could've punched him in the face and he'd have been less shocked.

They'd never talked about this, but Jasmine... Jasmine was allergic to commitment of any kind. She'd never had a relationship. Not ever. She hadn't been joking, all those years ago, when she'd told him that she didn't date.

She had fun, she fucked, she left.

So it had never occurred to him that she'd want... well, a family. She loved her dad, she kind of liked her dad's wife Marianne, and she cared for her friends. That was it.

He stared at her. Knew he was staring, but couldn't stop. She looked more than a little embarrassed at her words, her eyes skittering away from his. She wasn't even looking around for more random shit to put in the basket. Her hands were folded in front of her, fingers laced together.

"You want kids?" he asked, because he kind of felt like he might have just hallucinated.

"Yeah," she said quietly. "Why wouldn't I?"

Because you avoid human connection almost completely might be a little blunt. Rahul went for humour instead. "So you're taking the sperm donor route, I assume."

She smiled. "Obviously." And then, after a pause, she added, "Let me know if you'd like to volunteer."

He coughed. Cleared his throat. "What?"

"Well," she said seriously, "I don't know where I stand on

the nature/nurture thing, personality-wise, but physically you've got a lot going for you."

"*What?*"

"Solid immune system, good teeth..." She gave him a sly look. "You know. All that."

She was taking the piss. She was taking the piss, but he felt like she had him by the throat, and as fucking always, he liked it. He barely even thought before saying, "So how would I donate?"

She stopped walking. But interrupting the stream of traffic in IKEA was always a bad idea, so Rahul caught her arm and pulled her off onto one of the little side paths.

She looked up at him with wide eyes, her tongue sliding over her lips. She was nervous. That fact sparked through him dangerously. Why would she be nervous with him? Why would she be nervous over a joke?

If there's too much truth hiding here...

He tried to squash the hope. It was beyond ridiculous.

Still, he found himself leaning close, found himself murmuring softly, "Well?"

"I... What?" Her voice sounded hoarse. Her gaze flicked to his mouth, unmistakeable, then snapped back to his eyes. "What do you mean?"

"You want a baby? Tell me how to give you one." He had no idea what the fuck he was saying, or doing, or thinking. His mouth just kept moving, words just kept coming out, and he could barely even regret it. "People do it. We could do it."

He watched her throat shift as she swallowed. He waited, every muscle in his body tense, for the moment when she'd brush him off. When she'd laugh and turn away.

And it came, just like it always did. She stretched her lips into a smile and swatted at his chest, stepping back. "You're ridiculous."

He grinned. It was easy now, hiding the effects of every harsh reality check. "I know," he said, as if he'd been joking. As if he wouldn't give her anything she wanted and enjoy it.

Her smile became a little more real. She pulled him back into the stream of people and said, "You couldn't have kids anyway. You work too much."

Whatever IKEA-induced lunacy had caused him to start this conversation clearly hadn't gone away. Because he found a truthful response tumbling from his lips, one he'd always hidden from Jas. "I have to."

She gave him a sideways sort of look. She was walking more slowly right now than she had since they'd entered the damn building. Jasmine had never been subtle. When she finally said, "And why is that?" she sounded so much like a TV psychologist he had to bite back a laugh.

Then he realised that he was actually going to answer her, and the laughter died in his throat. "You know I've always wanted to be successful. You know I like getting things right."

"I know you like controlling everything because you're too hard on yourself," she said.

He stared down at her. She—what? How the fuck—

"But I think you're worse now. Worse than you used to be."

His throat tightened. He thought he knew what she'd say next, only his instincts must be wrong, *had* to be, because there were things he and Jas didn't talk about. Touches, moments, mistakes they filed away because it was safer. And there was no way she'd pull out one of those moments in the middle of fucking IKEA.

"Since he died," she said softly, "you've been working much too hard."

Rahul let his eyes slide shut for a moment. A tainted sort of relief bloomed inside him. She wasn't going to mention his...

mistake. The thing they never discussed. The thing he'd done the day of Dad's funeral.

But she *was* talking about the death itself.

While they'd walked, the busyness of the store had forced them closer, and their hands had brushed numerous times. So it took him a second or two to register the fact that she was touching him on purpose now, that her fingers were twining with his. He looked at her, and she smiled gently, squeezing his hand.

He was clearly weak, because that was all it took to release the prickly knot of pain in his chest.

"I'm the head of the family now," he said quietly. He wasn't sure she'd hear him over the general noise of the shop, but somehow she did.

"That would be your mother," she said.

"No."

"You're not even the eldest."

"You know what Dad would say. I'm the head of the family."

For once, she didn't argue about patriarchal norms or whatever. She just gave a slow nod, because he supposed she must know that, principles aside, this was his reality.

They walked in silence for a while, hands swinging gently between them, before she said, "Your mother wouldn't like this."

"I know," he gritted out, his jaw tight. "I—I feel..."

When he didn't finish, she didn't push. Just waited.

"I feel guilty. I feel guilty for feeling under pressure, because she didn't do anything to cause it. Neither did my sisters. They aren't asking me to take the responsibility. I just... did it. I feel it. I act on it."

It had been less than a year since Dad died, but Rahul had slid into his place almost seamlessly. He wasn't just himself now; he was a role model to his younger sisters, a support system for the older ones. He was the person his mother sat with quietly when she wanted to cry or fall apart, but couldn't let herself. He cushioned every blow he could for his family, and always he felt the drive to become more successful—more powerful—so that he could do a better job of it. Everything had to be right.

He'd always thought like that. *Everything has to be right*. But Jasmine wasn't imagining the fact that he'd gotten worse since Dad died. What had been motivational was now a steel collar.

The only time he didn't feel it was when he was with her.

She was watching him thoughtfully, familiar calculation in her eyes. Trying to figure out a way to fix him, as was her usual style. He didn't mind. She'd never guess that she managed it, if temporarily, just by standing at his side.

They were nearing the end of IKEA's path when she said, "Your dad would be really proud of you." Then she released his hand and walked ahead to check out a chest of drawers she couldn't possibly need.

And he stood, frozen, irritated customers manoeuvring past him with barely-hidden glares. He would move, he told himself, in just a minute. Just a second. Or however long it took for him to stop feeling like those words had burned him alive and made him new.

"Your dad would be really proud of you."

———

She caught him after IKEA, when he was still dizzy with the sheer amount of crap they'd bought, and cajoled him into poker with M&Ms as chips. They played for time again. She was a shark and a sugar addict and he knew from the start she would get exactly what she wanted. Which she did.

So the next day—Sunday—it was her turn to surprise him.

"*This* is how you're using your win?" Rahul stared at the items cluttering his kitchen counter. A small mountain of junk food—microwave popcorn, Ben & Jerry's, tortilla chips, and a six pack of Pepsi—stared back.

Jasmine drank Pepsi instead of Coke because, apparently, it was Beyoncé-approved.

"Yep." She flashed a cheerful grin at him and waved the DVD in her hand. "Double feature, baby."

"That's way more than an hour."

"So was IKEA, if we're being pedantic. But my hope is that you'll be having so much fun, you'll forget all about the time limit." She tapped the plastic-wrapped case against his chest. It contained, according to the cover, a copy of both *Lara Croft* films. *Tomb Raider,* and... whatever the other one was called. He couldn't quite make it out.

He could already tell that Jasmine wouldn't change her mind about this—but he felt the need to put up a token protest anyway. "I believe you won an hour of *fun.* Not an hour of me eating my bodyweight in saturated fat."

She widened her eyes. "But that's what fun is all about."

For a moment, his mind got caught up in the look of mocking innocence on her face. She captivated him at completely inappropriate moments, for no reason he could discern—not necessarily when she was prettiest. Just when she was completely herself.

"Anyway," she said, her easy smile returning. "Do you have any cheese in this house?"

He forced his mind to process her words instead of getting caught up in the way her mouth moved. Then he realised that she was starting the fucking cheese argument again. "You know I don't."

"Well aren't you lucky, then?" She held up the Tesco bag

from which she'd produced all that junk food and pulled another item from its depths. "I picked some up!"

Rahul sighed. "Why?"

"Because you can't have nachos without cheese, dinkus. Call it a cheat day."

He didn't do cheat days.

Although, if he *did*, he supposed Sunday was as good a day as any. And maybe he should. Maybe it would be fun to relax, and eat cheese, and watch shit.

But he certainly wasn't admitting that to Jas, because he'd never hear the bloody end of it. He'd spent years telling her that cheese was practically poisonous.

Instead, he rolled his eyes and leant against the counter. "I thought you were working today. When did you get time to plan out an evening of torture?"

"I wasn't working," she said, stowing the ice cream in the freezer. "I was volunteering at work."

"Isn't that the same thing, since you work at a charity?"

She rolled her eyes as she emerged from the freezer. "Sure. Only I don't get paid."

He resisted the urge to point out that she was barely paid anyway. She had a first class law degree and could probably get any job she wanted, yet chose to remain at a place that offered, amongst other things, pro bono rep to those having trouble with housing.

But she didn't like to talk about her job. She came over all embarrassed and uncomfortable if anyone dared to suggest that she was doing a good thing. So he dropped the subject and said, "*Tomb Raider?*"

She smiled slightly. "Let's do it."

Jasmine sat cross-legged on the sofa like a little kid while he fed the disc into the DVD player. By the time he sat down beside her, she'd already devoured a significant amount of the cheesy nachos they'd made.

"This film was, like..." She chomped on another nacho. "My spiritual awakening."

He gave her a sideways look as Lara Croft's mansion came into view. "I hope you're not referring to all the magical brown children and the exotic monks."

She snorted. "Shut up. I'm talking about the power of tits."

"How is that spiritual?"

"You don't think tits are spiritual?" She smiled slowly. "That's disappointing."

He licked his lips, then felt painfully conscious of the action. Couldn't help it. But he tried his very fucking best not to look at her chest, or think about the dark shadows beneath her T-shirt that might be her nipples. He waited for her to laugh, or flick the back of his head, or call him *kitten*. She didn't. Her gaze held his, and he saw what he always saw there: challenge.

But it felt different. It felt dangerous.

Then she blinked, and in a sweep of dark lashes, whatever he'd seen disappeared. A smile curved her lips, and she turned back to the TV. "Camera quality really has improved, huh?"

He managed to grunt something that sounded vaguely like agreement. Then he grabbed a bowl of popcorn from the coffee table and proceeded to stuff as much as possible into his mouth.

That seemed like the safest course of action.

Chapter 7

Now

The TV had turned itself off. To save energy, he supposed.

They'd fallen asleep. They must have, because outside, the city was early-morning quiet. The kind that only existed between blackest night and breaking dawn, all soft and shadowed and echoing.

Rahul kept his breathing slow and even, because he knew from experience that Jas slept light. And she was asleep on top of him, her body sprawled over his, the weight comforting and warm. How they'd gotten like this, he had no idea.

Maybe, sometime during the first film, he'd gotten carried away and let himself lean a little too close to her. And maybe, as they started the second and laughed about Lara's choice of wetsuit, she'd crossed the last of the space between them to let her head rest on his shoulder.

She'd been tired, clearly.

Now her head lay on his chest and strands of her hair brushed his face, tickling. That was probably what had woken him up. He was in two minds about the whole 'being awake' thing.

See, on the one hand, he had work tomorrow—or rather, today. Spending all night on the sofa would land him with a cricked neck and a late start, and really, he was lucky that his glasses were still safely on his face and completely unbent. Yes; it was better to wake now, to nudge Jas into the land of the living and head to bed.

Separately. They'd go to separate beds. Obviously.

So he should've been glad to wake up. But a worryingly large part of him was... pissed. Because she was so fucking perfect, her skin warm against his, her hand curled around his biceps as if she were actually holding him. Because his cock was half-hard and the pressure of her weight was delicious, and now he felt guilty for even acknowledging the fact, but fuck it. Because—this was his favourite part—his hand was resting against her arse.

If he'd been asleep, his hand could've stayed there. He wouldn't have been conscious to enjoy it, but some part of his sleeping mind would've known, he was sure. The part of him that had secretly, shamefully lusted after Jasmine Allen for years would've rejoiced and sent him wonderful dreams involving bottom-heavy, curly haired, brown-eyed women.

But he wasn't asleep.

Rahul moved his hand to the safe zone of her lower back and stifled a sigh. He already missed her arse.

And of course, that tiny movement fucked up the entire, delicate arrangement. Because seconds later Jasmine gave an odd little huff, the sound muffled against his chest, and began to stir. Rahul stared at the shadowed ceiling above, because if she woke up to find him staring at *her*, it might push their current position from awkward to disturbing.

Although, he supposed, she was the one lying on top of him. Technically, he was innocent in all this. The fact that he happened to be enjoying it was neither here nor there.

At least his dick was calming down. Maybe she wouldn't notice.

He felt the exact moment when she woke up completely and realised where she was. Or rather, who she was on top of. Jasmine's whole body stiffened for one taut heartbeat—but then she relaxed. Softened against him, just as she had in sleep.

Rahul abandoned his study of the ceiling. He looked down to find those big, brown eyes staring at him, slightly narrowed with sleep, fine lines fanning the corners.

She had a crooked little smile on her face, nothing like the biting smirk he'd expected. Then she pressed a kiss to his chest, just above the neckline of his T-shirt. Which didn't mean anything; she kissed him all the time. On the cheek, or the forehead, or the back of his hand.

But not on the mouth, he remembered. He'd been inside her, but he'd never kissed her on the mouth.

Don't think about that.

"Jas?" he murmured, his voice hushed like the pre-dawn city.

"Rahul," she whispered back, sleepiness making a soft word softer. Like a cat, she stretched, all smooth and sinuous. She held his gaze as her curves rolled over him. She was like a river, forging its path through earth and stone; so soft, so fluid and seemingly gentle, but powerful enough to mould the world to her will. Jasmine knew how to get what she wanted.

God, he loved her. He loved her.

He didn't want to. He shouldn't. It was useless. It was true.

She was looking at him with that pure focus that made him feel like the most powerful thing in the world. He knew it was an illusion—that it was just one of the many things that made her magnetic. She picked up every needle in the haystack and she didn't even try. She couldn't help it. Rahul told himself this, and yet, under her gaze he became a king.

His hand felt too big and too clumsy against the small of her back, even though there was plenty of space for it. If he moved that hand lower again, where he'd found it when he'd first woken, would she object? An hour ago he might've said yes. Now he saw something bright in her eyes, bright like the spots of light dancing across the darkened city. What did that mean?

He tangled his fingers in her T-shirt, as if that would give him more of her—the kind of more he needed. It wouldn't, but sometimes desperate people tried pointless things because it was better than sitting and wanting. He thought, *Kiss me. Fucking kiss me. Give me something, give me a reason, give me permission, and I'll give you everything I have.*

Maybe she heard him somehow. Maybe she saw it on his face because he was fucking obvious. Either way, the result was the same. She trailed her fingers up his arm, and he felt fire-works spark and fly in her wake. His core tightened and his balls grew heavy, just because she'd touched his bloody arm. He had no idea how she did this to him, had never understood and doubted he ever would, but he didn't want her to stop.

And yet, she did. Her weight shifted as she leaned towards him, raising her chin until their mouths were level. Close. So damn close. So close that there was no space for light between them, so close that he barely saw her in the almost-darkness. He felt her, though. Felt her like a promise. And then she stopped.

His pulse was racing, his blood burning its way through his veins like wildfire, his nerves singing in anticipation, but he held himself still. Kept himself quiet. Had to be sure.

She licked her lower lip again, the tip of her tongue sliding over that plump curve. Ripe fruit. He wanted to sink his teeth into it.

Her whisper sliced through the night air like a knife. "God, Rahul. You're so... *fuck.*" Her fingers caught his T-shirt, tightened as if to pull him closer.

Rahul told himself, *Control*, only he'd lost the meaning of the word somewhere along the line; he didn't recognise it anymore. So instead he thought, *Fuck it*.

He closed the space between them. His lips slanted over hers, barely touching, and that was enough to steal the air from his lungs. God. *God*. In the silence and the shadows, the brush of their lips felt like something holy. Like prayers whispered into the earth, like purifying flames. This was the closest he might ever be to perfection.

But no. She pulled away, laughed softly. Whispered, a dare in her voice, "Like you mean it, my love."

She was fucking impossible, and *that* was perfection.

Rahul slid a hand into her hair and pulled her back to his mouth. What was control, anyway? There was only one thing he desired, one thing he needed. *More*.

This time, when their lips met, the flames didn't purify so much as devour. He kissed her hard and ruthless, the way he'd always dreamed, and she responded like a fantasy except it was so much better—*so* much better—because it was real and it was Jasmine and he couldn't fucking believe it. She kissed him as if she were starving. He'd die just to let her consume him. Her breath came in short, sharp little gasps, and her whole body rocked into his, the pressure painfully sweet against his aching cock.

Her hair felt like a raincloud in his hand, thick and cool and fresh. He tightened his grip because right now, for who knew how fucking long, he could. He *could*. As long as she kissed him like this, she was his. His other hand slid from her back to her arse, and the ache in his cock sharpened. She was wearing a skirt; she always wore skirts. So he dragged up the fabric, and she arched her back as if in invitation, and nothing had ever turned him on more in his fucking life. Nothing except the sight he'd never forgotten, the sight of her sinking onto his cock.

He already knew that whatever this moment was, it would ruin him all over again.

Rahul slid his palm up the bare skin of her thigh, traversed the soft ripples of her flesh until he reached heaven. Grabbing one cheek, sinking his fingers into the ripe curve of her arse, actually made him moan against her lips. Fuck. He could feel the fabric of her knickers, cotton and unexpectedly plain and in his fucking way. He pushed as much aside as he could, and she laughed against his mouth.

"Just take them off," she whispered.

He shook his head, though he burned to do just that. "If there's something you want me to do," he murmured, "ask for it. Nicely."

He expected her to laugh or tell him to fuck off, but Jas never did what he expected.

"Take them off," she ordered softly. "Make me come. Kiss me until we fall asleep." She was slightly breathless, but there was no laughter in her voice, no bright, teasing spark. She recited her little list with something like desperation, and she moved as though she couldn't be still. Rocked against him, rolling her hips over his erection.

He caught her chin in his hand, held her tight because he wanted all of her formidable focus. "Still demanding, even when you do it sweetly. Do you know how to ask, love?"

"No." She bit her lip.

"That's okay." Rahul's heart seemed to melt in his chest, the soft warmth taking precedence over the need in his gut. He kissed her gently, almost chastely. "I'll show you." He hadn't imagined showing her anything. He hadn't expected Jasmine Allen to want or need a thing from him, but the fact that she might was sending a surge of electricity through his veins.

He sat up, pulling her with him. She clutched his shoulders, ended up straddling his lap. His cock was screaming for relief, straining against his waistband, but he couldn't even bring himself to touch it because that way lay madness. Instead, he focused on the woman in his arms and how much he wanted her. Wanted to make her smile, to make her sigh, to make her scream.

He raised a hand to her face, ran his thumb over her cheek. "Asking," he whispered, "is hard. Taking is easy. Doing is easy. But asking for what you want... asking is showing someone everything, and trusting they won't use it against you. Asking is about feeling safe."

"I know that." The words were ragged.

"You don't feel safe with me?"

There was a pause. Then she said, "Not with anyone."

His thumb traced the curve of her lips. "You don't want it like this?"

"I want it like *you*. I want it like last time. Do you remember?"

"You think I don't remember? You think I could forget?" His head fell forward to rest against hers. "You are unforgettable. You must know that, Jasmine."

She swallowed hard. Then she caught his hand, the one sitting at her waist, and moved it lower. Over the swell of her belly, the gathered-up fabric of her skirt, until his palm came to rest against her mound.

Rahul squeezed his eyes shut as the last of the blood in his brain evacuated. He couldn't stop his hand from moving if he'd tried; couldn't stop himself from feeling every inch of her, from stroking her plump folds through the fabric of her underwear. She made a soft little noise in the back of her throat, rocking against his palm. *Yes.* That was what he wanted; for her to understand the need, to feel it the way he did. He wanted her hungry.

He shoved his hand beneath the waistband of her knickers,

and then he kissed her. He couldn't get enough of kissing her. He never thought he'd get the chance. As his fingers tangled in her soft curls, as he nudged at the tight little bud of her clit, his tongue slid over hers. She sank her fingers into his hair, and the part of his mind still capable of sensible thought was grateful that he'd done as she always asked; he'd washed 'that shit' out of his hair. Because now she was pulling, hard, and the sharp pain danced down his spine like something heaven-sent.

"You have no idea," he managed to choke out. She kissed him, and he kissed her, and he said between gasping breaths, "*No* idea."

"What?" she panted. Bit his lower lip.

"How much I want you. How much I've wanted you—"

"You can't be serious." She was laughing now, still kissing him, and she'd knocked his glasses almost off his face, but he didn't need to see anyway. Not when he was touching her.

He circled her clit, gave her the firm pressure that made her breath hitch. "Of course I'm fucking serious. Don't say you didn't notice."

She moaned, arched in his arms. "I thought... I mean, you always seem so... Well, I've noticed now."

"I should hope so." He lowered his lips to her throat, tasted her, wanted more. Licked, bit, sucked.

She gasped. "You can't... you can't leave a mark."

He pulled back. "There? Or anywhere?"

"There. Or anywhere someone could see."

"Hmm." He kissed her, quick and hard. "People see quite a lot of you in those dresses."

She snorted. "Are you complaining?"

"Nope. I'll just have to get creative." And he'd enjoy it too. But he hoped, next time she went out barely dressed—next time she walked into a room and made half the occupants fall in love —that they might see his mark on her.

The thought brought his passion to a shuddering stop.

See his mark on her... and then what? Fuck her anyway. Because Jas always got what she wanted, and she'd never wanted to be contained.

"Hey." Her voice interrupted his thoughts, soft and hesitant. "Everything okay?"

He looked up and met her gaze. In the low light, her eyes were gleaming obsidian. He slid his hand out of her underwear, let it rest against her hip. "Jasmine... What are we doing right now?"

She stiffened. He felt every inch of her harden, pull away from him as if repelled. "I think it's rather obvious what we're doing."

"Don't," he said. "Don't do that."

"Do what?" Her weight shifted as she moved to get off him.

He wrapped a hand around her wrist and pulled her back. "*That.* I want to know what you're thinking. I want to be clear. That's all."

She huffed out a quick, sharp breath. But then she stopped herself. He could practically see her cooling down, forcing herself to stay calm. When she finally spoke, her voice was quiet. "I don't know. I don't know what we're doing."

He swallowed down the lump in his throat and tried not to think too hard. Tried to wait for her to work through whatever else she had to say, because her gaze had become vacant and that meant her mind was churning.

"Maybe..." She hesitated. "I've been thinking. And I wondered—I mean, living with you—"

His pulse pounded loud in his ears as she broke off. Trust her to come over all quiet and cautious at the exact moment he was desperate for every word she had.

"Living with you," she said finally, "has made me think that we could try the... erm, the friends with benefits thing."

And there it was. Reality swinging for him like a fist. The hit connected and it fucking hurt. His brain vibrated in his skull. "Friends with... benefits," he repeated dully.

She shrugged. "You know I don't usually... I mean, I don't like to blur lines. But you know what we are. And I want you."

God, what the hell had he been thinking?

Jasmine, that's what. Jasmine and nothing but. So caught up in the way she felt against him, he'd forgotten who she was and how she loved.

Or rather, how *he* loved.

He'd never gotten over her at all, had he?

She must feel him pulling away, even though he hadn't moved yet. His body stayed frozen while his mind raced. What was he supposed to say? *I'm sorry, but I can't handle that. I can't fuck you and leave you alone. I can't touch you and pretend I don't love you. I know what we are, but I wish we were something else entirely.*

He only managed to choke out the very last of his thoughts: "We shouldn't have done this."

She pulled back. Her voice sounded higher than usual and oddly uneven when she said, "What?"

Rahul shook his head, trying to push the starshine from his eyes. Straightened his glasses, cleared his throat, wished his cock wasn't still hard and pulsing beneath her. Wished the memory of her soft, warm pussy against his palm wasn't imprinted on his brain. Wished he'd touched more of her—but no. That would only make things worse.

He scrabbled for some reason, a lie that she'd believe, a lie that wouldn't hurt her. "We shouldn't... complicate things. We're friends. And we're living together."

The words could've come from Jasmine's mouth instead of his—yet he thought, for a moment, that he caught a flash of pain on her face.

Probably a trick of the light.

After a pause, she said, "I don't think it would be complicated. You're a very sensible man."

The unspoken end to that sentence was something along the lines of, *And* I've *never complicated anything in my life*. That was Jasmine. Eternally free. He loved it about her, even if it meant he'd never have her the way he wanted.

In fact, it meant he'd never have her at all. Because one thing Rahul absolutely could not do with this woman was half-measures. If he ever got his hands on Jasmine Allen, for real, he'd be all in.

He didn't have to think too hard to find the next excuse. "I only do exclusive. You know that."

She gave a drawn-out, airy sigh. "I do what I want."

"Exactly," he said, the word firm. "We wouldn't—we wouldn't suit." Biggest fucking lie he'd ever told.

Tension burned through the silence. Then, finally, she said, "Perhaps you're right. Perhaps this was... a mistake."

And he must be the biggest prick in the world, because hearing her say it made him want to argue.

"They're your rules," he said. Pointlessly. Foolishly. "I know you hate blurring lines." Every word tasted like ash in his mouth. Blurring lines? He couldn't even *see* the fucking lines. He'd kissed *her*. He needed *her*. He was the problem, and he wanted to punch a wall.

She gave a laugh that was soft and light and grating to his ears because it wasn't real. He'd watched her deploy that fake charm often enough to know the difference, but she'd never used it on him before. She stood and said with false humour, "You've saved us from ourselves, my grave muffin."

"Jas—"

"It's so late. We should really go to bed."

She was hurt. He wasn't surprised. It was unavoidable.

He still hated it.

But he forced himself to stand and tried to sound convincingly unaffected as he said, "Yes. You're right."

Chapter 8

Four Years Ago

I t had seemed necessary.

Rahul stood by the window of his brand new flat, looking out onto the city below, and repeated that truth to himself. It had seemed necessary. It had *been* necessary. And it had worked. It *had*.

He'd spent two years in London; two years away from home, right after graduation. Ostensibly for a graduate scheme in the City with a top accounting firm—but really, he'd done it to get away from Jasmine.

Or rather, to get away from the fact that he'd fallen quite horribly in love with her.

As plans went, it had been a wild one. But his problem had been extreme, so the solution had to be extreme too. Since they'd met, he'd gone from lust, to infatuation, to soul-destroying, unrequited love—the kind that would've decimated their friendship if she'd ever found out. So he'd done what he had to do. He'd cut himself off. Cold turkey.

His plan had worked. Bit by bit, like the sluggish drip of old blood, he'd gotten over his best friend. He'd gained professional experience, built the foundations of a strong career, made friends with people she'd never even meet. Now he was back home, and he'd spent a week being smothered to death by his family, and decorating his new place with his dad, and—

And he was waiting for her.

When it came, the knock at his door shot through him like an electric shock. He'd been expecting her—had *invited* her— but all of a sudden he felt uncertain. It wasn't like he hadn't seen her over the last two years; he had. Of course he had.

But carefully. He'd seen her very carefully. Never for too long. Never in London, the place that had become his chrysalis. Never alone, because Jasmine alone was a different person entirely, and Jasmine alone was so much harder to resist and so much easier to want, and Jasmine alone felt like his own fucking heart reflected back at him.

No. No, he reminded himself, smoothing back his already-smooth hair. That was then. This was now. He'd cured himself of inconvenient love; he'd done what he had to do. She was just a friend. She was just Jasmine.

He opened the door, and she slammed into him like a heat-wave. His skin tingled as she wrapped her arms around him and squeezed tight.

"You're back," she said, her voice muffled against his chest.

Fuck. He hadn't expected this. For all her casual touches and easy smiles, Jasmine wasn't exactly the sort to act like she'd missed someone.

Even if she had.

The thought struck his heart like an arrow. *What if she had?*

Rahul swallowed and allowed himself to hug her back. Hugging was a friendship thing. Hugging was not inappropriate and would not necessarily lead to awkward feelings.

But as he buried his face in the soft, scented cloud of her hair and breathed deep, his heart seemed to swell.

Friendship, he told himself firmly. He was experiencing feelings of extremely innocent, very platonic, *friendship*.

She pulled back slightly and beamed up at him. "Good Lord! I thought you'd be gone forever! It felt like you were!"

"I told you I'd come home again," he said lightly. "You know Mum would kill me if I ever moved so far away for good."

"True. I'd help her hide the body." She winked at him and stepped aside, wandering off into the flat. "Oh, this is nice," she called from the living room. "But you need candles. Every good flat needs candles. Tea lights! And maybe some plants..."

She wasn't about to feign politeness and let him show her around, then. That pleased him. He'd been worried, somewhere in the back of his mind, that after two years of relatively little contact the connection they'd had would be... cut.

You wanted it cut. At least partially. The part where you felt things she never would.

Regardless of what he'd wanted, it was good to know she hadn't somehow transformed. That the easiness between them hadn't disappeared. That he hadn't ruined the best friendship he'd ever had.

Rahul shut his front door and followed her inside.

She was running her finger over some of the paperbacks on his bookshelf. When he came into the room, she turned a judgemental eye on him—but she didn't say a word about his collection of *James Bond* novels. Which was just as well, since he'd never said a word about all the useless knick-knacks she used to cram into her uni flat.

"What do you think about the tea lights?" she asked.

"No."

"What about a succulent?"

He rolled his eyes. "You know what dad calls this place? He calls it my bachelor pad."

Jasmine snorted. "I see. You're far too masculine for succulents, then." She moved away from the bookcase, stepping closer to him, a little smile on her face.

"Most definitely," he murmured, his eyes tracking her movement. His heart pounding as she came closer.

Stop it, he snapped at his own nervous system. Didn't help. Happiness thrummed through his veins.

"How about a cactus?" she asked lightly. "Much more appropriate, if you want to be all cis-hetero-caveman."

"Because of all the—?"

"Don't be awful." But her grin widened, and she came even closer.

"The pricks?" he finished.

She laughed. Something about the sound brushed away the last vestiges of reserve between them, the hesitance that had formed at the edges of their friendship like cobwebs.

They were less than a foot apart now. Smiling at each other in silence like fools. Her eyes flitted around the room, from him, to the window, to the kitchen just behind him. She rose up on tip-toe and craned her neck, peering over his shoulder.

"Nice table," she said. "Shall we break it in?"

His mind presented him with an image of Jasmine perched on the dark wood, holding out a hand just for him.

He blinked and the image disappeared.

"Yeah," he said, his voice steady. "Let me get the cards."

They were in his room because he'd hidden them from Dad during the move. He wasn't a good Muslim like his father, or a good Hindu like his mother, and everyone knew it. But he did not need the father he worshipped to find out about he and Jasmine's gambling habit.

When he came back from his room with the old, worn deck, she was already sitting at the table, munching a bag of M&Ms. Apparently, she had no problem going through his cupboards.

"Chips," she explained, waving one of the colourful little chocolates.

"You want to play poker?"

"I'm in the mood." She smiled. She'd cut her hair—just a little, but he loved her hair so much it felt like a momentous change. Instead of floating around her shoulders, it bounced around her jaw, the curls seeming even springier. Somehow, the length drew his eyes to her mouth. He had no idea why—no idea how the mysteries of haircuts worked—but it was ruining one of his many don't-look-at-Jas-like-that resolutions.

He hoped her hair would grow fast.

Rahul sat down at the little table, opposite her, and they swapped: she took the cards, he took the M&M's. Because she was a show off, she shuffled like some big-time dealer. "Three hands," she said. Her hands were moving rapidly. She was pulling every trick she knew, it seemed; overhand, sure, along with the dovetail and the kutti.

She nodded down at the M&Ms. "Do your thing."

Right. Rahul was faster at sorting their pretend chips, because he had an odd ability. He could look at a group of things and know, without counting, how many items were there. He could look at twenty dots on a page and say, *Twenty*.

The minute Jas had found out, she'd become mildly obsessed with making him perform. He hated doing it for other people. He liked doing it for her because she acted like it was a skill instead of an unnatural ability.

He emptied about half the pack, split them, and pushed hers across the table.

"How many?"

"Twenty-eight each." He put five of his M&Ms in the centre of the table. "Your deal."

She put a card down in front of him, put one down for herself. Repeated the action.

"What are we playing for?" he asked.

"What do you want?"

"How about... some of those caramel things your dad makes?" Eugene Allen's super secret dessert, which he only wheeled out for birthdays and Christmas.

Jasmine rolled her eyes. "Fine. In the spirit of your bet, should I win, I require some of your mother's dosa."

"I'm sure that can be arranged." He checked his cards. A pair of queens.

She looked at hers, and then her dancing, midnight eyes met his. Her cat-got-the-cream look could be an act. Could also be pleasure over the game.

Or even pleasure that he was home at last, for good. He'd known, over the years, that he was hurting her. With every visit he didn't make, every call he didn't take, he was hurting her. But he'd had to do it.

And now look at them. Sitting down, playing like the old friends they were, and he didn't want her at all. Not even a little bit. Not even when she tapped the cards against the soft pillow of her lower lip. Not even when she gave him a sphinx-like look he could never hope to decipher because she was so bloody good at this shit.

No; he didn't want Jasmine anymore. He'd definitely done the right thing.

He laid out his bet and she matched it with a feline sort of smile.

"You didn't improve your pokerface in London," she murmured. "I thought you might return with a few more skills. Like, I don't know—the ability to tell a lie."

He raised the bet, flicking a few more M&Ms into the centre of the table. "Isn't honesty a virtue?"

"So you're virtuous now?"

"Maybe."

She reached out, picked up a few of his makeshift chips, and tossed them into her mouth.

"Jas," he said, his tone warning.

She smiled. "Sorry, buttercup."

He rolled his eyes and took more sweets from the bag.

Jas called, then dealt the flop. Three cards, face up, in the centre of the table: a jack of spades, a four of hearts, a six of hearts.

Hmm. This could go either way for him, really.

Jas was smirking slightly, twisting one of her curls around her finger. Sometimes her hair looked black, but when she stretched it out like that, he could see all the colours at play; deep chestnut and cool earth, with spider-fine flashes of bronze.

She arched a brow. "Rahul?"

Right. Right. "Five," he said, and pushed his M&Ms forward.

She smiled slowly and said in her silkiest voice, "Are you sure about that?"

He gave her a hard look. "Do you really think that *thing* you do will work on me right now?"

"Thing?" she echoed, her smile widening. And then, as if the significance had just hit her: "*Right now?*"

Oops.

Rahul leant back in his seat and folded his arms, keeping his face blank. In what he hoped were dry, long-suffering tones, he said, "Stop fishing for compliments."

She ignored him, of course. "I have a thing?"

"You know you have a thing."

"And it works on you? Rahul Khan, Master of Wisdom and Reason?"

"Now you're just being obnoxious."

"I'm always obnoxious, love. I thought you knew me." She grinned. She was so fucking gorgeous.

Control.

"Come on, Jas. Bet."

She winked, matched his bet, and laid out the turn card. Queen of spades.

Well, fuck it. Without a word, he pushed ten of his M&Ms into the centre.

She pushed hers in too. "So what did you learn in London, then? Since you didn't improve your pokerface?"

She was just ribbing him. He wasn't *that* bad. "I learned how to use that pesky Accountancy and Finance degree. No big deal."

Her hand hovered over the deck, but she didn't draw. "Did you do what you needed to do? Do you feel better now?"

He froze. His gaze shot to hers. "What?"

She smiled. "Have you met your own ridiculously high standards, now that you've lived, worked and learned in London?"

He relaxed all at once, though he tried not to show it. Didn't want her to realise the tension that had gripped him at her words, at the suspicion that she might somehow *know.*

Of course she didn't know. He'd been so careful. And now he was cured.

"You know me," he murmured. "When it comes to work, I've never quite met my own standards."

She snorted. "That's what you need me for." At his arched brow, she explained, "We balance each other out. Since I have no standards whatsoever."

He didn't like the way she talked about herself sometimes. But she said it with a smile and a wink, and since he wasn't in love with her, he shouldn't want to protect her from every little thing. He shouldn't want to protect her from her own harsh words. So he nodded towards the deck and said, "Draw."

"Nervous?" she asked. And suddenly there was nothing playful in her tone whatsoever; just pure confidence.

She'd nailed him. He knew immediately.

And fuck, he like that. He liked the fact that when it came to games like this, even games that relied on little more than chance, she would almost always screw him into the fucking ground.

"Go on," he said.

She picked up the river card and laid it on the table. Two of hearts. "No shame in folding," she said softly.

As if he'd back down now, when she was watching him like that. He'd never been drunk, but he knew that she was it. She was inebriation. He pushed all his bloody M&Ms towards her, and she matched him.

"Show me what you've got," she said crisply, amusement tugging at the corners of her lips.

He put his cards on the table. He'd had a pair of queens; three of a kind. A decent hand.

But of course, she laid down an ace of hearts and a jack of hearts and said, "Flush."

He sighed. Looked down. For a second, his gaze caught on the delicate curve of her wrists, the smooth, brown skin of her arms, the edge of her scar that was visible. Then he dragged his attention back to the cards. "You played me. Like a fiddle."

"It's what I was born to do."

Oh, she wasn't wrong.

Chapter 9

Now

R ahul woke up naturally and cursed himself for it.

No alarm. Which meant he hadn't set one, which meant he'd overslept. *Fuck.*

He rubbed a hand over his still-tired eyes before squinting up at the ceiling. Soft light filtered in through his curtains, a comforting, fresh sort of glow that might have made him smile if he wasn't horrified at the prospect of arriving to work late. He'd never been late in his life.

This was the price of Jasmine's *fun,* he thought grimly, sitting up with a bone-cracking stretch.

Jasmine. Jasmine lying in his arms, Jasmine's hands in his hair, Jasmine's mouth against his.

The pain in her voice when he pushed her away.

Okay. That was his daily pining allowance all used up.

Rahul found his glasses and stood, shoving his hair out of his face. It didn't help. The hair proceeded to behave exactly as it wished. He hoped that he'd have time to beat it into submission.

A glance at his phone dialled down his panic somewhat. It was almost eight, true, but he could get to work within half an hour. He certainly wouldn't have time for the gym, though—and would therefore be a mess of energy all day, unable to concentrate for more than five minutes.

With a sigh of resignation, Rahul headed for the shower.

Jasmine's bedroom door was slightly open. Maybe she'd already gone to work; he had no idea. It occurred to him that he didn't know a thing about her morning routine, even though they were technically living together.

That was a weird phrase. *Living together*.

He *did* know that she'd probably hate him after last night, that she couldn't understand what the hell his problem was, and he certainly wasn't about to explain it. He'd kissed her, and then he'd... well.

He pushed the bathroom door open, a headache already threatening the back of his skull.

And then he frowned.

Because there Jasmine stood, in the shower... fully clothed?

She saw him, and screamed with entirely too much drama, in his opinion—unless she'd been doing something really fucking weird in there, and he'd just caught her, and she was hysterical with shame. She *was* in an odd position, come to think of it, her skirt hiked up and one leg propped against the tiles.

Then she hissed, "*Fuck*," and dropped something. Something small and pink. She staggered backwards, and Rahul leapt to grab her like a fool—because how could he cross the bathroom and open the shower door and stop her from falling in time? He couldn't. But he still tried.

He failed. Luckily, she saved herself, windmilling her arms enough to regain her balance.

He yanked open the door and grabbed her anyway, pulling her out of the shower. "What the fuck are you doing?"

"What the fuck are *you* doing?" she shot back. "Jesus, I thought you were at work!"

"Overslept," he said grimly. He knew, logically, that she was a solid sort of woman, but her arm still felt uncomfortably fragile in his hand. He loosened his grip slightly.

She wobbled.

He looked down to find that she was standing on one leg. "Why are you hopping? And why were you in the shower wearing clothes?"

"I was shaving my legs," she muttered. She was refusing to meet his eyes, and he missed her somehow, ridiculously and insensibly, and his chest ached, but he understood.

Control.

Rahul raised his brows. "I'm not an expert on that sort of thing, but I thought it usually involved nudity and running water."

She smiled, and then she looked at him. Her gaze was dark and sharp and dancing. "Are we still talking about shaving?"

Rahul swallowed. His throat felt suddenly, painfully dry. He wanted to ask what she was doing, *sparkling* at him like that. He wanted to ask if this meant they were okay.

Instead he decided to go with it, and said, "Behave. Why the hopping?"

"You made me cut myself," she sniffed. "Barging in here like a pervert."

"A—what? There's a lock on that door, you know! Use it!" Rahul guided her firmly, but, he hoped, gently towards the toilet. Not ideal, but needs must. "Sit down."

"Why?"

"Let me see."

She rolled her eyes. But she sat. "It kind of hurts."

A spark of alarm shot through Rahul. Had he ever heard Jasmine use the word *hurts*? Or *pain*? He wasn't sure. He remembered the time she'd broken her arm in two places, hiking with her friends. Rahul had brought her a chocolate bouquet and asked how she was feeling. She'd said, *Metal as fuck.*

He knelt down, took her left foot in his hands—and swore.

"What?" she demanded.

"Nothing." He rubbed his blood-stained palm discreetly on his pyjamas. His mother had gotten them for his last birthday, and he'd started wearing them since Jasmine moved in. Now her blood stained the fabric. *Sorry, Mum.*

"Don't bullshit me." Jasmine twisted her ankle so that she could see the side where she'd cut herself, bending slightly to look. "Oh, shit. *Shit.* Shit, shit, sh—"

"Stop it. Close your eyes. It's not as bad as it looks."

"Piss off!" she snapped, her voice cracking slightly.

"Close your fucking eyes," he barked.

And, miracle of miracles, she did.

Her face had paled slightly, brown skin turning ashen, and her lips were pressed tight together. Her fingers were twisted in the fabric of her skirt. At least he knew she wouldn't faint. She'd rather die than faint.

Rahul turned his attention back to the ankle. It was... unpleasant. She'd managed to shave off a four-inch-long strip of skin. Blood flooded the pink wound. A lot of blood. In fact, it was dripping down her foot like something out of a horror film.

But, he reminded himself, the cut was shallow, and the blood thin. Capillary damage. It was a shaving nick with an unusually large surface area, and at least it wasn't wide as well as long. There was no reason for his heart to pound like she'd been attacked by a fucking bear.

It pounded anyway.

Rahul undid the first button on his pyjama top before yanking it over his head. Wrapped the fabric around her ankle as many times as it would go. Then he crouched beside her, slid an arm under her knees and said, "Ready?"

"What?"

"We're moving." He picked her up.

She gave an odd little gasp, more a sharp exhalation really, and then her arm snaked around his neck. He could smell whatever it was she put in her hair—something light and summery—and the soft, clean scent of her skin.

She'd opened her eyes. Her tongue slid out to wet her lips, and he tried not to remember how it had wet *his* lips. "You can tell me," she said solemnly. "Am I going to die?"

"Stop being dramatic."

"*I'm* being dramatic? You've taken your shirt off, for Christ's sake!"

"For practical purposes. I needed something to stem the bleeding." He shouldered open his bedroom door.

"Because I *am* going to die."

"Because I don't need your blood all over the hardwood."

She huffed as he set her down on his bed, the side he hadn't slept on. It was mostly undisturbed. He probably should've taken her somewhere else, like her room or the sofa, but he wasn't thinking.

"What a charmer you are," she muttered, settling against the cushions. "Your concern warms my heart."

"I bet. Don't move."

"Thank God you said that," she called as he went in search of the first aid kit. "I was going to get up and dance the cancan."

He found the green and white box in the kitchen and hurried back. "Wow. High-level comedy in here. I'm in awe."

She was staring across the room, towards the window and away from him. Obviously trying to hide her alarm. Rahul came to stand beside her. Before he could think better of it, he reached down and cupped her face, his hand nudging her jaw, forcing her to look at him. Panicked eyes met his.

She dragged in a breath. "I don't—I don't like bleeding. I mean, it stresses me out. To see so much."

"It's bleeding a lot," he said, "because razors are sharp. I promise you, it's nothing."

"I know," she said, in a voice that was a little too light and unconcerned.

"Good." He released her and focused his attention on her ankle. Quickly, he found alcohol and gauze, and got to work. But he didn't miss the way she rubbed the scar on her forearm.

"Since when are you Mr. First Aid, anyway?" she asked, her tone accusatory. As if he'd been hiding first aid skills from her with nefarious intent.

"Took a course at sixth form. Put it on my CV to take up space. So every place I worked at decided to make me the first aider, and they sent me on even more courses." He shrugged. "The amount of time and money that's been spent on my first aid skills, I should be a nurse by now."

Jasmine snorted. "I think there's a bit more to nursing than plasters and anti-bacterial wipes, poppet."

There was his girl. He flashed her a grin. "But I'd look so good in the outfit."

"You're a pain in the arse," she said. "I'm going to be late for work. This is entirely your fault." Her voice barely hitched as he applied the alcohol.

"Hey, I'm late too. You should be honoured. If you were anyone else, I'd have let you bleed all over the bathroom just so I could be on time."

"Sadly," she deadpanned, "I believe you."

"You know, you still haven't explained why you were shaving your legs fully-clothed."

She huffed out a breath. "I forgot to do it in the shower."

"Ah." He secured the gauze around her ankle, then wrapped a shit ton of surgical tape around it for good measure.

The added pressure would help. "I don't know how you feel about this idea, but I'd like it if you didn't go to work today."

She looked at him as if he'd suggested playing football with a hedgehog. "You want me to stay off work for a... a scratch?!"

"Oh, now it's a scratch?" He tried, and failed, to hold back a laugh. "Five minutes ago you thought it was fatal."

"Don't be pedantic. I can't just call in!"

"Sure you can," he said calmly. "Tell them your evil room-mate sabotaged you and now you're gravely injured."

She gave him a narrow look. "I'm not taking the day off. I might take the *morning* off."

"That works too."

"*If* you do the same."

Rahul raised his brows. "I beg your pardon?"

She gave him a smug little smile and settled back against the pillows, clearly making herself comfortable. "If I need time off work, surely I also need supervision?"

He blinked. That didn't sound completely illogical, but it was coming from Jasmine's mouth, so it was almost certainly some sort of trap. Then again, he *was* worried about her. She looked a little too grey and clammy for his liking.

Still..."I can't just take a day off," he said, the words automatic.

"A morning," she corrected. "And if I can, you can. Unless you're suggesting that your job is more important than mine."

"No. No. I just..." The thought of breaking from his professional routine made him feel more than a little adrift.

But then he looked at Jasmine and the feeling faded.

"Okay," he said. Then, again, his voice a little more firm: "Yes. I suppose you're right."

She gave him a superior sort of look. "I usually am."

———

Jasmine didn't think she'd ever had so lovely a morning. Excluding the part where she sliced a decent chunk of her own skin off.

Ick. The thought still made her shudder.

But that minor horror was almost completely eclipsed by the near-perfection that had followed.

Rahul lay beside her on his bed, actually relaxing for once. He was so close she could feel the warmth radiating from his body. The sheets smelled like him. She hadn't realised until... well, until last night actually, when she'd woken up with her face on his chest, that he had a very specific smell, and that it made her feel both comfortingly safe and mildly aroused all at once. But it did. Cloves and fresh paper and ink and tea. She'd been working hard, in the back of her mind, to identify every part of the scent, and she thought that was rather accurate.

He'd propped her leg up on a pile of pillows, and then he'd brought more pillows from *her* room to make sure there were enough behind her back. He'd brought her toast even though she'd already had some—not that she was complaining—and then, when she'd asked very nicely, he'd stopped clucking around like a mother hen and taken five fucking minutes to chill.

That had been hours ago. Somehow sitting beside her had turned into lying beside her, and talking about *Lara Croft,* and then *The Good Place,* which he'd somehow only just discovered, the poor sod. It was all quite adorably mundane. And she was unbelievably glad that she'd convinced him to actually take time off work. Now he knew that the sky wouldn't fall if he took a break every so often.

It should be easy, in the midst of all this happiness, to forget that he'd rejected her last night.

Which is for the best. You can't have everything you want.

She knew that. But all she wanted was him, so suddenly and

so fucking badly. She had this idea that if Rahul would just touch her like he had last night, everything in her world would hit that elusive, perfect balance she'd spent her whole life falling just short of.

Except it *wouldn't*. It wouldn't it wouldn't it wouldn't— because he was too good for her to use and discard, and she'd been over this a thousand times, and what the fuck was she on right now?

"Hey," he said. "You've gone quiet."

She turned her head to smile at him. "Thinking. Even I do it sometimes."

Instead of laughing, he smiled gently back. "You do it a lot." He'd taken off his glasses. His face was a hand's width from hers, and she could see flecks of honey-gold in the warm brown of his eyes.

"Not as much as I should," she murmured.

"Maybe you don't need to think as much as everyone else," he said. "You know, because of your mighty IQ score."

"I don't believe in IQ scores."

"Only people with high IQ scores say that." His voice had become a laughing whisper. She watched a network of fine lines form around his eyes, watched smile lines bracket his mouth. What a fucking mouth. When his smile faded, she realised he'd caught her.

Jasmine met his eyes, not with embarrassment, but with a sense of inevitability.

"What is it?" he asked, his voice low.

She wasn't good at denying truths. She wished he hadn't asked. "It's you."

The words hovered between them like cigarette smoke and secrets between the lips of teenagers. Like promises you break, and never forget, and always regret. Like the capsule eternity of that pin-prick moment before a first kiss.

She barely remembered her first kiss. She remembered *their* first kiss, though, better than she'd like. In fact, she had a disturbing feeling that, unlike all her other firsts, it was one she wouldn't forget.

"Jas," he whispered. "I'm sorry about—"

"Don't say you're sorry about last night." She made herself smile. "That's usually my line."

He laughed. "I don't know what to do with you."

Oh, yes you do. "Look; I should apologise. You didn't want to, and I hope I didn't... make things awkward."

His expression flickered. "What? No. It's not like that. I mean, it's not that I don't..." He trailed off, pressed his lips together. A familiar little furrow appeared between his brows. She could kiss that furrow. She could kiss his ferocious frown.

Weird.

"I'm sorry," she said. "That's all. You don't owe me an explanation. Saying no is enough."

He nodded. "Well, I—I shouldn't have kissed you."

She swallowed and tried not to wince. "I get it," she said, hoping her voice sounded casual. "You don't want to complicate things."

He raised his eyebrows. "*You* don't want to complicate things. And I don't want to lose your friendship."

That... was an interesting way of phrasing it. A way that made her palms itch, made her skin hot and prickly with possibility. But she was probably reading too much into things. *And,* she reminded herself, he'd been right to refuse her. She'd been talking nonsense last night, rubbish about friends with benefits as if that could ever work. Jasmine avoided complications for a reason.

"You're such a nice boy," she said lightly, searching for a way to change the subject. "No wonder your mother is so proud."

He snorted. "I don't know about that. If she is, she tells everyone but me." He said the words with fond amusement, rather than any kind of resentment. It was an old joke. The look on his face was soft and... secure. It was the look of someone who was loved.

She attempted a smile in return and tried not to sound painfully jealous. "Whatever. She brags about you all the time."

"Maybe."

He hadn't shaved yet. The permanent shadow on his jaw was darker than she'd ever seen it. Jasmine stared at the stubble, remembered the harsh rasp of it against her skin, and the softness of his lips soothing the burn. She wanted both. Again.

She wondered, if she called someone else and tried to feel what she'd felt last night, would it work? Usually, she'd try. Just to see.

But she felt so sure that it wouldn't.

"Can I ask you something?" he murmured.

She blinked, dragged her attention back to reality—the reality where he'd said no. "Maybe. Ask and we'll see."

He gave her a half-smile. His hand found her arm, traced over her scar the way it always did. "You never told me how you got this."

She stiffened instinctively, then forced herself to relax. "The usual way."

"Hmm." His hand kept stroking. "You don't have any other keloids."

She didn't like thinking about it. She also didn't like coming off all eternally tortured and damaged when she was actually completely fucking fine, so she said, "I had an accident when I was a kid. Cut myself."

"Badly?"

"I suppose so."

"How?"

She gave him a sideways look. "With a knife, genius."

"I mean, if you were a kid—"

"I wanted a sandwich. My mother wasn't going to make me a sandwich. I thought I could cut cheese on my own." God, she didn't want to talk about this. It was exhaustingly pointless.

He took a breath. The sort of breath that meant he was about to be Very Serious. Which wouldn't do at all.

So she forced herself to sit up, to check the clock. Then she pinched his cheek and said, "You know, I think we have time for a quickie. If you've changed your mind."

He rolled his eyes and moved away from her, rising up on his elbows. "Actually," he said, "I think we've gotten carried away." His deep voice had the sort of implacable tone that might've gotten her wet if he wasn't using it to reject her.

Or was he?

He got up off the bed and strode to the window.

Yeah, he was.

Oh—but he'd picked up his glasses. And instead of putting them on, he was cleaning them with his shirt a bit too hard.

Hmm. Maybe the situation bore further investigation.

And maybe she was being ridiculous.

"You're right," Jasmine said. "We should start getting ready to go."

Rahul put on his glasses and turned to peer at her with a frown. He looked, in a word, suspicious.

So she added, "Be a doll and make me some lunch first, would you?"

He rolled his eyes, all suspicion erased. "If life were a game, pushing your luck would be your special ability."

She gave him her sweetest smile. "It would, wouldn't it? And I bet I'd win."

Chapter 10

Now

"Hello?"

"Hello, Jazzy."

Jasmine grinned; she couldn't help it. Then she cleared her throat, wiped the emotion from her face, and cast a suspicious look around the office. Everyone was working, focusing on their own shit—even Asmita, sitting at the next desk over. Still, Jasmine said politely into the phone, "One moment, please," and locked her monitor. Then she got up and hurried out of the room.

Once she was a few metres down the hall, she let every inch of her pleasure show. "Dad!"

"How are you my love?"

"I'm good!" *Except I made out with Rahul three nights ago, no big deal.* "How's the cruise? How's Mari?

"Ah, we're living the life. Every damned day, that woman's dragged me down to the spa. You'll not know me. I've had my pores cleansed."

"That's great, Dad." Jasmine leant against the corridor's cool wall and cradled the phone to her ear, savouring her dad's familiar, easy happiness. She wished she was like him, but she wasn't. She just pretended to be.

She was like her mother.

"And what've you been up to, my little muffin?"

"Oh, you know..." *Don't tell him. Don't tell him. Don't—* "I had a bit of a problem with my flat."

Sigh. This was why she'd been avoiding his calls. Jasmine was physically incapable of hiding things from her father.

Most things, anyway.

"Problem?!" She could practically see his screwed-up face, his frown of outrage at the idea that his daughter should ever face a problem again. "What problem?"

"Well, there was a flood." She didn't go into detail. "The water damage in my room was pretty bad."

"I hope you told that tosser Potter-Baird—"

"Don't worry, I'm handling it. They called me the other day actually, and said the room should be fixed in a month."

"A *month*?" he bellowed. "And what are you doing in the meantime? Where the hell are you?"

Well, at least she had an answer he'd like. "That was a while ago, so it's just a couple of weeks now. And don't worry, I'm staying at Rahul's."

There was a pause. A rather long one, actually, which she hadn't expected; Dad wasn't one for pauses. When he finally spoke, he didn't sound as brash and uncomplicated as usual. He huffed out an odd sort of sigh and said, "I don't know why he does it to himself."

Jas blinked. For a moment, treacherous thoughts hovered at the edges of her mind. *You're a burden. Even your own father thinks so.*

Then sense kicked in, a bright flame scaring off the shadows. *It's a joke. You're not a burden. And even if you were, Dad's the last person on earth who'd see you that way.* She made herself laugh and said, "Poor him, right?"

"Right," Dad said wryly. She heard humour in his tone and wondered how she'd missed it before. Her pounding heart slowed. "Well, I'm glad you're somewhere decent," he said. "I might give Rahul a call. To thank him."

"I said I'd pay rent but—"

"Oh, he won't have money off you." Dad sounded like his usual self again. "He doesn't need it, and he's your friend. You know what friendship means, don't you, Jazzy?"

"Mmm," she said awkwardly. Because really, no matter how many friends she managed to acquire, she'd never trusted the concept. Sometimes, thinking badly about herself required her to think badly of other people, too. To imagine cruelties and ulterior motives and falseness behind every smile.

But when her insecurities tried to twist Rahul into that mould, the idea wouldn't stick. He was so... difficult.

Maybe Dad could tell she was having one of her minor internal crises, because he changed the subject. As he recounted the most recent evidence of his mini golf expertise, things slowly returned to normal. By the time Jasmine said goodbye, she'd almost forgotten her emotional blip.

Almost.

And then, on her way back to the office, she found Asmita.

"Where've you been?" Asmita asked suspiciously. Her arms were full of folders, so she flicked her glossy hair over her shoulder with a shampoo-advert sort of swish.

"Talking to my dad," Jasmine said. She crossed her arms and leant against the wall. "He's on a cruise."

"Right. Are you okay?"

"Yeah," Jasmine said, her tone shamefully unconvincing.

Asmita arched a brow. "You sure?"

She meant to say, *For fuck's sake, yes,* but when she opened her mouth, "I don't know," came out instead.

Asmita's eyes widened in alarm. "Okay. What's up?"

Jasmine tried to come up with a decent answer, even inside her own head, and failed. "I think... I think I'm having feelings."

"Oh my," Asmita deadpanned. "How disturbing."

"I know!" Jas was momentarily pleased that Asmita understood. Then she saw the sarcasm written all over her friend's face and deflated again. "Oh, piss off, you cow. It's alright for you. You have a girlfriend now. You're deeply in love and living happily ever after."

"Yes," Asmita said dryly, "it's definitely that simple. Completely uncomplicated."

Jasmine felt herself blush. "Whatever."

"So you're carrying on like a pantomime dame over a girl? Or guy? Or otherwise categorised person?"

Well, when she put it like that...

Jasmine became suddenly aware of how very embarrassing her behaviour was. She stood up straight and cleared her throat. "No. No, I was just having a moment."

Asmita pursed her lips. "Don't clam up on me, sweetie. I want to know."

What simple words. "*I want to know.*"

That wasn't something Jasmine heard often. Then again, she didn't have conversations like this often—or ever.

Sometimes she'd forget to keep things light and get all emotional—usually when she was drunk. And whoever she was with might say something like, *Are you alright?* Or, *Is everything okay?* Because human beings were conditioned to pretend to care about each other's trivial bullshit. But no-one actually wanted another person's sadness vomited all over them. No-one liked a whiner. So she'd cut them off, avoid the issue, change the subject, and everyone was happier for it.

Except Rahul. She told Rahul everything. She couldn't tell Rahul about this.

"I'm just... confused about something," Jasmine said.

Asmita's brows shot up. "Okay, wow. Wait a second. Just processing the fact that you're actually going to answer."

She snorted. "Shut up."

"Please, don't let me distract you. Do go on."

Jasmine bit down a smile. She opened her mouth, frowned, closed it. Where to go from here?

I've spent three days tip-toeing around the most important person in my world because he doesn't need the only thing that I know how to give. I can't want something without trying to take it. I'm struggling not to ruin everything, as always. I don't know why I'm wasting your time. What do I do?

"Don't ask questions when you have no intention of listening to the answer." A tutor of Jasmine's had said that once, a barrister who spent her Thursday and Friday afternoons guiding students. Olivia. She was rather brilliant, in every sense of the word.

Jasmine didn't ask the question. Instead she said something that felt, in that moment, more important.

"I'm sorry if I'm ever... kind of a shitty friend?"

Asmita blinked. She appeared genuinely surprised. "You're not a shitty friend. You're a distant and mysterious friend, sometimes, but not shitty." She smiled gently. "But if you wanted to be less distant and mysterious, that would be great too."

Jasmine huffed out a laugh. "I'll take that under advisement."

"Good. Hey, are you busy this evening?"

Um... *Busy trying not to desperately want something I cannot have.* "No. Not really."

"Why don't we have a girls' night? With Pinal, maybe?"

Jasmine widened her eyes in mock astonishment. "You still want me around her now she's your super-official girlfriend?"

"Be cool, or you're disinvited."

"Does *cool* mean I can't tell her about the time you threw up pure vodka on your Mum's—"

Asmita slapped a hand over Jasmine's mouth. "I shouldn't have invited you, should I?"

———

"Are you alright?"

Rahul wondered vaguely why his jaw ached, then realised it was because he'd been clenching his teeth for... God, how long?

Three days fucking straight.

"Rahul."

He looked up. Blinked. "Oh. Jo. Ah... Yes. Thank you. What've you got there?"

The small, round woman came into the room with a wary look, a stack of files in her arms. "Ian said you wanted the Hubbard Services assets on paper."

Had Rahul asked for that?

Oh, yeah. He had. For reasons he couldn't quite remember. Oh—because he was going over the Hubbard account, because Ian was an incompetent prick. Rahul pulled off his glasses and ran a hand over his face. The past three days had been a sunset-red haze of frustration and confusion and...

"Why did Ian send you? I told him to do it."

Jo gave him a look. "Probably because you've got him and half the office shit-scared. What's up with you?"

"Nothing," he said, the word automatic.

She snorted, perched on the edge of his desk and dumped the files. "You're a shitty liar."

Jo had seven thousand grandkids and silver—literally *silver,* like starlight—hair. She wore floral shirts with linen trousers and slip-on shoes. She swore like a sailor and was the only friend Rahul had ever made at work.

"I'm not lying," he lied. Badly.

"Right." Jo gave him a skeptical look. "Where's your stress ball?"

Everyone loved to laugh about his stress ball. It wasn't really a ball, because it was shaped like a unicorn's head, but it served the same purpose.

He should never have brought it to work, except Jasmine had given it to him, and it made him smile, and he was absolutely pathetic. The stress ball was shoved in his drawer today. He wished hiding away thoughts of *her* were that simple.

"Never mind my stress ball," he said, with what he hoped was at least a scrap of dignity. "Tell Ian he is an unchivalrous pig for sending you in his place."

"It was a calculated choice," Jo smiled. "Everyone knows you won't shout at an old woman."

"You're not an old woman," he muttered, rifling through the files. "Could you shut the door when you leave?"

She clucked her tongue. "Hark at you. You're such a misery."

"I'm aware." He studied the first few pages in his hands, hoping some issue or other would leap out at him—something he could use to occupy his mind, to push out almost-painful thoughts. Nothing appeared. But he had plenty more pages to go.

"Enjoy whatever it is you're doing," Jo snorted, pushing herself to her feet.

"I'll try. Thanks, Jo."

"No problem. Just... try and leave the office before ten, would you?"

There was no chance of that. Today's strategy was to stay at work as long as possible, to avoid home at all costs. But he glanced up and flashed Jo what he hoped was a reassuring smile. "I'll do my best."

She gave a highly skeptical *humph* before shuffling off. And she shut the door behind her.

Rahul let himself relax. Or rather, deflate, safe from prying eyes.

He had no fucking clue what to do about Jasmine.

She'd clearly meant her apology, because from that morning on, she'd left him alone. Or rather, she did her best to annoy him, and forced him to play poker, and *beat* him at poker, and wasted his time with far too much TV—but she didn't call him anything outrageous, or touch him for just a little too long, or watch him watching her with that sharp little smile.

And he wanted her so fucking much his teeth hurt. His *everything* hurt.

She wasn't even doing anything to cause it. She was just Jasmine with her hair up and her words blunt and her laughter uncontrolled, all the fucking time. It was painfully perfect and it left him achingly thirsty. He had no idea how he was supposed to resist her.

The figures in front of him blurred as if he'd taken off his glasses, so he gave up completely and actually took them off. Now she'd disrupted the cool simplicity of his beloved numbers, and he couldn't even resent her for it, because it was *his* fault. Rahul squeezed his eyes shut, rubbed a hand over his face, and was barraged with memories of the past few days.

He felt her lips every time he closed his eyes. Sleep was for other people now; Rahul lay in the dark and lived through desperation until the sun rose. His cock felt like it had been hard all week. Hard and begging him to do something about it— but he couldn't, because if he touched himself he'd think of her and that would make things worse. If he called a woman, and he could, he'd still think of her. And that would just be disgusting.

Holy fucking shit, he was so sick of this. Rahul surged to his feet and strode to the door Jo had closed. Hesitated. Locked it.

He leant a hand against the cool wood, and shut his eyes, and tried not to hate himself. It wasn't easy.

Why can't you just fuck her? Why?

Because I've lasted this long. Because she'll eat me alive.

So enjoy it.

His right hand moved to his belt without permission, just like his mind moved to that night without permission, over and over again. He felt himself undo the belt with jerky movements, unzip his trousers, shove them down, and grab his aching cock through his briefs. Rahul exhaled hard, shuddering at the pressure—at the relief.

Thoughts couldn't hurt anyone. Thoughts didn't mean anything. He dragged down the waistband of his underwear, releasing a low hiss as his dick sprang free. He'd do this, and he'd feel better. His head would be clearer. He could focus on his work, go about his business—without his thoughts straying to the taste of her lips every five minutes. He'd just take the edge off...

He saw her come into his office. Fuck it; naked. She came into his office naked. He pieced her together with scraps of memory. Her body had changed since he'd had her all those years ago; he knew that. He'd seen some of it. Most of it. He knew how her arse shook with each step and how the muscles in her calves moved, and he knew how thick her waist was and how her tits were almost non-existent. He knew that her nipples begged to be taken into his mouth, and God he fucking wished he'd done that, but he hadn't.

He should have. Years ago, when he'd had the chance, or even last night. He should've taken those hard little points gently between his teeth—but he was getting ahead of himself. She'd just come into his office. So he'd kiss her first.

He kissed her, tasted tea with too much sugar. He wrapped an arm around her waist and pinned her to him, felt every inch of her nakedness. Rahul's thumb and forefinger squeezed the head of his cock so hard it was almost painful. He opened his eyes and watched pre-come seep from the swollen tip, slick and clear. Used his thumb to spread it around, and groaned at the sensation.

He couldn't wait, and he couldn't go slow. He took himself firmly in hand and started the rhythm that always worked, fast and hard along his shaft. When his eyes closed again, he saw Jasmine pull him towards the desk, heard her beg for him because she knew how to ask, he'd taught her, and she knew what he liked, because he'd taught her that, too.

He felt her push him onto the desk, and then she climbed on top of him, took him inside her sweet cunt—fuck, he could've had her like that. Rahul's hand moved faster. Just a few nights ago, if he hadn't stopped, he could've pushed her onto his cock and come inside her.

No, he couldn't—she wouldn't have let him do that. Would she? Didn't matter. This was his fantasy, so he did it anyway. He fucked her raw, felt her squeezing his cock as she came, felt her pull his hair and kiss him and demand more—

The release that tore through him was almost violent. He felt half-destroyed, almost revived, light-headed with relief. And breathless with the realisation that it wasn't enough. His spine tingled, his blood sang, his come was hot and wet in his palm— and it wasn't enough. He needed her.

Rahul focused on his breathing, focused on slowing down the pounding of his heart. He had no idea how long he stood there before he became aware of the fact that he was... well, first of all, standing. Leaning against the door of his office. His *office*. He'd just come in his own bloody hand at work.

He was absolutely fucked, wasn't he?

Rahul straightened, found his handkerchief, cleaned himself up. He yanked his clothes into place with something close to fury, though he wasn't quite sure at what—or whom.

Himself, perhaps. Yes. Almost certainly himself.

He raised a hand to his hair, and was relieved to find it in order. Adjusted his glasses, as though it were necessary. Realised that the mild headache he'd had for the last couple of days had receded. He rolled his shoulders, working the tense muscles.

This was ridiculous.

Why should he feel like this, like such a fucking mess? Why was he denying himself the only thing he needed?

Rahul ignored the irritating voice in his head and went back to his desk. Except now, his desk reminded him of Jasmine, and he hadn't even had Jasmine on it. Fantastic. Perfect. Brilliant. All the pain, none of the pleasure.

His temper snapped.

"Fuck it," he ground out. The empty room listened in silence. "I want her. She wants me."

Common sense told him that human beings weren't as simple as basic equations. Rahul decided he'd had enough of common sense.

He'd take Jasmine instead.

Chapter 11

Now

Asmita and Pinal had graduated from 'cute' to 'painfully adorable'. Jasmine had declined drinking anything alcoholic, because the couple-ness made her dangerously nauseous, and combining it with gin and pub snacks was probably a bad idea.

She felt rather proud of that decision.

But she wasn't proud of the fact that she came home vaguely deflated, oddly flat and childishly envious. Because feeling anything other than ecstatic about the fact that Asmita was in love made her an evil human being.

Probably. She wasn't sure. She'd make some toast and think on it.

Jasmine let herself into Rahul's flat and kicked off her shoes by the door, fanning herself slightly. Her white shirt and long skirt combo had seemed fine in that morning's cool air, but the day had ripened into unexpected heat, and now she felt... not sweaty, exactly. But in need of a cold glass of water. Maybe an ice lolly.

Ha; as if Rahul would have ice lollies.

She dumped her bag in the living room and found the man

himself sitting at the kitchen table. Her smile came quick and automatic, as it always did with him, and some of her lurking dissatisfaction started to fade.

"Hey," she began. Then he looked up at her, and she stopped. Couldn't speak. Practically lost the ability.

He'd never looked at her like that. Not ever. His eyes seemed almost harsh, framed by the thick slashes of his brows, by that furrow between them. He raked his gaze over her, from head to toe and back again, and she felt as if he'd just ripped her clothes off.

She licked her lips. "Rahul?"

He drummed his fingers against the table. Long, strong fingers that had felt so fucking good tangling in her hair and delving between her legs. His voice was even deeper than usual, rougher than she'd ever heard it. "Where've you been?"

She laughed. "What?"

His scowl deepened. He drew in a breath. "That sounded... I was just asking. I'm sorry."

She raised her brows. "Okay. Where are your glasses, by the way?"

"I don't know. Somewhere. Bathroom."

He was shirtless, which wasn't so very unusual. Shirtless, and wearing a pair of those basketball shorts; she caught sight of them under the table. His skin glowed slightly, enough to let her know that he'd been working out. But he usually went to the gym for that, and in the morning too.

She moved past him to get a glass. "You want a drink?"

"No."

"Is everything alright?"

"Yes."

Liar. She went to the sink, sneaking looks at him. She could see the tension in his back, in his shoulders, just as easily as she could hear it in his voice. She knew that he exercised because controlling his body helped him concentrate, burn off frustration, and handle stress. She wondered if something had happened at work. She poured him a glass of water, though he claimed he didn't want one.

Then she put the glass firmly in front of him. "Water helps everything." For him, anyway. For her, the equivalent was vodka.

He glared.

She sat down across from him, and her hands moved to the pack of cards they'd left there the night before. Jasmine pulled out the cards and shuffled, the movements absent. "Want to play? The mood you're in, you might actually win."

He stared at her. For a moment he seemed alien, unnaturally still, every muscle in his body coiled, as if he were a predator waiting to strike. His eyes shone almost amber, so much brighter without his glasses. She tried not to look at his chest, at the expanse of lean muscle and warm skin and dark curls, but her gaze disobeyed for a moment. Flicked to the brown nipples, the taut abs, the thick line of hair that pointed down, down, down...

He pulled the cards from her hands. His fingers brushed hers, and she had to stifle a gasp—because she'd been surprised. Because he'd moved so quickly. Not because the brush of his skin against hers made her palms tingle and her mouth dry.

He shuffled the cards himself, his hands moving fast but his eyes holding hers. And he said, his voice a harsh challenge, "Wanna bet?"

Jasmine swallowed.

She was good at reading signals. At least, she liked to think she was; and she had plenty of evidence to suggest her belief was correct. A girl didn't get laid as much as Jasmine without learning to pick up a few signs.

But this was... confusing. Confusing because he'd said no,

and she wished he hadn't, and she'd stopped trying to change his mind, but *fuck*, she wished he'd change his mind, and now here he was, looking at her, shuffling those fucking cards, waiting for an answer...

"*Wanna bet?*"

She bit her lip and let her gaze travel over his chest—not surreptitiously this time, but bold as brass. Then she said, "Yes. I do."

He put the pack in the centre of the table. "One chance. High card. Draw."

"What are we playing for?"

"Time," he said softly. "Same as always. You win, you get an hour to do whatever you want with me."

She'd won before, but she'd never done what she wanted with him. She'd made him watch *Riddick* or go to a nightclub, or something else he'd typically avoid. But she'd never done what she *really* fucking wanted.

"Alright," she said. "And you?"

"The same." His voice was quiet, but raw. "I get an hour."

Now, why did that sound like a promise?

This isn't happening. He doesn't want—

He nodded towards the cards and said again, "Draw."

She reached out, tension thrumming through her body. She felt almost giddy, as if she were at the top of a rollercoaster waiting for the drop.

Jasmine had always liked rollercoasters.

She slid a card off the deck and laid it on the table. "Eight," she said, because he probably couldn't read it without his glasses. Her chest felt tight. She became hyper-conscious of each breath, imagined she could feel her own heart beating.

Through the open window at the back of the room, she heard a snatch of blaring music as a car drove by. The air felt thick, the tension thicker.

Rahul took a handful of cards. She frowned. "What are you—?"

He held up a hand to silence her. Used the other to fan out the cards. Then he picked one out and threw it down.

A nine.

"Look at that," he said. "I won."

Then he stood, crossed the table in one stride, and dragged her out of her chair.

Jasmine was feeling more than a little dazed, but her body, at least, caught on fast. She practically jumped on him, wrapped her legs around his waist, and he caught her with a grunt before finally, finally kissing her.

The painful interlude between their last kiss and this one had been, frankly, torturous. Jasmine only realised how torturous when his lips took hers, desperate and insistent, and his hands grabbed her arse, and the thing inside her that had been restless and bitter and ravenous actually *relaxed*. This was all she'd had to do, all along? Kiss Rahul again? Well, shit. Good to know.

She ran her fingers through the thick curls of his hair, like so many ribbons of silk, and kissed him with everything she had. The desire, yes, and the longing, but the confusion too, the tenderness she didn't know what to do with, the recklessness, the fear. There were things swirling inside her that she didn't recognise, couldn't identify, things that appeared without permission or apparent reason. Usually, she buried them. Now she gave them all to him, because he would know what to do. He'd handle it. He could handle her.

And he did. He carried her out of the kitchen, and if they moved slowly, if they bumped into a counter or a wall or a bookshelf, she understood, because really she had no idea where she was—which way was left, which way was down, if she was right-side up—and the fact that he could walk at all was kind of amazing. When he sat down on what must be the sofa, and her knees came to rest against soft cushions, she felt like giving him a round of applause. Might have, if she weren't busy running her hands over his bare skin, over the defined muscles of his back, his shoulders, his biceps.

Now that he wasn't carrying her anymore, his hands moved just as freely. His fingers traced gently over the bandage on her ankle, his touch delicate even as his lips and tongue dominated hers. Then he moved higher and his hands grew hard, demanding. He dragged her skirt up over her hips, until it was just a band of useless fabric around her waist. She felt his hand delve between her thighs, felt him stroke her through the cotton of her underwear, and dragged her mouth away from his.

He stared at her, panting, black pupils swallowing the brown of his iris. "What?"

"Two things," she murmured, breathless. "First... You understand that I want—"

"I know what you want," he said. His fingers toyed with the edge of her underwear, sliding along the seam where her thigh met her mound. "Let me give it to you."

"Okay," she said, her voice cracking.

"But I have a rule," he added.

"What?"

"As long as we're doing this," he said, a hand tangling in her hair. "You can't have anyone else."

She licked her lips. *Why the fuck would I want anyone else?*

His grip tightened. "Say you agree."

"Why?"

"Jasmine." A muscle in his jaw ticked.

She smiled. "Whatever you want, buttercup."

"Good." He relaxed; she could see tension roll away from him. "What was the second thing?"

For a moment, it was almost a struggle to remember. But

then she did. Jasmine reached for her bag at the end of the sofa, rifled through the zipped pocket inside, and produced a condom. "Second thing." She put it on the arm of the sofa. Wouldn't want it to go disappearing. The rest were in her bedroom and that was just too far away.

A slight smile softened the harsh look of need on his face. "You take condoms to work?"

"Preparation is key."

He laughed. Full lips, white teeth, strong jaw; there was nothing prettier than Rahul laughing. Actually, there was; the way he bit his lip when he came.

She remembered that. She remembered everything.

Jasmine shuffled back slightly and started to pull down his shorts. He choked on his laughter and caught her hands. "You can't wait?"

"Clearly," she said, "I cannot."

His smirk was infuriating and arousing all at once. "You never learned patience, did you, brat?"

"I suppose not." She tried to tug her hands from his grip. He didn't budge.

"I think I'll have to teach you."

"If you think *now* is the time to teach me—"

He released her, only to grab the front of her shirt with both hands. He dragged her forward, kissed her again—oh, she felt so good when he kissed her, as if her body had been slightly out of sync with her mind but now everything was *just* right. He sucked her lower lip into his mouth, and each strong pull tugged at something hot and electric inside her. Jasmine's toes curled.

Then he tore her shirt open. She let out a rather embarrassing screech as the buttons flew, scattering across the floor, and he laughed. If she'd thought his laugh was sexy before, hearing it while he shoved off the remains of her shirt was... well, it was something.

She wore bras to work as a matter of principle rather than necessity. Rahul appeared to be a fan of today's underwear: white, of course, and thin and lacy and sheer. He stared at her chest for one long, taut moment, a hunger in his eyes that she'd never seen before. Then his arm came around her waist like a steel bar. He dragged her closer, bent his head and sucked her nipple into his mouth through the lace.

Jasmine sank her fingers into his hair and moaned, desire rushing through her. *Fuck.* His tongue, so hot and soft and wet, made the lace seem suddenly rough. His free hand found her knickers, and he yanked them down her thighs. Then, abrupt and deliciously rough, he pushed her back so that her body arched away from him. Jasmine braced herself, her hands resting behind her, on his knees. She panted hard, slightly dizzy, her underwear tangled around her legs, one of her bra cups damp and her nipples tight, her pussy growing hot and wet.

He raked his gaze over her, hunger in his eyes. "Look at you," he whispered.

None of her insecurities arose to whisper misinterpretations in her ear. She heard the reverence in his tone loud and clear.

She liked it.

Chapter 12

Now

Rahul fisted his cock through his shorts as he took in the—admittedly blurry—sight before him. The living, breathing manifestation of all his wildest fantasies. Jasmine Allen, gaze heavy and lips parted, her nipples hard and dark beneath that sweet lace, her legs spread wide for him. Her thighs were soft and rippled with stretch marks, like waves across an ocean's surface. He was more than ready to drown.

One of his arms held her secure on his lap. He studied her face as his free hand moved between their bodies. He'd barely seen her face last time. He cupped his palm over her pussy and slid his middle finger through her plump folds. Felt slick skin and heartbreaking softness. Wanted. Watched.

She bit her lip, hard enough to make the deep rose pale. Her eyes were almost shut. When his finger ghosted over her clit, she made a sharp mewling sound that shot right to his cock. So he did it again, rubbing the hard bud gently, and her hips rocked towards him.

He pulled her closer, because her body was something to look at, yes, but it *felt* even better. She clutched his shoulders and pressed herself against him, and moaned as he stroked her, and it was heaven.

"Fuck," she panted. She was breathless. He made her breathless. Rahul kissed her neck, tasted the slight tang of salt on her skin, and was filled with savage pleasure when she whispered something that sounded like his name.

The pad of his finger still circling her clit, he asked. "What was that?"

"Nothing."

He released her waist, sliding his hand up to cradle her throat. Her gaze, suddenly sharp and defiant, met his. Rahul smiled. "Liar."

She stuck her tongue out. So he dragged her forward and kissed her, thrusting his tongue against hers, devouring her mouth, trying not to wonder how the reality of Jasmine could be so much fucking better than every single one of his fantasies. Weren't fantasies untouchable? Wasn't reality disappointing?

But he'd never *felt* this much, not inside his own head. He couldn't have. She held his face as they kissed, frantic and desperate and messy. He'd never been so free in his fucking life, and nothing had ever been so perfect. He slid his hand from her clit to her entrance, found it slick and swollen, and pushed a finger inside. She moaned into his mouth, the sound ragged, and God, she was so fucking hot, and so tight, and his cock was so hard it hurt.

He dragged his mouth from hers and ordered in a voice he barely recognised, "Touch me."

It was as if she'd been waiting for permission. Her hands finally strayed from his face, his hair, his shoulders, to the place he needed her most. She reached between them and pulled at the waistband of his shorts. Rahul raised himself up slightly, and she laughed and almost lost her balance on his lap—but he caught her, and he kept stroking her, adding a second finger to the first. Somehow, in the midst of all the clumsy, urgent need, she managed to release his cock.

He hissed with sharp relief as she wrapped a hand around him. Spread his thighs wider, because his balls ached so badly. Then she reached down with her free hand and massaged his sac gently, and he thought he might just come all over her.

Control.

She caught his earlobe between her teeth for one sharp second, then released it. "Your cock is almost as pretty as you."

Rahul bit back a moan. "You're the only one who's ever called me pretty."

"Don't know why." She stroked him steadily, twisting her fist over the sensitive head. "You're sickeningly pretty. The first time I saw you, all I wanted to do was sit on your face."

"Don't say shit like that." He tightened his grip on her throat, just enough to remind her he was there—and yet, he felt like the one at her mercy.

"Why not?" she asked, her voice hitching as his fingers brushed over a yielding, tender spot inside her.

"Because," he said, and repeated the action. "I'm trying to last longer than I did the first time."

She cried out, her pussy clenching around him. "Oh my God, keep doing that. Holy shit."

He watched as her face twisted, beautiful and uncontrolled. She writhed against him with every shallow thrust of his fingers, her breath coming in gasps, and all he could think was, *Mine.* But he'd never be foolish enough to say that aloud.

Did it matter, as long as he knew? *Mine. Now. Always.* "Give me the condom."

Even as she gasped, even as her cunt tightened and released around him, she managed to laugh. "You're so fucking bossy."

He caught her jaw in his hand, his grip hard. "You can talk

back to me when you're on my cock and not a minute before. Give me the fucking condom."

She came. Her gaze pinned to his, her hand on his dick, and *his* name on her lips. Whether she liked it or not, whether she wanted to admit it or not. Rahul felt her tighten around his fingers until it was almost painful, and then her wetness flooded his hand. His hand, his wrist, his forearm. He raised his brows as he watched the clear fluid trail along his bare thighs. Then he looked up to find Jasmine biting her lip, chest heaving, cheeks dark.

He gently pulled his fingers from her and raised them to his mouth. She tasted like raw fucking heaven. "Did you just squirt?"

She gave him a look. "What do you think?"

A smile tugging at his lips, he shook his head. "So you do that a lot?"

"Only sometimes." She shrugged. Her gaze skittered away from his. "I probably should've—"

He slid a hand into her hair and pulled her close, until their lips were just a breath apart. "So you can do it again?"

"Yes," she said softly.

He kissed her, not as hard or as desperate as before—even though he was still just as hungry, needed her just as much. He kissed her as if he had all the time in the world to do it, because it suddenly occurred to him that he did. She hadn't put a time limit on things. She wanted friends with benefits, and they'd been friends for years. They'd be friends for years more.

And he'd have her. As long as he didn't fuck it up.

Don't. Don't overthink. Just do.

He helped her climb off him and stood. The look in her eyes was questioning, but she didn't speak. Just waited while he got the damned condom himself, and followed when he twined their fingers together and pulled her towards the door.

He'd wanted this for a very long time, and he certainly wasn't going to do it in the fucking living room.

When they came to the pseudo-crossroads of the hall, he looked once at the blurry door to her room before settling on his own. When she left—*the flat,* he told his wincing heart, *not me*—her room would be empty, but his room would always be his. And he wanted the memory of her in it.

"Sex in a bed," she murmured, as he pulled her through the doorway. "You're spoiling me."

She wore the sort of tiny, focused smile that suggested she was more pleased than she'd like to let on. Probably not about the bed—or at least, he hoped not. If she was happy about the bed he'd have to seriously question everyone she'd ever slept with. But she was happy about something. Maybe about him. The possibility swelled in his chest.

He pulled her closer. Her eyes were bright and her hair was all over the place—she'd definitely complain about him touching it so much, as soon as she remembered to care. She'd lost her knickers somewhere, but her clothes were still half-on. The sight of her skirt around her waist and her pretty, flimsy bra turned useless was almost as arousing as the thought of her naked.

Almost, but not quite. Rahul led her to the foot of the bed, turned her to face it. Stood behind her. Close.

He felt her shiver. Then she said, trying and failing to sound unaffected, "I take it we're not done?"

He threw the condom on the bed in front of her. "Do you want to be done?"

"Well, I suppose you..." Her words broke off as he trailed his fingers along her sides, grazing the sensitive skin. She sucked in a breath when he eased down her skirt. Then she tried again. "I suppose you've made it worth my while so far."

"I'm glad to hear that." He crouched down to help her step out of the skirt. For a moment, he became oddly fascinated with the backs of her knees. The skin seemed impossibly fine, dangerously soft and delicate. He bent his head and kissed one leg, then the other, just because he loved her. He would never say it, but he could kiss the backs of her knees and know exactly what that meant in his own head.

Before his thoughts could spin out of control again, Rahul slid his palms up her thighs, then cupped her arse with both hands. "I want to bend you over," he murmured, "and fuck you until you can't stand."

Just like that, she bent forwards, resting her forearms on the bed. Her back arched, pushing her flesh more firmly into his hands. She looked over her shoulder with a smile that went straight to his cock and said, "You always have such good ideas."

He avoided her intoxicating gaze because he was trying to control himself. But the alternative view was the plump curve of her pussy, exposed by her wide stance and right in line with his face. Fuck.

His hands slid from her cheeks to her lush folds. He spread them wider, drank in the ragged moan she released and the way her hips shifted. Her inner thighs were still damp and gleaming from her orgasm. He wanted to give her another. He wanted to taste her, straight from the source, to lap her up like she was the fountain of fucking immortality, but—

Control.

He wrapped a tight fist around the base of his cock and winced. "Up. I haven't finished undressing you."

"Oh, is that what we're doing?" Her voice was teasing. "I thought you were just going to stay there and stare at my—"

He stood and dragged her up with a growl that was half-laughter. Her back hit his chest, and he wrapped an arm around her waist and kissed her shoulder. "Quiet, brat."

"I like this," she said, out of nowhere. "I like you." Her voice faded on the last word, as if she was unsure, or surprised by what had come out of her mouth. He was, too. He knew Jasmine. He wouldn't expect her to say something like that at the best of times. Right now, when they were in the middle of complicating everything—*no, it doesn't have to be complicated*—when they were traversing relatively new territory... Rahul felt like he'd witnessed a minor fucking miracle.

But if he reacted that way, she'd freak out. So he pressed a kiss to her neck and murmured against the heated silk of her skin, "Of course you do. Everyone likes me."

She snorted. "Shut up." And then when he kissed her throat again, open-mouthed with the threat of teeth, right over her pulse, she moaned.

God, he loved making her moan.

Rahul reached between them to undo her bra, and she exhaled as the clasp came free. He eased the straps down her arms, and then his hands rose to cover her tits. Her nipples tightened against the centre of his palms, and somehow just that tiny sensation made his cock jump.

She laughed softly, arching back against him. "Just fuck me."

"I'm taking my time."

"Would it help if we agreed to do this again? Repeatedly?" She turned to look at him, and her gaze was as heavy as her tone was light. There was a breath between their lips, a whisper of space that shouldn't have even mattered, but felt like a canyon.

He crossed it, his brow bumping hers, his lips brushing hers, everything about him hungry for her. It was beginning to dawn on him that this absolutely would not be enough, so yes, her words helped.

Still, he whispered, "I already knew we'd do this again, because you can't resist me." He spoke right against her lips. Into her mouth. Felt her smile in response.

"I had no idea you could be this cocky."

"That's what happens when all the blood my brain needs travels elsewhere."

"Nice to know I'm responsible for loosening you up." She angled her head slightly, turned the almost-kiss into something deeper, and swept him under. She was everything. She was a hurricane.

He turned her in his arms, and the feel of her body against his was something like euphoria. His hands returned, inevitably, to her hair, sinking into the thick curls, and he used his weight to push her slowly back until she sank onto the bed. He followed, kneeling on the mattress with her soft body beneath him.

She lay back and kissed him harder, deeper, her nails digging into his shoulders and her hips arching into his cock. Heat rushed up his spine as he felt her come slowly undone beneath him, *because* of him—but he couldn't think like that. Thinking like that was one of the many, many things that would end up getting him hurt.

Still, when he pushed her up the bed, and she broke the kiss, and smiled at him with those fucking eyes and said, "Condom, love?" it was hard to maintain his control. His distance. Maybe he was foolish to try.

How could he separate loving Jas from loving her body—Jas, who *was* her body more than anyone he'd ever met, who was present in every sense of the word, who'd had her soul in her eyes when she'd come for him?

Maybe he couldn't. Maybe he was doomed to suffer. Everything came at a price.

He rose up for a moment and didn't miss the way her gaze slid down his abdomen, the way it settled on his erection. When he found the condom lying bright against his sheets, and tore it open and rolled it on, she bit her lip. He liked that. He wanted to bite it for her.

Instead, he lay over her again, and savoured the way she

spread her thighs for him. Her legs rose up to wrap around his hips and she reached between their bodies and grasped his cock.

He squeezed his eyes shut. Looking at her and feeling her all at once might be the definition of too much.

"You remember last time?" she asked, voice low.

He choked out a laugh. "You ask me that like I could ever forget."

Her answering chuckle was soft. She shifted slightly, guiding his cock until he could feel the heat of her, the promise of perfection hovering so fucking close. Her hand was warm and firm, but he wanted more, and he knew she'd give it to him.

"I wonder, sometimes," she said, "if you ever think about it."

His eyes opened. "You can't be serious."

"What? You're the one who didn't want to keep doing it."

That's what she thought? That he hadn't wanted more?

He huffed out a breath. "For such a smart woman, you can be unbelievably obtuse."

As if in response, she dug her heel into his thigh. Urged him forward. He'd like to deny her, just to hear her beg for it, but frankly, he wasn't physically capable. He felt like he might die if he didn't fuck her right now. Immediately. This second.

She must have felt the same, because when he sank into her, just a little, just an inch, she whimpered. Oh, he wanted more of that. Slowly, Rahul eased forward, felt her stretch to accommodate him, felt the delicious friction and impossible glide all at once. As searing pleasure tore through him, his hands cupped her cheeks. Her gaze met his, holding him together when he felt like he might unravel. Anchoring him. Always.

And holy shit, this was just as good as he remembered—only better, because she was so much more *Jasmine*, and he'd wanted her so badly and for so fucking long and never expected to have her.

"More," she gasped, her hips jerking. She was hot and wet,

tightening and releasing around his cock. Gentle and rapid as a butterfly's wings.

He kissed her, tracing his tongue over hers. "Say please."

She sucked his lip into her mouth, then bit down. "No."

So Rahul pulled out. Not all the way, not completely. But he pulled out, and then he thrust back in part-way. She shifted her hips to meet him. He repeated the motion, giving her sharp, shallow strokes, never truly filling her, and it was the purest pleasure and the harshest pain he'd ever known, because it was so fucking good—but it wasn't everything.

At least, it wasn't until she choked out, "Fuck. Please. Rahul, please."

Yeah. That was good. Good in the sort of deep and satisfying way he rarely felt. He moved a hand to her hip, his fingers sinking into the soft flesh. Then he filled her to the hilt in one stroke, and cried out at the perfection, his voice ragged. He saw stars for a moment before they faded to reveal Jasmine's face, her brows furrowed, her lips parted on a silent gasp. He kissed her and she clung to him, her cunt like a fist around his cock.

"So," she panted, as his lips moved from her mouth to her jaw. "What do you think? Better than last time?"

Ah. That reminded him. He buried his hands in her hair again and enjoyed it, enjoyed the fact that he could. Then he tugged until her head tilted to the side, the line of her throat exposed to him. "That was then. This is now."

Her laugh turned into a gasp as he kissed her neck, worshipping the tender spot just above the curve of her shoulder. "Oh, fuck, Rahul..."

"Jas," he sighed. Then he thrust into her again, and savoured the way she tightened around him, the way her lashes fluttered at the feel of him. "It is better than last time," he admitted. "This time I get to kiss you. This time you say *my* name."

"I didn't know if you'd want to kiss me," she said. "I didn't know you then."

He pressed an achingly soft kiss to her lips. "You know me now." *You want me now.* The thought was too much. He rose up and pushed her legs wider, opened her further, fucked her deeper. His hands clutched her hips, holding her in place as he thrust hard and fast, her rising cries urging him on. He felt sweat bead at his brow, felt his capacity for reasonable speech drain away at the sight of her body beneath him, her slight breasts and round belly shaking with every thrust.

And her face. Her fucking face. Her full lips were parted as if ready to scream, her eyes burning into him. He watched as she rubbed her own clit, her hand moving just above the place where his cock stretched her open. God, he loved the sight of that. And loved the way her frown deepened as she drew closer to orgasm, as she clenched around him.

He slammed into her with every year, every month, every fucking day of pent-up desire he had. That was a lot. With every thrust, he thought, *Mine*, and then he realised that he was saying it aloud, growling like an animal. "Mine. Mine. Jasmine—"

"Fuck," she gasped. "I need you."

His body settled over hers again because he didn't know what that meant, but he knew he needed to kiss her. Desperately. His thrusts sank deeper as his mouth explored hers in a way he'd never dreamt of doing, a way that spoke of the possessiveness burning through his bloodstream. When she raked her fingers through his hair, he groaned, pleasure shooting down his spine.

He slid a hand between their bodies and stroked the folds of her pussy, swollen and slick and spread open for his cock. She moaned low in her throat, and he felt a shiver roll through her.

When his fingers found the plump bud of her clit, she cried out, "Oh my God, please."

Her hands tightened in his hair and the sensation went straight to his cock. As if it wasn't going through enough already, fucking the sweetest cunt in the world, coping with the feel of her. He slid his fingers, covered in her wetness, over the tight bundle of nerves—*gently*, so gently even as he pounded into her. He forced himself to concentrate, to keep steady, to work her as she writhed and moaned until finally, finally—

She didn't scream when she came; she gasped out his name as if it were air, and moaned helplessly, and shifted her hips beneath him. It was so fucking sexy, he stopped trying to hold off the inevitable and let himself come too. Something inside him came apart in the best way possible, and he groaned as relief pulsed through him. When he slumped over her, he realised that every inch of the tension he'd been carrying had finally faded. *That* was an orgasm. A fucking good one, one that left him drained and breathless and almost dizzy.

She relaxed her grip on his hair, combing through the curls lazily. The motion soothed him. He felt weightless, better than he ever had in his life. If the world ended right that second, he wouldn't be surprised; something so perfect had to be followed by something as terrible. Otherwise reality would be out of balance.

Only, nothing terrible came. When he finally raised his head to look at her, she wore the sort of sleepy smile that reflected everything he felt in that moment.

Well; maybe not everything. But the pleasure, and the comfort. Definitely that.

"Rahul," she murmured.

"Yeah?"

She trailed her fingers from his hair to his neck, tracing the indent of his spine. "We should've done that before."

Chapter 13

Now

J as leant back in her seat and muttered, "You vile motherfucker."

"What was that, darling?"

She turned from the damning words on her computer screen to find Asmita looking over from the next desk, brows raised. Since the shared office was fully occupied, Jasmine should probably try to sound professional right now. But she'd never been great at 'professional'. The truth was more her thing.

So she didn't hide her fury as she stabbed a finger at the computer screen. "Look at this shit. It's from CPP Housing."

Asmita sighed. "I hope you're not getting worked up over a group of known arseholes behaving like..." She widened her eyes in mock surprise. "Arseholes!"

Jasmine snorted. There was little humour in the sound. Lowering her voice to a self-conscious hiss, she turned the monitor towards Asmita's desk. "*Look.*"

Rolling her eyes, Asmita stood and came over. Her long, glossy hair hung between them like a curtain as she studied the email. Jasmine tried to keep her outrage under control—she wasn't particularly friendly with the other three women in the office, and she didn't want to disturb them, either—but it was frankly impossible. Within seconds, she was quoting the damn email as if Asmita wasn't reading it herself.

"Dear Ms. Allen," Jasmine recited, her tone low and biting. "We regret to inform you that, under our records, there is no evidence of the claimed agreement between one Mrs. *Pentergast* —they couldn't even spell her fucking name right!—and our representative. In light of this fact, we see no grounds whatso- ever—*no grounds whatsoever,* the cheeky sods—to continue this line of investigation, and have thus closed the case." She huffed. "*Closed the case.* Who the fuck do they think they are? Like it's some TV court scene."

Asmita straightened, her expression grim. "They're trying to bluster their way out of trouble."

"They're amoral pieces of shit. They're throwing Mrs. Pren- dergast and her kids onto the street."

"We got the Prendergasts emergency housing," Asmita reminded her.

"Yes, but *they* don't know that!" Jasmine snapped. "Good Lord! Who the fuck raises these people? How do they get like this? We should—we should sue the shit out of their arses, just to teach them a lesson."

"No," Asmita said calmly. "We should exert just enough pressure to force them to compensate Mrs. Prendergast for the breach of contract, because court costs are not in the budget."

Jasmine took a deep breath. "Yes. Obviously. You're quite right."

"Of course I'm right. Are you okay?"

Now, *there* was a question. "I'm fine. Just... got a bit of a headache."

Also, I slept with my best friend last night, several times, and again this morning, and I'm not quite sure what that means, but I liked it, and everything about my life feels suddenly strange and...

She'd stick to the headache story.

"Oh, dear," Asmita murmured. "Would you like some codeine, darling?"

"No," Jasmine sighed. "I've decided to stop using other people's prescription drugs."

"How... unusually sensible of you."

Jasmine grunted in reply.

"Anyway," Asmita said airily. "Speaking of Rahul—"

"Which we absolutely were not."

"Fine." Asmita flicked her hair irritably, like a horse, before clarifying. "Speaking of housing, and therefore your flat, and therefore your temporary accommodation, and therefore your flatmate-slash-landlord Rahul—"

"Don't you have work to do?"

"Don't be boring, darling. I'm trying to cheer you up. In fact, I was wondering if the two of you might like to come for a drink with Pinal and I?"

Jasmine stiffened. *The two of you?* Did Asmita know what they'd done last night? Was her guilt written all over her face? Her mouth felt dry, and the headache she'd invented suddenly materialised with a vicious thump at her temple. Which really served her right for telling the lie.

Eyes narrowed, suspicion dripping from her words, she said, "Why would you ask that?"

Asmita arched a brow. "Why would I ask you to come for a drink?"

"Why would you ask *me and Rahul* to come for a drink? We're not a couple, you know. I'm not his keeper. We're not a crime-fighting duo. We're not a pair. You can't stick our names together like Jasmine-and-Rahul—"

"Alright!" Asmita raised her hands with an expression of mild alarm. "Are you okay? You're being incredibly weird right now."

Fuck. She was, wasn't she? Jasmine gnawed at her lip, then realised *that* probably seemed weird, too. She may have... overreacted slightly to Asmita's wording there. Because usually, people *did* stick Jasmine and Rahul together, and she didn't mind, since they were best friends.

Only now they were... what? She had no idea. Orgasm buddies? Live-in sex companions? She raised a hand to rub her aching temple. "Sorry," she muttered. And then, as if it bore repeating: "Headache."

"Right," Asmita murmured skeptically. "Well, let me know. Unless all this weirdness is because, I don't know... Rahul tripped over a rogue scented candle somewhere in the house, and hit his head and died, and you panicked because it was your candle, so you chopped him into tiny pieces and are currently storing him in his own freezer. In that case, feel free to reject the invitation. I don't need that kind of drama in my life."

Jasmine raised her brows. She noticed Pam, who worked two desks over, squinting at Asmita with a combination of alarm, disbelief and vague disgust on her face.

Asmita swished her glossy hair over one shoulder and widened her eyes innocently. "What?"

―――――

Jasmine's headache disappeared before the end of the day. Her foul mood wasn't nearly as accommodating.

By the time Rahul came home that evening, she'd worked herself into a state of general unhappiness that felt heavy and cold and sodden, like her own personal storm cloud.

She sat and listened to the sound of his key in the door, of him kicking off his shoes. He stepped into the living room with a ready smile, but as soon as he laid eyes on her, everything about him turned still.

She huffed and sank deeper into the sofa cushions.

"Jas?" he said, the beginnings of a frown creasing his brow. "Are you okay?"

Inexplicably, his instant concern only pissed her off further. "Yep," she gritted out. "Fine, thanks."

He came to sit beside her, arching a single brow expertly. Irritating fuck. His weight shifted the soft sofa cushions, sliding her towards him. "You were *fine* when I left this morning," he said. "You're not fine right now."

Despite herself, she felt her cheeks heat at the mention of that morning. Yep; she'd definitely been alright when he'd left. Rahul had made quite sure of that.

He pulled at her curled-up legs until she allowed tense muscles to release. He wrapped strong fingers around one of her calves, just above the gauze still dressing her ankle, and pulled it closer for inspection.

The warmth swirling in her belly dissipated; irritation returned.

"Stop that," she snapped, pulling her leg back.

"Stop what?"

She spluttered, searching for the words. The words to describe his caring hands, his gentle eyes, the sensation of sun-ripe fullness that burst in her chest at his touch. "Stop checking on me."

He sighed slightly, sprawling back against the sofa with an easy confidence in his own body. The sight of him in those austere work suits always threw her. The staid, grey outfits didn't match the tightly coiled power that vibrated though him.

141

Or, she thought wildly, the things he could do in bed.

And now she was horny again. And irritated. Bad combination. Especially since she had no fucking clue how to handle what they'd done last night.

And this morning.

Several times.

Not that she was fixating or anything.

He studied her for a moment, his gaze almost painfully sharp, spearing the flimsy protection she'd built around her tender self. She sat still, trapped by his attention, unreasonably afraid that he was somehow seeing right through her.

It was a senseless fear. She wasn't hiding anything. She told herself that several times, and almost believed it.

Finally, he spoke. "Alright, then. If you say you're okay, you're okay."

"Yep," she said tightly. *Nope*, she thought.

He smiled and stood. "I'll make dinner."

"What? You just got in. I can do it."

"I'm in the mood." He shrugged off his suit jacket and headed towards the kitchen on the other side of the room. Then he paused, looked back at her. "Jas?"

"Yeah?"

"You should change."

Slowly, as if in a dream, she looked down at herself. She'd been home for over an hour, but she was still wearing her work clothes.

She *should* change. They felt too tight, too... heavy, somehow, even though that didn't make any sense. She stood and began to walk out of the room, already working at the buttons of her shirt. She'd shower, too. Her skin felt like it was suffocating beneath a layer of the city's grime and—

Wait.

She stopped in the doorway, turned and scowled. "Don't tell me what to do."

Rahul was already rifling through cupboards, his back to her. But he glanced over his shoulder and raised his brows. "God forbid."

"Piss off."

He looked at her. Just looked. But something about the fire in his dark eyes and the firm set of his jaw made her swallow. And then, without a word, he turned back to the cupboards.

She glared at his broad, shirt-clad back for a moment. Then she went to take a shower.

It was better than she'd expected.

The hot spray pummelled Jasmine's muscles until she felt as liquid as the water around her. She leant back against the cool tiles and felt them warm up as steam filled the room. Her hair must be frizzing terribly. She hadn't taken off her mascara, and it was no doubt smudged in rings around her eyes, but that was okay; all of a sudden, she was in the mood for her elaborate skin-care routine. She might even deep-condition her hair.

Jasmine held out a hand and watched the water bounce off her palm and smiled.

When she eventually returned to the living room, squeaky clean, with her curls piled on her head and slouchy pyjamas clothing her aching bones, dinner was almost ready. Veggie lasagne. *Real* lasagne, with cheese. She hadn't even known Rahul could make something like that. But clearly he could, and well, because she curled up on the sofa with a huge steaming slice and devoured it in ten minutes flat. It was really fucking good.

She put her empty dish on the coffee table and mumbled, "Sorry," and hoped he'd know what she meant.

He did. He pulled her towards him, dragging her onto his lap, and she came without resistance. But she kept her eyes closed, because the scorching cauldron of emotion bubbling in her chest could not be allowed to boil over, and his face was so dear, it had a way of undoing her sometimes.

When she felt him press a gentle kiss to her cheek, she shivered in his arms. Knew that he felt it. Was too exhausted to be self-conscious.

"It's okay," he murmured. "Now, will you tell me what's wrong?"

She sighed heavily. "Bad day at work. Nothing serious. Just being dramatic."

"And?"

She meant to ask him what the fuck *and* meant, but what escaped her lips was, "I miss my dad."

He held her tighter. "I thought you might."

She hadn't. She hadn't thought that at all. Yes, she and Dad were close, but it wasn't like she saw him every day. She was a grown woman. And sure, he hadn't gone away this long since she was a kid, since he'd taken all those business trips, since before...

She slammed the door on those memories and the dark emotions they stirred.

"For God's sake," she muttered. "I'm being childish. Ignore me."

"No. There aren't many people in this world who have your love. One of them is far away and will be for a while. If you want to miss him, miss him."

The bone-deep sadness in his words was like a slap. Because of course she was complaining about her father, who would be home eventually, to Rahul. Rahul, whose dad had died less than a year ago.

She opened her eyes and pressed her lips together. Almost against her will, she found herself cupping his cheek. "I'm sorry."

When he closed his eyes and leaned into the touch, his handsome face seemed suddenly vulnerable. Something warm and soft and simultaneously electric sparked in her heart. She let her head rest against his shoulder, let his cheek, rough with a day's stubble, fill her palm, and somehow... somehow, peace snuck up on them both.

After a moment, he murmured, "What else?"

And she was so relaxed, she said without thinking, "I don't know what we do now."

As soon as the words left her mouth, she stiffened. But he shifted her around on his lap until he was almost cradling her, his hold comforting, protective. His eyes open now, and gleaming with gentle humour, he said, "We do whatever you want, brat. Just like always."

"What does that mean?" She winced at the words. She sounded like... well, like the kind of person *she'd* drop like a hot potato. *What does that mean? Where do we go from here? What are we?* It wasn't that she wanted definitions or titles or a *relationship*—the idea made her feel slightly sick. But... fuck. This was Rahul. She needed to know what was going on. She needed to know where things stood. And she wasn't going to bite her tongue.

If she'd thought about it for five minutes, she'd have realised that he'd never expect her to. His expression turned serious. He traced a finger over her cheek, his eyes steady, and murmured, "It means you're still my best friend. And if you want to..." He took a breath, his exhalation heavy and his brow furrowed. "If you want to repeat last night, we will. If you don't, we won't. And whichever you choose, we'll still be us."

Jasmine thought about that for a moment. It couldn't be that easy. It shouldn't be that easy. People never were.

But she wanted it to be easy, so badly. And it had felt so simple, so natural, being with him.

Despite herself, she smiled. Reached out. Slid her hands over his shoulders, her gaze falling to the lush curve of his lips. "Whatever I want?"

She felt him shift beneath her. His voice was a little less even, a little less calm and controlled than usual, when he said, "Yep."

Her smile widened. "Okay. I think I can work with that."

Chapter 14

Two Years Ago

"Step right up, sweetness. I've got something special for you."

Rahul snorted and rested his forearms against the house's little bar, watching Jasmine screw the cap off a mysterious bottle. "Another of your tooth-ache-inducing concoctions?"

"The best virgin cocktail in the world, you mean? How did you guess?" She grabbed a fancy glass and started pouring, but her eyes, sparkling with humour and half a bottle of Malibu, stayed on him. They'd been at this rented holiday home in Norfolk for four days now, and Jas already had the bar well-stocked.

Behind them, Mitch hollered, "Special treatment!"

Jasmine looked past Rahul's shoulder and winked. "You're damn right, Mitchell. You know this one's my favourite."

"Bitch," Asmita called lazily. She started to say something else, too—but her voice was muffled suddenly.

Rahul didn't bother turning round. He arched a brow, met Jasmine's eyes and murmured, "Emily?"

She rolled her eyes. "Emily."

Asmita's latest girl. Very giggly. Had a habit of grabbing

Asmita and kissing her in the middle of conversations, snooker games, races on the beach, and—most disturbingly—meals.

"Next thing you know," he said, "they'll be sharing oxygen."

Jas stifled a laugh. "Behave yourself."

"You're telling me? How the tables have turned."

She gave him an arch look and grabbed another bottle, this one bright green and fizzy. Rahul watched in alarm as she poured the luminous crap into his glass, on top of all the other shit she'd put in there already.

Jas liked to think of herself as a cocktail 'artist'. According to the others, she was damn good at mixing drinks that involved alcohol.

Not so great on those without it, though.

"You know," he said as she bent to rifle through the mini fridge, "you really don't have to make me anything."

She popped back up, her hair bouncing, a box of strawberries and a wicked little knife in hand. "I do. I make them for everyone else."

"I'm happy with lemonade." He pulled the knife from her fingers and tutted at her grumbled protest. "You're too drunk to be chopping shit up. Tell me what you want."

With a huff, she pushed the strawberries over to him. "Just cut one, you know... halfway in half."

He arched a brow.

With an exaggerated sigh, she picked up a strawberry. "Like this, you see? Just up to here." She made an imaginary line.

"Alright." He followed her directions carefully and presented her with the result. She plucked the ripe, red fruit from his hand with a smile so bright, you'd think he'd just given her the sun.

Moments like that were the hardest. When she flashed all that endless, innocent happiness around, it became really fucking easy to love her.

But he didn't love her. Not anymore, he reminded himself. He was done with that now.

She slid the strawberry onto the rim of the glass and pushed the drink over to him with a flourish. "*Voila!* Your virgin 6 a.m. Sunrise."

He eyed the green cocktail skeptically. "You trying to poison me?"

"Would I ever?"

In the background, Mitch's brother whooped. Some Arctic Monkeys song was on the radio. The music grew louder, and Jasmine's grin grew wider as she watched their friends over his shoulder.

Rahul didn't want to turn around yet, though. Didn't want to see everyone sitting there in the centre of the room, no matter how hard they laughed or how loud they shouted or how much fun they were undoubtedly having. He would, in just a minute. Just one more minute.

But for now, he picked up Jasmine's awful concoction and took a sip.

Her gaze snapped back to him. She watched with obvious anticipation. He tried to hide his grimace as the bitter-sweet, far too fizzy liquid travelled down his throat.

"What do you think?" she asked. She looked so earnest. She had a thing about 'including' him, like he cared that all their friends drank and he didn't. He'd never cared, never would.

But she did.

So he lied, just like always. "It's great."

She clapped her hands together. "Really? You like it?"

"Oh, yeah." He took another sip. Forced his face into a smile when it wanted to screw up in a wince. "I love it."

Her eyes lit up. "Tell me when you want another one!"

Aaaand now it was time to turn around. "Sure," he said, and

started drifting—slowly, so slowly—back towards the others. "But not just yet. Want to dance?"

She practically flew around the bar. "Fuck, yes!"

Jasmine loved to dance. Drunk Jasmine loved it even more. So they danced along with everyone else, and talked and laughed and sang, and she barely even noticed when he poured his virgin 6 a.m. Sunrise down the nearest bathroom sink. Nor did she ask if he wanted another.

But if she had, he would've said yes.

———

Hours later, Jasmine woke up in time to see scarlet sunrise peeking through the window. She picked her way through the passed-out bodies of her drunken friends, sprawled across the carpet. She told herself she was going outside to watch nature's miracle.

Which was bullshit. She was looking for Rahul.

She found him, too, in the most predictable place: the pool sunken into the house's massive deck. He'd left his glasses by the side, but somehow he still saw her coming. By the time she reached him, he was grinning up at her from the water.

"You're never still," she called, as if she didn't love that about him.

"Too much energy," he told her. "If I don't do something about it I'll erupt."

"You mean you'd lose control." She said it carefully, absently, purposefully not looking at him. Because Rahul hated when she dragged the inner workings of his mind out of the shadows and into the light, when she ruined his strict stoicism. But he was more likely to let her do it if he didn't feel cornered.

Her tactics didn't work this time. He ignored her words completely and said, "Come in."

She snorted "I'm not getting in there. It's fucking freezing."

So cold, so blue, so different to the sunrise. Right now, the morning sky was scarlet. She knew, logically, that it should seem pretty. That the birds were chirping, and the temperature was mild, and she was still a little drunk, and this should all be idyllic. But red only ever reminded her of blood.

She wasn't a fan.

"Suit yourself," Rahul said. She didn't buy it for one minute. She sat on the deck while he swam leisurely through the little pool, its spotlights casting strange, shifting shapes beneath the water's surface. Chlorine-colour looked good on him. But the water was so cold she could feel it from here.

Maybe that was an exaggeration. Whatever. Cold water was for drinking.

Rahul swam closer to the edge, closer to her. Then, without warning, he dunked his head beneath the surface. Came back up in a cascade of water and shining, soaking-wet curls. When he shoved his hair out of his face, her gaze snagged on the muscles working in his arms. On his shoulders, his chest.

Then she caught herself and looked away.

"Hey," he said. "Bet I can hold my breath longer than you."

Jasmine arched a brow. "You think you're so smart."

"I do." He grinned.

The word *bet* sank into her skin, flesh, bone, and he knew it. Not even the word itself really—but the challenge. The dare. The possibility. "I could just hold my breath out here," she said. But she was already standing up.

"You might cheat."

"You know I won't cheat."

He gave a helpless shrug, a smile playing at the corners of his lips. "Who can be sure? Get in the pool, and we'll do it properly."

She pushed her leggings down. It was summer, so the early

morning air was mellow and mild. As she stripped, Rahul ran his hand over the surface of the water. Stared at the pattern he'd made.

She pulled off her hoodie and said, "I'm not wearing a bra."

He looked up with a smile. "Neither am I."

"Piss off," she laughed. Usually, she'd go topless. But sometimes, when Rahul looked at her, she felt like more than just a body.

So she kept on the thin vest top she'd worn beneath her hoodie. Then she sat at the edge of the pool and stared at the water for a tense moment before throwing herself in.

She was submerged with a splash and a sharp intake of breath that almost choked her. When she shot up out of the water, she spent a good minute or so coughing. Then she spat, "Holy shit, that's cold."

Rahul arched one of those no-nonsense brows in her direction. "You're so dramatic."

"Fuck you. Are we doing this or what?"

They were.

She shouldn't be putting her head in at all, because it would dry out her hair something awful, but she couldn't turn down a bet. Bad habit, yes. She was working on it. Along with all her other bad habits. Jasmine submerged herself, closing her eyes underwater like she always did—partly because the chlorine stung slightly, but mostly because she didn't like the tricks that water played. When she studied herself beneath a pool's surface, she felt alien. Not as if she'd changed, but as if the world around her had—and really, didn't it amount to the same thing?

When strong hands closed around her upper arms, she jerked up out of the water. Swatted at him blindly because she couldn't open her eyes just yet. "What are you doing?"

"You won," he said. She could hear laughter in his voice, but he wasn't panting or gasping for air, and neither was she, because she'd barely been down there ten seconds.

He brushed drops of water from her eyes with wet thumbs. Somehow, it worked. She blinked a few times, then gave him a skeptical look. "You didn't even try."

"Prove it." With that infuriating statement, he pushed himself onto his back and swam off down the pool.

She scowled. She wasn't the greatest swimmer in the world; she didn't like feeling weightless, without anchor. But she was on the taller side, so she walked—or rather, bobbed, slow as an astronaut—in his direction, until the water hit her chin.

"Swim," he called from the other end of the pool.

"Don't tell me what to do," she called back.

He laughed. Then he came towards her, faster than he had any right to be, his arms arcing out of the water and spraying drops of cold light. She rolled her eyes because he wasn't even trying to show off. He was just kind of sickening.

When he bobbed up before her with a smile, her heart stuttered. Nothing prettier than Rahul smiling. And he always smiled for her.

He wrapped his arms around her waist and drew her into his body. "Hold on to me."

Do I ever do anything but?

She clasped her hands behind his neck. Her thighs caged his hips. They were close enough to kiss. If anyone came outside right now, they'd think she and Rahul were... well. They weren't. So it didn't really matter.

He carried her, painfully slowly, to the far end of the pool. When the water got higher, he pushed her up until her chest was level with his face. And even though her vest was thin, white cotton and soaked all the way through, he didn't look. He kept his eyes on hers like a good boy. Which was slightly infuriating and completely expected.

The pool wasn't full size, so he carried her almost to the end before the water covered his mouth. When her back hit the side and her arms came up to rest along the edge, he released her. She could half-float there for as long as she wanted, supported by the deck and the water.

But he closed the gap between them. His hands came to rest on either side of her, and his body pressed against hers, and her legs closed around his hips again.

"Hey," he murmured.

She smiled, because the sight of him filled her heart with something soft and warm, and she couldn't *not* smile when he was carefree like this. She could see tiny drops of water dotting his long, dark lashes like jewels, could see herself reflected in his eyes, could see his stubble growing in, thick and defiant as always.

"Hey," she whispered back.

And for a single, reckless moment, she thought he might... *do* something. Something he shouldn't, something that would be a fucking disaster, and something she might—sort of—want him to do.

But he didn't, of course. Which was a good thing.

He said, "You know you're my best friend, right?"

She laughed. "Very mature."

"I know. We should make a secret handshake."

"We should make a vow," she corrected. "And become blood brothers."

His teasing smile disappeared for a moment. "You're not my brother."

"Don't be pedantic, love. We don't have to be related. It's a blood vow thingy."

He snorted. "Blood vows sound vaguely demonic to me."

"You're so closed-minded." She raised a hand to ruffle his hair, the movement playful—but as always, she got distracted.

Even wet, his hair felt like satin. She ran her finger over the drenched waves. "I like your hair."

"I like yours," he said.

She frowned, meeting his gaze. "That doesn't make any sense."

"What?" He actually looked surprised. He pulled back slightly, a furrow appearing between those fierce brows of his. "Why doesn't it?"

"Weeeelll..." she said slowly. Stalling. Because she didn't think he'd want to talk about this, and really, she shouldn't have said anything at all. Her gaze strayed from his face up to the wounded sky. But then he cupped her cheek and made her look at him again. His expression was disturbingly serious.

"Tell me," he said.

"Well, you hate your hair," she blurted out. "Because it's curly. My hair is extremely curly. Therefore—"

"I'm going to stop you there," he interrupted. "First of all, I don't hate my hair."

She couldn't bite back a snort. "If you don't hate your hair, why are you always trying to... to suffocate it?"

His features, already so sharp, hardened. He stiffened against her. Not in the good way, either.

But then he sighed and relaxed. "I just... I like to keep it under control."

There was that word again. *Control.*

"You should take a leaf out of my book," she said lightly.

"I could never be like you."

She tried not to take that as an insult. There was no reason for her to take it that way. She'd been working, recently, on not expecting the worst from those around her. Actually, she'd been working on that for years—but she wasn't always very good at it.

This was Rahul, though, and she trusted him more than

most. So she tamped down her knee-jerk response and waited for him to go on.

He sighed. "You're... brave and confident and charming. You command attention." He caught one of her curls between his fingers and pulled. Released. Even wet, it sprang back into place. "Your hair suits you. But I'm nowhere near as interesting as my hair seems to be, and I don't like people looking at me, or touching it, or asking about it, and it just doesn't suit me. So I keep it under control."

She studied him for a moment. He seemed worryingly sincere. She considered approaching the issue delicately for half a second, then remembered that she was as good at delicacy as she was at swimming. "That's bullshit."

He snorted. "How I live for your nuanced and considerate analyses."

"Shut up. Your hair has zero connection to who you are." She held up a hand as he began to protest. "I know people act like it does, but it doesn't. And I know you don't like attention, but... Rahul, *you're* brave. You're confident. You're charming." She paused. Winked. "Thanks for that, by the way."

He looked pained. "I should never compliment you out loud."

"Oh, no, you definitely should. But anyway... if you feel comfortable keeping your hair under control, that's fine—"

"Good, because I do."

She smacked him on the shoulder. "Shut up. I'm delivering an inspirational speech."

"Sorry." He cleared his throat and attempted a solemn expression. It wasn't especially believable, considering the light in his eyes and the way his lips twitched.

Jasmine gave an exasperated sigh. "Fine! My inspirational speech ends here."

"Oh, no, please. I was so enjoying it."

She put her hands on his shoulders and shoved him under the water. Managed to hold him down for a good few seconds, too, but in the end, muscle overpowered bodyweight. He emerged with a look of laughing outrage, and before she could say a word, he shoved *her* under.

They didn't talk much, after that. Not about hair, or confidence, or each other—or themselves. They just played like kids in a freezing pool under the rising sun, and it was good.

Chapter 15

Now

The days passed slowly, all at once. Summer dripped over the city like spilled honey. Jasmine found herself disturbingly and unnaturally happy, and it was all Rahul's fault.

She would come home after work, and shower the sweat and grime of her commute away, and stare out of the window and convince herself that she wasn't waiting pathetically for Rahul to arrive.

And then he'd be there, and it would be painfully clear that she *had* been waiting pathetically. But the shame and embarrassment that usually arose when she realised she'd wanted someone—someone specific, not just a body—would disappear when he grabbed her as soon as he stepped in the door.

Rahul's body was magic in that it had the ability to pack all of her clamouring thoughts into a box, shove them into the back of her mind, and entertain her so beautifully, she didn't even hear them screaming for attention. Rahul himself continued to be the only person she could talk to without considering every word that left her mouth.

She only considered every *fifth* word. Give or take.

On this particular, sticky Saturday afternoon, she didn't

consider her words at all. It was the second weekend since she and Rahul had started... well. She liked to call things exactly what they were, because reality had a way of crushing you if you tried to avoid it. So it was the second weekend since she and Rahul had started fucking.

The first weekend, he'd brought a thousand bottles of water and a ton of protein bars to the bedroom and told her she wasn't wearing clothes again until Monday. He hadn't exactly been joking, and she hadn't particularly minded.

This weekend, she felt like she should be bored, but she wasn't, and it was stressing her out. They'd woken up that morning in his bed, which she hadn't intended—she didn't like to sleep with him. She preferred to shag him and shove off. But sometimes, when they were done, he'd say something that made her laugh. And then she'd say something that made him laugh. And then they'd start talking, and slip from fuck buddies to best friends like it was easy as pie, and she had no problem falling asleep beside her best friend after laughing in the dark.

Then the morning sun would wake her, and she'd open her eyes and see how beautiful he was, and they'd be fucking again.

When she'd woken with him that morning, the strangeness of wanting him and needing him all at once had kind of punched her in the face. She'd freaked out, and he'd opened his eyes and caught her freaking out and said, "You're freaking out."

She'd nodded jerkily. He'd found her hand and put it on his chest and said, "Breathe with me."

It was a thing they did sometimes; mostly when she was drunk and having a minor panic attack over something that didn't matter to anyone else. And maybe it should've felt different, or worked less, because now his chest was naked and she was lying in his bed. Or perhaps because, the night before, he'd made her scream a thousand times with nothing but his lips.

Except, none of that mattered, and everything worked fine, because he was still Rahul.

So she breathed with him, but while she felt the rise and fall of his chest, she couldn't help noticing the beat of his heart.

Now, about five hours later, she was stressing out again. And somehow, as if he had a magical fucking connection to her brain, Rahul knew.

He was sitting in the armchair, reading the finance section of the newspaper because he was an adorable nerd. She was reading a Canadian law journal, but that was neither here nor there. She'd put the paper down anyway, once the weird, choking stress hit. Once her brain had whispered, *You're far too content right now. You know you'll pay for it later. You know he can't possibly be enjoying this as much as you are, and eventually he'll break down and admit it, and you'll feel like more than a fool.*

Across the coffee table, Rahul put the newspaper down and looked her in the eyes and said, "You're anxious today."

She forced herself to snort. "How would you know?"

He didn't smile. Just kept watching her as he said, "We should leave the house."

The words sounded odd. They'd spent the last ten days only leaving for work, texting their friends instead of calling. It was as if all the years they'd spent *not* sleeping together had to be made up for. She was starting to wonder when he'd get bored. Maybe he was bored at that very moment.

She wasn't. In fact, she had this terrifying suspicion that she might never be.

"You're right," she murmured. "We should leave the house. Um..." She trailed off, an odd sort of embarrassment choking her. It was funny; that embarrassment came at the weirdest times. She rarely felt it—not even when she arguably should. If fifty of Jasmine's closest friends were asked to describe her in a word, more than a few would probably say 'shameless'.

But sometimes, she was so embarrassed she couldn't even think straight. She wasn't entirely sure that *embarrassed* was the right word, either; but she didn't know what other word to use. Her skin heated and prickled uncomfortably, and she became conscious of her every breath and blink and fidget. All of her words seemed wrong, their meanings magnified until her intentions were all twisted up in her chest, and it was better not to say anything at all. The embarrassment didn't come often, but when it did, it gutted her.

Rahul waited for her to finish, and when she didn't, he said, "What?" Not with impatience, but gently. She got the impression, from the way he leaned forward, that he wanted to move— to come closer. But he didn't, and she was oddly grateful.

"I was just going to say," she managed, "do you mean we should leave... you know, go out separately, or—"

Jasmine thanked God when he interrupted, because she hadn't been sure how to finish that sentence anyway. "No," he said firmly. "I meant we should go out together. In fact, I have a place in mind."

If she'd felt hot before, she was boiling now. Like a lobster. She'd never blushed so hard in her life and was vaguely disgusted by it, but that disgust couldn't overwhelm the odd, fluttering feeling in her chest. She nodded.

He sat back in the armchair, his posture relaxed and oddly masculine in a way she couldn't identify, but really fucking liked. She briefly considered going over to him. Felt discomfort creeping back. Vetoed the thought.

It was funny; since they'd started sleeping together, she'd felt the embarrassment more often. If she'd felt it this much around someone else, she'd have pushed them away. But around Rahul, there was an underlying safety net that always turned the nerves into a warm sort of giddiness. Into something positive.

"Come here," he said softly.

There. That was it. That was the safety net.

She stood and came towards him. He was shirtless and wearing the basketball shorts he'd usually save for the gym, because up until an hour ago, he'd been naked. Plus, it was fucking hot. She was wearing a loose vest, and some comfy cotton knickers that he shouldn't be eyeing as if they were silk lingerie.

He did, though.

His gaze tracked her as she came closer. When she was within his reach, he wrapped those long fingers around her wrist and tugged her into his lap.

"So," she said, resting her head on his shoulder. "You have somewhere in mind."

"Yeah. You'll love it." He looked down at her, and she couldn't resist. She pulled his glasses off gently and rubbed the slight indent they'd left on the bony bridge of his nose. His eyes crinkled at the corners as he smiled, their chocolate depths melting into caramel under the sunlight.

She smiled back automatically. "I will?"

He brushed his lips over hers, sending an odd sort of shiver swooping through her belly. With one arm, he cradled her against him, and with his free hand, he pushed her thighs gently apart.

"Rahul?" she breathed against his lips.

"Mmm?" He reached between her legs and stroked his fingers along the cleft of her pussy, his touch burning even through her underwear. When she let out a choked sort of moan, he deepened the kiss, his tongue sliding into her open mouth. His fingers kept sliding up and down, the pressure devastating and not nearly enough.

"I—*oh*. Um... What did you—I mean, where did you... Oh, fuck." Jasmine gave up on the whole 'direct train of thought' attempt and kissed him back, tilting her hips towards his palm. For a moment, as his mouth took hers, he pulled his hand away. Didn't break contact, exactly—just didn't let her push into his touch. She growled in frustration and felt his answering laughter vibrate through his chest.

And then, finally, just as she was considering dragging her mouth from his—but Christ, once she started kissing him, it was hard to stop—he touched her. Really touched her. Palmed her mound, his hand big and warm and insistent, building pressure over her aching clit.

Then *he* stopped the kiss, and she whimpered and realised the embarrassment was gone. Vanished. All she felt was happy and horny.

"It's a surprise," he panted.

"What's a surprise?"

His smile was sharp and satisfied. "Tonight. We're going out, remember?"

"Oh. Oh! Yeah, of course. Wait—it can't be a surprise." She cleared her throat and tried to pull herself together, tried to hide the obvious fact that he'd just wiped her brain clean with a kiss and a touch.

Rahul didn't look convinced by her charade. "I assure you, it definitely is."

"No, I meant—how will I know what to wear?"

He increased the pressure of his hand over her pussy. "Dress like... like we're going to a half-decent pub."

"*Are* we going to a half-decent pub?"

"It's. A. Surprise. Take these off." He tugged at the fabric of her underwear.

And even though Jasmine wasn't big on surprises, and even though she loved a challenge, she forgot to badger the truth out of him. Because he kissed her again, and touched her again, and put all her thoughts in a box.

———

They drove with the windows down and the music loud because Jasmine had been put in charge. Rahul was clearly regretting that, but she'd won control fair and square.

Well; he claimed that using her mouth hadn't been fair. But he hadn't specified that when they hashed out the terms of their orgasm-related bet earlier.

Now she belted out the latest crappy pop song while he grimaced in the driver's seat. Jasmine had a terrible singing voice, and on top of that, Rahul had never learned to appreciate crappy pop. He probably couldn't see how tinny beats and over-produced vocals were somehow perfect for a lazy summer evening, how plastic music matched the capsule happiness that was warm wind blowing through wild hair.

But when she looked over and caught his eye, his scowl melted away, and he actually managed to smile. And it didn't just feel like he was smiling at her, but like he was smiling *for* her.

Sometimes Rahul made her feel like perfect wasn't just a performance. Like someone could be seen as something special without constantly *trying*, as long as the right person was doing the seeing.

Which was gross and emotional, and irrelevant, since she didn't care how people saw her. She looked out of the window at the industrial estates and car showrooms speeding by, and sang louder.

If she had to guess by their location, she'd say they were going to the cinema—except she didn't see why that would be a surprise. Suddenly impatient, she turned down the music and narrowed her eyes at him. "Where are we going?"

He didn't look away from the road. Just sprawled in his seat, a hand on the wheel, sunlight picking out the gold in his hair. "We've been over this." But a little smile curved his lips. It was the kind of smile he wore right before he dragged her into the shower with him or knelt down and lifted her skirt. And, like it was an ingrained response, she felt heat curl low in her belly.

But he couldn't be allowed to know that a certain smile from him was enough to get her hot, so she scoffed and rolled her eyes. "Stop being all mysterious. You realise I'll be able to see once we get close?"

"I don't know if you'll figure it out," he said. The car slowed as they turned a corner. They *were* headed to the cinema, or maybe one of the few restaurants that shared its industrial estate. Or the bowling alley across the way? But she hated bowling, because she was terrible at it.

"Why wouldn't I figure it out?"

"It's not exactly obvious."

She pondered that for a moment. "Are we going to the strip club?"

That got his attention. He coughed so hard she thought he might choke. She was not exactly qualified to take the wheel if he passed out, so she really hoped he didn't.

After a moment, he caught his breath. Half-laughing, he asked, "The strip club?!"

"You know. There's the casino down there—" she pointed "—and it has that strip club."

"Jas." They swung into a huge car park just after the turning for the cinema. "We're here to get out of the house. I don't think sitting in a darkened room watching other people dance is a cure for restlessness."

"So *we're* going to dance?"

"Stop asking."

"Hmph. Well, I suppose we're not going to the casino, either, since we're... here." As he parked the car, she squinted up at the huge building standing at the front of the lot. It had an enormous, flashing neon sign in bubblegum shades that read, LUCKY'S WHACKY ADULT EMPORIUM.

She arched a brow. "Is this a sex thing?"

"Nope." He un-clicked his seatbelt and flashed a grin at her. "Do you think about anything other than sex?"

"Shut up," she snorted. "That sign is giving me mixed signals."

They got out of the car and wandered across the tarmac, weaving through oddly parked cars—although there weren't many. Not enough to fill the huge lots that dominated this part of town, anyway. A light breeze swirled through the skirt of her white dress, soothing the intensity of the low-hanging sun against her skin.

She kept meaning to wear suncream this summer, and she kept failing. The upside was that she had tan lines Rahul seemed to like. A lot. The downside was the fact she'd be wrinkled like a prune by the time she hit fifty.

As they walked, Rahul slid an arm over her shoulder. "How are you feeling about your surprise so far?"

"I'm pre-surprised," she murmured, trying to figure out why the familiar weight of his arm and the softness of his skin was making her feel slightly dizzy.

"Pre-surprised?"

"I'm not surprised yet because I don't know where we are, but I'm ready to be surprised when I find out."

"Ah. I see."

"Has this always been here?"

"Nah. It's new. If it wasn't, you'd already know about it."

She arched a brow and squinted up at him, the sun stealing

half her vision. She was about to ask what he meant, but then she noticed the sunglasses tucked into the front of his T-shirt. "Uh... what are those?"

He looked down. "Oh. They're for you."

She watched in astonishment as he pulled them free and handed them to her, his movements casual. "You... you brought sunglasses for me?"

He smirked. "Well they're not for me, are they?" Rahul's mother, Deepika, was always telling him to get prescription sunglasses, and he continued to refuse. Apparently, it was a waste of time and money.

Jasmine slid the glasses on, and the world was sepia. She looked up at Rahul, his skin washed a deeper brown. "Um... I... I forgot mine."

"I thought you might."

"This... is... good."

He laughed. "Are you trying to say 'thank you?'"

"Oh. Yeah. That."

They walked in silence for a moment longer before he said, humour dancing through his words, "Go on, then."

"Hmm?"

He grinned down at her. "Say 'thank you'."

"Oh. Right. Yes." Why was this entire conversation making her chest tight and her cheeks warm? Jasmine wasn't sure, but it was annoying her. She took a deep breath and ground her teeth for a second before forcing herself to say, "Thanks."

Before she could register what he was doing, Rahul pulled her closer into his side and kissed her forehead. That was...

Fine. That was absolutely fine. Just because they happened to be sleeping together, and she liked him possibly more than anyone else in the world, didn't mean everything between them had to be so heavy.

In fact, right now, she felt lighter than air.

They came to stand before the outdated metal doors at the front of the building. They looked like fire exits, minus the push bars and flashing green signs. Rahul paused for a moment, as if for effect—and Jasmine stared skeptically at the rust-edged hinges and the smeared glass windows, swiped with some translucent white substance that stopped her from seeing through.

"What a palace," she said grimly.

"Yep." He sounded unsettlingly cheerful. With one hand, he shoved the heavy door open and moved aside to let her walk in.

She stepped into heaven.

Chapter 16

Now

"Holy fucking shit balls," she murmured.

Oh, that was perfect. That was exactly what he'd wanted.

Jasmine was walking ahead of him, unselfconscious, moving deeper into the renovated warehouse that had recently become the city's strangest arcade.

In fact, she wasn't walking so much as skipping, and swearing a blue streak while she did it. He couldn't blame her. He'd heard a lot about Lucky's, and the place didn't disappoint.

Across the sprawling, red-carpeted space, the flashing lights of old-school arcade machines and more modern games competed with the colourful graffiti art splashed across the walls; art that featured the adventures of an Alice-in-Wonderland-alike with a pink dress and brown skin. He saw Jasmine stare at the art, then the games, then rise up on her toes to see the huge, circular glass counter at the centre of the room. The counter that held a few chatting employees in baby-blue uniforms, plus the arcade's myriad prizes.

Should've known she'd zero in on that. He grinned.

She turned back to him with the biggest fucking smile on

her face, and Rahul's heart stopped. Stopped as if it was simply done—purpose achieved, life goal met. *"Jasmine Allen looks so happy she could die; mission accomplished. Over and out."*

Then she ran to him, her arms thrown wide. The jolt as she slammed into his chest restarted his heart again—or maybe it happened when she looked up, the sunglasses he'd given her slightly askew, and said, "You're kind of amazing."

He pulled the glasses off gently, which was usually something she did to him. But he didn't mind the role reversal. "Yeah?"

"Oh, yeah." She looked so bright and alive and excited, and all he wanted to do was kiss her. Maybe, if he'd done it quick enough, a light brush of the lips, he could've gotten away with it. But Rahul realised he was staring down at her, and had been for a while, probably displaying every inch of his adoration.

Couldn't kiss her now.

Instead, he twined his fingers through hers and pulled her forward. "Come on. Let's play."

The journey to the circular counter would've been a long one anyway, but it ended up longer because Jasmine stopped to stare—and point, and gasp—at every cool thing they passed. And almost everything was cool.

"Is that Donkey Kong? Oh my God, that's Kung Fu Fighter. Holy fuck, Rahul, is that a bar?"

He glanced over at the American diner-style counter and chairs that quite clearly constituted a bar. "Yeah. You see the big sign that says—"

"Alright, arsehole, I see the bloody sign." She was grinning uncontrollably, swinging their joined hands. "Lucky's Sugarshot," she read. "Sweetest Bar in Town."

"Apparently, they make shots based on different sweets," he said, already waiting with a smile for her response.

She didn't disappoint. "Oh, sweet baby Jesus. Are you serious? I'm going to get absolutely smashed—"

"Not yet," he said gently. "You have to give me a few decent games, first."

Jas snorted, spearing him with a look. It was her competitive look, half adorable bravado and half gleaming, star-bright confidence. "I'd beat you with a bottle of vodka put away."

"See if you can beat me sober, first."

She laughed, and then she was off again, dragging him along as she practically flew through the room. She kept pointing out games she wanted to play, but Rahul's attention wandered.

What would she do if he pointed out that this was essentially a date?

He wouldn't, of course. He wouldn't risk wiping the carefree smile from her face, erasing her excitement or the casual comfort between them. He wouldn't put pressure on her.

Especially since he'd started to think that Jasmine might be reconsidering certain things. Things about the two of them. About relationships.

Maybe it was just wishful thinking. But the way she looked at him sometimes...

She stood ahead of him, running her fingers over the migraine-bright art of the nearest pinball machine. She was beautiful. And her fucking dress was killing him slowly.

It was pure white, bright against her dark skin, the soft cotton fabric imprinted with tiny leaves. The skirt was long and loose, but the top part was tight. Very tight, with thin straps at her shoulders that he could push down easily, and a sort of bow thing over her chest. He had this idea that if he tugged at that bow, the front of the dress might come undone—but he wasn't sure if it worked that way.

He intended to find out.

"Come on," he said, pulling her gently away from the pinball machine. "We need tokens to play."

When they reached the counter, he bought a ton of blue and pink coins. Jas glared at him as he pushed the basket of tokens into her hands.

"You told me not to bring any money," she said accusingly.

"Yep."

"So what are we going to do? Spend your money all night?"

"Yep."

"Rahul—"

"Jasmine." He shot her a look. "Choose a game, would you? Unless you're scared of losing."

She huffed out a sharp breath. "I'm not that easily distracted."

"Yes, you are."

She gave him the finger and stalked off towards a first-person shooter.

He followed, smiling like a fool.

———

"So... One week left."

He didn't know why he'd said it. Everything was so fucking perfect. But then, maybe that was why.

Jasmine looked up from the reams of tickets they'd won, her brows raised. "Until what?"

Rahul cleared his throat. "Until your room's ready. At Tilly's."

"Oh. Right." A shadow passed over her face, the glee that had been there as she trounced him at every game fading away. And even though he hated the loss, the implication sent a flash of hope through him. Why would she look unhappy about going home?

Maybe because Tilly's irritating, and your flat is nicer.

Or maybe because she was going to miss him the way he'd miss her.

"I suppose," she said, folding up the tickets and shoving them into the little basket they'd been given. The pink and blue tokens were fading fast now, replaced by a small mountain of paper strips. He should've known she'd be amazing at this. She had the luck of the gods, and she was good at pretty much everything.

"Have you seen it recently?" he asked, leaning against a pinball machine.

She gave him an odd look. "The room? When would I have seen it? I'm either at work or with you."

Ah. Right. It occurred to him that he had been monopolising her time recently. He'd never known Jasmine to spend weekends in rather than partying with her friends. Maybe this was the part where he gave her more space and encouraged her to go, but he didn't want to do that because he was a greedy, selfish fuck, and they'd both have plenty of space soon enough, anyway.

Instead, he said, "We should look together. Sometime this week. Check things are going okay."

"Maybe," she murmured, wandering ahead of him, passing one of those capsule RPGs. Two people sat inside, sharing a fake motorbike, the screen's flashing display cutting through the shadows. They were kissing.

Jasmine stared for a moment, frozen mid-step. Her gaze darkened, her chest rising and falling with each breath.

He curled his hands into fists. If he didn't, he might touch her. If he touched her, he might drag her off somewhere dark and barely-hidden, just like the couple she watched.

The moment lasted a second or two before she turned,

shaking her head slightly. She flashed him a rueful smile, then walked away.

Towards the bar.

"I think I've beaten you enough sober," she said, her voice light. "Time to make things interesting."

Even though he wanted to push, even though hope and worry warred in his chest, he couldn't resist the mischievous smile she flashed him over her shoulder. He loved her shoulders. Was that an odd thing to love? Didn't matter.

She perched on one of the blue and cream leather stools, leaning against the glass surface of the bar. He came to join her and found that beneath the glass, what seemed to be a hundred flavour options were displayed in a bar-long sort of menu. There were different liqueurs, and then various sweets, chocolates and desserts, along with suggested combos. Jas stared at the bubble writing and illustrations like a kid in a sweet shop.

"Bailey's cheesecake," she muttered, her finger tracing over the letters. Then, her eyes flying over the next few options: "Jelly bean vodka! Oh, God. I hope you're ready to carry me to the car."

He laughed. "If necessary. But I need to talk to you first."

She arched a brow. "That sounds serious. You know I hate serious."

"It's not serious. I just want to talk. Outside."

She gave him a suspicious look, then turned to catch a bartender's eye. The guy had been waiting for her, that much was clear. He leapt forwards as if she'd called him by name, his smile blatantly flirtatious. Jasmine tended to have that effect.

"Hey," she said. "You do virgins?"

For a second, Rahul thought she was making some kind of outrageous sexual reference. Then he realised she was talking about alcohol.

The bartender shrugged slightly and said, "Tell me what you want, and I'll do my best."

"Something with Snickers. Also, a jelly bean vodka. Thanks."

While the bartender attempted to show off, throwing bottles around like an accident waiting to happen, Jasmine turned to look at Rahul. Her smile was hesitant and the kind of sweet he'd like to taste. But he had no idea what she'd do if he kissed her in public.

He'd find out, though. Soon.

"I thought you might want a sugar... thing," she said. "A sugar drink. Thingy. Not a shot."

"Technically," he said, "as long as it's in a shot glass, it's still a shot." Hopefully his teasing tone hid the fact that he was unreasonably touched by her thinking of him. It was ridiculous. She did things like that all the time. She was his friend.

But if he'd thought he'd known infatuation before, he'd been sorely mistaken, because ever since the moment he'd gotten her naked, nothing had felt the same. Everything was brighter, louder, almost too much to handle, except shutting out his senses would mean shutting out *her*. Ignoring the fact that this might end in disaster would mean ignoring the fact that he knew how to make her scream his name. The danger and the perfection were entwined.

Life was tough. What else was new?

Their drinks were presented with a flourish, and he watched as Jasmine tossed hers back. He liked watching her do shots. It was one of the many weird obsessions he'd developed while they were at uni together: studying the line of her throat as she threw her head back, the way her muscles shifted as she swallowed, the brief look of shock on her face before she slammed down the glass and her eyes lit up.

Rahul swallowed his without tearing his gaze from her.

When she smiled and said, "Good?" he grunted in response. Then he stood, and caught her hand, and pulled her with him.

She laughed as he tugged her out of the little bar area and onto the main floor. "Wait, where are we going? Slow down, sugar. Oh, crap, we left our tickets!" She didn't sound too upset about that, despite the amount they'd earned. And she didn't stop walking or break his grip on her hand.

No; she followed him all the way, right out into the thick, heavy heat of the night. Somehow, the sun had fallen and the moon had taken its place while they'd been playing inside. He had no idea how long they'd been at it and didn't care.

Rahul turned sharply, finding an alleyway between Lucky's and the side of the next abandoned warehouse. He pulled Jasmine into it with him.

Chapter 17

Now

A thrill coursed through her as Rahul pressed her into the wall, the concrete cool against her back. His lips grazed her throat, his big hands sliding up her ribcage, heat burning through the fabric of her dress.

"Jasmine," he whispered. Took a deep breath, as if he could inhale her, his face buried in the curve between her neck and shoulder. That was her spot. He knew it was. He knew all of them.

She knotted her fingers in the raw silk of his hair and let the perfection of the moment sink into her bones. Stars above her, darkness around her, Rahul against her. She'd been satisfied for so long with feeling almost-right, but after this? She had a sinking suspicion that she'd never be satisfied again.

This thing between them was something she'd never had before, something that danced at the edges of her vision, that hung from the tip of her tongue. But when she looked at it straight on, when she tried to name it, she felt a sick sort of pressure in her gut. So she wouldn't look and she wouldn't speak. She'd feel.

"Kiss me," she murmured.

He didn't move, didn't raise his head; just pressed his lips against her skin. His tongue was hot and lush, and then she felt the slight bite of his teeth and the pull of his mouth and knew he was marking her. Didn't matter. He'd already marked her in every other way.

Don't think like that. It's nothing. This is nothing.

As if he'd heard the lie, Rahul released her and looked up, his eyes glittering in the sex-soaked shadows. He studied her in that way he had, as if he was seeing something no-one else did. She needed that look. It sustained her. Had for years, even when she'd turned away from it and pretended it wasn't there.

"How long have you wanted to do this?" she asked softly.

He kissed her then. Kissed her mouth. The world around them sank into nothingness, her senses dulled as if she'd been submerged in an ocean, with no way to tell where the surface was. So she floated, directionless, and enjoyed it. She'd read somewhere that drowning was euphoria. It was true.

But the question bit at her. Because the way he looked at her—she hadn't understood it, not for years, so she'd ignored it. Pretended it wasn't feeding her and stoking her flames and leaving her wanting in the most painful way. But she couldn't do that now, because over the days since they'd started this fucked up thing, she'd learned his desire. And now she recognised it.

"Rahul," she said, panting softly. "Tell me. How long?"

For a moment, she thought he wouldn't answer. Thought he'd sink his hands into her hair and drag her close again, and she'd have allowed that because God knew she'd hidden in his arms often enough. But Rahul never hid. He swallowed and rasped, "Forever."

Her breath hitched. Her mind barely began to race, struggled to grasp the fine edges of those implications, when—

"Don't panic," he said softly. "You're beautiful. That's all. Don't panic."

She dragged in a breath. Drank in the familiarity of his gaze, his kiss-swollen lips. Her pulse calmed a little, and she thought, *There's no need to make it something it's not. So he wanted you. You wanted him, sometimes, too. What's a little lust between friends?*

Explosive, if they were anything to go by. But she pushed that thought away with a smile and the slide of her body against his.

"Jas?" he murmured.

"It's okay. It's cute." She leant hard against the wall at her back, hooking one leg around his hips. "You think I'm beautiful?"

She saw a flicker of relief cross his face before he answered. "It's an objective fact."

"True." She tugged at the bow resting over her chest.

His eyes fell to watch the show. His hand grasped her thigh, holding it against his hip, as if she needed the encouragement. As if she wouldn't do whatever he fucking wanted in a bloody alley because he was perfect—no. Because she wanted to come, and he always made it so fucking good. That was why. That was the reason.

His fingertips grazed the inside of her thigh in slow, swirling strokes. She undid the bow and he bit his lip, white teeth sinking into plump flesh. She wanted those teeth sinking into *her.* Wondered if he'd managed to mark her suntanned skin or if he'd have to try harder. She wouldn't mind him trying harder. When the two halves of her bodice fell apart like tissue paper, she heard his harsh, sucked-in breath. Everything about his face looked sharper in the dance of shadow and moonlight.

He slid his free hand over her ribs, over her bare skin this time. When he reached her breast, his thumb slid over her nipple, flicking the tightening bud gently. She heard a high, keening sound emerge from her throat, felt her hips jerk against his as if he'd already put his cock in her. Couldn't help it. He was electric. Too much. She'd thought lightning couldn't strike twice, but it hit everywhere he touched.

He slid down the straps of her dress, one at a time, until the entire bodice was hanging down around her waist, her upper body exposed. She should've been nervous. They were outside, hidden, maybe, but not hard to find. She could hear the rumble of an engine starting in the car park, could hear the distant hum of music inside the building she leant against. But she didn't give a fuck because she knew nothing bad could happen while they were together. As long as he was with her, disaster counted as adventure.

So she let her eyes slide closed as he bent down, crouching before her. When he growled, "Skirt," she gathered the fabric up in her hands and raised it out of his way. Anything he wanted. Anything.

Then he slid a finger down her slit, parting her already-swollen lips, and murmured, "No underwear?"

"Seemed like a waste of time," she whispered into the night air. Couldn't look at him. The strange way she felt tonight, looking at him might be dangerous.

But when he muttered, "Brat," she saw his smile in her head. Beautiful and teasing and familiar, and a surprise every time.

He hooked her leg over his shoulder. The air felt cool between her thighs, ghosting over her sensitive pussy. Every inch of her skin felt icy and feverish all at once. She shivered as his touch spread her wide. Then his tongue, firm and slick, lapped at her entrance. Sensation danced along her nerve endings, tightening her core and heating her cunt and forcing her to clench her thighs.

He licked her again, slow and exploratory, as if he didn't know exactly what he was doing. As if he couldn't make her come in minutes with that fucking tongue and those fucking fingers—as if he hadn't done it just yesterday.

She understood. It always felt like the first time, and the last.

His hands grasped her hips, tilting them forwards, forcing her against his face. He breathed deep. She heard him and felt him at the same time when he growled, "Why do you taste so fucking good?"

She couldn't quite manage an answer. Instead she slid her fingers through his hair and dragged him closer, a ragged moan leaving her lips.

He resisted, pulling back with a smile on his face that said he just wanted to prove he could. "Ask me," he said. "Ask for what you want, Jasmine."

He said that a lot. And she tried. Maybe she liked it. Maybe it got easier every time and it felt better than taking ever had, or maybe she just liked the results—because he always gave her what she asked for.

Either way, she managed, "Lick me. My clit. And—and put your fingers inside me," because *fuck,* that felt so good, when he filled her and played with her and worshipped her with his mouth. "Please," she breathed.

He pushed two fingers into her aching channel, and she clenched around him automatically, crying out as he thrust into her emptiness, as he took the edge off her rising need. His eyes held hers, his movements steady.

"You like that?" he murmured.

"Yes," she whispered, sensation tearing through her. "Yes. Please—"

"Say my name."

Her head fell back against the wall as his thick fingers curled inside her. He brushed against that place that made her want to scream, that made her arousal swell beyond anything her body could contain. "Fuck, Rahul."

As if he'd been waiting for that, he brought his lips to her pussy again. The tip of his tongue circled her swelling clit, occasionally licking it full-on. But the pressure was never too much, because in the next breath he was dancing away, his tongue sliding around the source of all that sensitivity. And all the while, he pumped his fingers into her, adding another when she groaned, "*More*."

The stretch was delicious, but it wasn't the best he could do. Not even close. She felt her orgasm rising even as she gasped, "Just fuck me. Please, just fuck me."

As if in response, he sucked her clit gently between his lips, and the pressure sent her eyes rolling back into her head. She came all at once, weightless and witless and a hell of a lot louder than she should be, and he stood and wrapped his arms around her and brought his lips down on hers.

Shudders rolled through her, and ragged moans fought to escape the cage of his kiss. He devoured her, taking everything. His palm slid possessively between her legs, cupping her mound as she arched against him. When the writhing need inside her faded, he released her gently and pressed his lips against her forehead.

His hand slid from her pussy, to her hip, to her arse. He squeezed one cheek roughly, as if he was trying to memorise the feel of her, as if he didn't want to let go. "You're so perfect when you come," he whispered. "When you're mine."

She swallowed down the wave of emotion those words dredged up, because she wasn't quite sure what the emotion *was*. Then his hand moved to the crevice of her arse, his slick fingers sliding down her cleft. When he brushed over her tight hole, a sharp exhalation escaped her. She arched her back automatically, her body demanding more of that tender pleasure, the sweet, barely-there pressure in her most private place.

He watched her, his expression fierce. "You like that?"

"Yes," she breathed. "I like that."

He bent his head and kissed her. His fingertips circled her back entrance as his tongue plundered her mouth. But she wouldn't be distracted that easily; she reached between them and undid his jeans, then remembered to slide a hand into his back pocket. No condom in the left; she found it in the right. She'd learned, since they started all this, that she wasn't the only one who liked to be prepared.

When she shoved down his jeans and underwear, his cock smacked against his belly, thick and hot and hard. He tugged the condom from her suddenly clumsy fingers, ripped it open and slid it on. Then he spun her around, his hands strong and sure. He pressed her against the wall, his weight deliciously insistent, his body surrounding her.

The rough side of the building grazed the sensitive tips of her nipples. His teeth sank into her throat. He slid a hand beneath one of her knees, dragged her bent leg up, and spread her open for him. Then she felt the fat head of his cock settle against her pussy, and a spark of pure need coursed through her. Jasmine arched her back, urging him to move, to thrust into her.

He kissed her jaw, then her cheek, his lips gentle. Too gentle. She forced her eyes shut, as if that would protect her from the surge of tenderness in her chest, from the reverence she imagined in his touch. She wanted more from him than she should. She knew that all at once, then wondered if she'd known it all along.

He pumped his hips and filled her with one hard stroke.

She heard a ragged cry tumble from her own lips, mingling with Rahul's groan. With one hand, he held her leg high; the other moved between their bodies and found the tight little star of her arse, stroking it achingly slowly. Just as slow, he thrust into her, his movements pressing her harder against the wall.

Then he rasped into her ear, "Play with yourself, Jas. I want to feel you come again."

He'd feel it fucking soon. Her hand shook slightly as she slid it between her body and the wall before her, fidgeting in a way that made Rahul breathe in sharply until she found the right position. She began circling her clit firm and fast.

He fucked her steadily, the motion of his hips sharp and forceful, his thrusts spreading her wide and filling her deep. The sensations of his cock, and his hands, and his breath against her cheek, and his chest against her back, all collided in a burst of blinding light, and she shattered with a deep, drawn-out moan.

"Fuck, yes," he panted, his thrusts growing faster, harder. His grip on her thigh tightened as he held her in place, rocking deeper. When he came, he pressed his face against her shoulder and pushed his heavy groan into her skin. She drank in the sound of his pleasure, the feel of his cock jumping inside her as his release filled the condom.

For a moment, they stood panting in the silence. Then he eased slowly from her heat and lowered her leg, and she shivered slightly as the warmth of his body moved away. He pulled down her skirt, then turned her to face him.

"Hey," she said softly,

He kissed her, too gentle again. But she couldn't bring herself to complain. What would she even say? *When you do that, it feels like my heart is breaking, and I don't know why, because I shouldn't have one?*

"Hey, yourself." He wore the kind of smile that said he thought she was being cute, but wouldn't dare say it. He tugged her dress into place, his hands sure, sliding the straps back onto her shoulders.

She laughed and tied up the bow and felt far too much. *Far too much.* "Do you... do you want to go back inside?"

"Well," he said wryly, "we lost all our tickets and didn't get a prize. Unless you're done for the night?"

She leant back against the wall, hands folded demurely, and a smile tugged at her lips. Something foreign filled her heart. "No. I won't be done for a while."

Chapter 18

Now

The bartender had saved their tickets

They went back inside, and as soon as the guy caught sight of Jasmine, he waved and held the little basket up. A grin plumped her cheeks, and she hurried over to him.

Rahul took his time. Watched her lean against the glass bar, the pink and blue light washing over her white dress, and tried to remember that he was the one who'd just made her come. Twice. If he got possessive every time someone looked at her the way the bartender was right now, he'd have a cardiac event within the next six months.

After a few moments of what he considered unnecessarily intense conversation, Jas turned around and searched him out. When her eyes fell on him, her face lit up. She motioned for him to hurry up, that flawless smile on her face.

He reached the bar and tried not to glare at the guy. Instead, he put an arm around Jasmine's waist and bent to kiss her cheek. It was barely a kiss at all, he told himself, just a brush of the lips. A reflex. Nothing.

When he pulled away, he studied her face for signs that she didn't agree. That she was freaking out or pissed. But all he saw

was a little smile and a glowing gaze that seemed almost...
pleased.

He knew that the hopes he'd started to nurture would eventually be crushed, but at times like this, he wondered if maybe
they'd have a chance.

"Rahul," she said, sounding slightly breathless. "This is Ben.
He's trying to do that thing you do."

Rahul's brows arched. He looked at the guy, studying his
pleasant features even as he murmured to Jasmine, "That thing
I do?"

It was Ben who answered. He seemed slightly bashful,
mostly charming, as he said, "Clean eating. Started going to the
gym, but I'm struggling to get enough calories in."

Huh. Jasmine patted Rahul's chest, and the action felt
almost proprietary. "You can tell him about that," she said.
"Can't you?"

Because she knew he loved talking about it, but she personally couldn't stand to listen. She was looking very pleased with
herself, like she'd just found him a particularly special form of
entertainment. Which she might have. No-one, not even Mitch,
was really interested in Rahul's gym routine.

Ben looked interested. But he said hurriedly, "I don't want
to interrupt your night or anything."

Rahul looked down at Jasmine's satisfied face. "Nah, it's
okay." He sat on one of the stools. "Jas, you want to go and play
without me?"

"Nope." She dragged a stool closer to his and sat, hooking an
ankle around one of his, lacing their fingers together on top of
the bar. Hope beat against his chest like a dove's wings,
pounding harder than his heart. She looked at the bartender and
said, "I would like some more shots, though."

Ben laughed. "I think we can manage that."

So Rahul talked while Jasmine downed the sweet surprises

Ben put in front of her. The arcade had been mildly busy when they'd come in, but a steady stream of people were arriving now, and the lights seemed slightly lower than they had before, the music louder. Ben was dragged away more and more, despite there being two other bartenders. When it got too busy for him to justify chatting, he scrawled his number on the back of a napkin and gave it to Rahul.

"Maybe you could text me about that stuff?" He shouted over the heavy bass of No Doubt.

"Creatine?" Rahul clarified. "Yeah. No problem." He gave Ben a little wave before picking up their basket of tickets and tugging on Jasmine's hand. She hadn't let go of him once, even when her eyes glazed over with familiar boredom and she started chatting to whichever stranger wound up next to her.

There were no strangers next to her at that moment, so she slid off her stool and followed Rahul onto the arcade's red carpeted floor. He paused as she drew close to him, as she pressed the length of her body into his side and rose up slightly on her toes. Her lips brushed his ear. "You made a friend!"

He bit back a laugh and brought a hand to her face, as if he was keeping her close so they could hear each other. Really, he just wanted to touch her. "I think *you* made me a friend."

"Well, if I didn't," she smiled, "you'd never have any!"

That was sadly true. Rahul went through the world with specific goals, and tended to bear those goals in mind to the exclusion of all else. It didn't leave much space for making friends, and *trying* never really occurred to him.

But Jasmine made friends by accident and occasionally palmed them off on him, like donating clothes to the community.

He kissed her cheek, just because it was there. It occurred to him that he was probably kissing her too much, but she hadn't complained yet.

In fact, she didn't look like she'd be complaining any time soon. She wore the soft, absent grin that suggested she was in the early stages of Jasmine Drunkenness. Slightly flushed, extremely enthusiastic, liable to forget her train of thought every five minutes. He slid a cautious eye over her and judged her stable enough, balance-wise.

Still, he asked, "You okay?"

"I am golden," she replied in extremely serious tones. "Let's play on the giant Pac-Man."

So they did.

Depressingly, she hadn't been wrong about her ability to beat him while drunk. By the time they came to the counter in search of a prize, Jasmine had strings of paper tickets draped over her shoulders like a scarf.

The 'Adult Emporium' part of Lucky's name didn't just refer to the bar. While there were the usual arcade prizes on offer, there were more than a few atypical items available, too. He leant against the huge, circular counter and watched as Jasmine grinned in delight at the bottles of flavoured vodka on display.

There was a tense moment when she hovered over a glass case labelled 'XXX', which actually did hold sex toys. He wasn't sure how to tell a slightly drunk Jasmine that taking a cock ring from a dodgy, if enjoyable, arcade wasn't the wisest decision.

Thankfully, she ended up choosing a pair of Chip and Dale soft toys. They were each the size of an average ten-year-old. Rahul wondered how he was supposed to get them in the car— until Jas turned to him with a huge smile, her arms wrapped around each chipmunk's neck. Then he decided he'd call the things a bloody taxi if necessary.

It didn't turn out to be necessary. He shoved one in the boot, its softness making it easy to compress, and lay the other across the backseat. Technically, Jas still had control of the music—but she spent the drive home dozing, her breathing soft and deep, her eyes opening every so often for a few bleary moments before they fluttered shut again. He wasn't complaining. Her music choices were questionable at the best of times.

By the time they parked outside his building, she'd managed to sleep away most of her drunkenness. She was now mildly tipsy, so she led the way to the lift as he carried Chip and Dale's remarkable combined bulk.

When they reached his door, she slid her hand into his jeans pocket. Looking up at him, her dark eyes glittering, she fumbled around for his keys. And it was an incredibly bad idea, but as she searched without looking, he bent his head and kissed her nose.

She smiled. Then she said, "Why do you keep kissing me?"

Now, there was a question he couldn't answer.

She found the keys and unlocked the door, but he didn't imagine he was off the hook.

He put Chip and Dale safely on the sofa, then came back to find her crouching down, fiddling with the little buckles on her sandals.

With a sigh, Rahul sat on the floor beside her and pushed her hands gently away. He felt her eyes on him as he undid the first strap.

"Well?" she said after a long, silent moment.

He sighed again. Apparently, sighing was his thing now. "I can stop," he said finally. "If you want."

"I didn't say that." Her voice was soft. He looked up sharply and met her gaze, sleepy and gentle and slightly more sober than he'd prefer for this conversation. "I just want to know why you're doing it."

He shrugged as he moved on to her other shoe. "I like kissing you. You're very easy to kiss."

"On my nose?"

"Anywhere." He tugged off the sandal and helped her to her feet. "Let's go to bed."

For him, that meant stripping and brushing his teeth. For her, that meant washing her face with seventy different products, and wearing one of those weird, white masks with the eyeholes cut out for ten minutes. But she skipped that tonight, probably because she was tired—so he wasn't alone in bed for long before she appeared, turning off the lights and sliding in beside him.

His arm curled around her waist as he dragged her closer. He would never get used to this; to touching her the way he'd always wanted, not just when they made love but at moments like these. Moments when her breathing slowed, when she was soft and vulnerable and their legs tangled together beneath the sheets as if they were one body.

The first time they'd fallen asleep together after sex, she'd been worried. He could tell. Her awkwardness, the tension in her muscles when she'd woken, had dragged a blade of regret across his heart.

But then it had happened again, and again, and again. And now she didn't bother sleeping in her own bed. She slept with him. She held him at night, and she didn't regret it in the morning. Not recently, anyway.

Maybe she never would.

———

Jasmine snuggled closer into Rahul's comforting warmth. She breathed deep, drinking in the scent of him from the sheets and his bare skin. Perfect. *Perfect.*

God, she was tired. And drunk, clearly, because she felt disturbingly content, and when she tried to search for dark thoughts and worries to ground herself, none were forthcoming.

It was as if Rahul had put all her stress in a box again, but he wasn't kissing her. He was just holding her, his face buried against the scarf that covered her hair, his thumb sliding back and forth over her hip.

She slid her foot up his calf, feeling firm muscle and warm skin. "Thank you for tonight," she whispered, her words disappearing into the dark.

He squeezed her slightly, his voice sleepy. "You don't have to thank me. You know I love being with you."

Fuck. He said it so simply. As if the words didn't bring tiny tears to the corners of her eyes. She really was drunk as hell. Suddenly she felt pure, almost golden gratitude, not towards him, but *for* him—like life had given her something far more precious than it should. Sometimes, she couldn't believe he existed, someone who made things so easy and told her he cared without being embarrassed. Sometimes, she imagined losing him because nothing so perfect could last forever.

She mumbled, "I'm so glad I saw you."

He sounded half-asleep as he said, "Saw me?"

"At—" she broke off. It occurred to her that she'd never told him this before. It wasn't hard to see *why* exactly—it was fucking weird. But she told him so many other things, so many other secrets...

"Jas?" He sounded a little more awake now. She felt him shift back slightly, imagined him squinting down at her in the dark.

She took a breath. Might as well. "At uni. I saw you going into the library one day, while I was leaving. You and that kid you hung out with. What was his name?"

He sank back against the pillows. "Ben?"

"Yeah, Ben. I thought you were..." Gorgeous. His hair had been wild—it always was, back then—and gleaming in the sunlight. His glasses were covered in raindrops because it had been drizzling non-stop, so he kind of jogged into the foyer with those fierce brows screwed up, dragging his friend along. Then, once they'd gotten inside, he'd pulled off his glasses to clean them. He'd smiled. The sight had gone straight to her head like champagne.

Maybe he sensed she couldn't, or wouldn't, finish her sentence. His thumb still gliding over her skin, he said, "When was that?"

Her lips stretched into an awkward smile he couldn't see. "The week before we met."

He stilled. But he didn't shove her out of bed or call her a stalker. Then again, why would he? All he knew was that she'd seen him, and then they'd coincidentally bumped into each other at a later date...

"What did you do?" he asked, laughter barely hidden behind his words.

Ah. She'd overlooked the fact that he knew her. He could probably take a guess at exactly what had happened.

Her cheeks heating, she mumbled, "I kind of followed you in, I suppose."

"Followed me?"

"Well, I planned on talking to you. I was going to ask your name or something. But I couldn't work up the nerve. Maybe I was having an off day."

"Right," he said slowly, drawing out the word. She couldn't tell if he was still laughing, but she also couldn't stop talking now she'd started.

"You guys went up to the Accounting floor, and I felt like I was being creepy, so I left. But the next day I decided to find you, so I..."

"You... went to the Accounting floor?"

It was easier, now that he'd said it. "Yes. And I saw you, but I chickened out again. So I left. I came back the next day, and you weren't there. So I just... sat down. I thought you might turn up and sit next to me."

He hadn't. Not at first. And she'd tried not to be disappointed, and wondered why she was being weirdly hesitant and kind of pathetic over one random guy. She certainly couldn't be *shy*, she'd told herself; that wasn't in her vocabulary.

So what was it? She'd never been quite sure.

For a moment, Rahul was quiet. Then he said, his amusement clear, "So you hunted me down using your A+ spying techniques to... what, seduce me in the library?"

A reluctant smile tilted her lips. "I suppose. I mean, I wanted to make sure you weren't an arsehole, so I could... you know. Shag you senseless."

He laughed. Relief floated through her at the familiar sound. She had no idea what had possessed her to tell him any of that, except the mighty power of alcohol and an odd certainty that he wouldn't hate her for it, or push her away. That he'd laugh and tease her and want her anyway. That he wasn't searching for a reason to get rid of her, because he wasn't. He *wasn't*. She told herself that and meant it.

His laughter faded as he pulled her closer. "I can't believe you. Actually, I can. Why didn't you tell me that before?"

"I shouldn't have told you now," she mumbled. "I'm mortified."

"Are you blushing?" She felt his smiling lips brush over her cheeks. "Don't be embarrassed, Jas. Maybe I'm flattered."

"*Are* you flattered?"

"I don't know. Did you secure all your uni conquests like that?"

"Oh, for God's sake. Of course I didn't."

"Okay." He slid a hand over her jaw, angled her head slightly. "Then I'm flattered." His kiss was as light and teasing as his words, just the gentle glide of his lips against her own.

Then he pulled away and bumped his forehead against hers. "You know, you were my first time."

Reality came grinding to a halt. So many thoughts flooded her mind, she could barely speak; it felt like opening her mouth to let one thing out might cause a typhoon. Eventually, she managed to splutter, "I beg your pardon?"

He snorted. "What? Are you surprised?"

"Of course I'm bloody surprised!" She whacked at the place where she judged his arm to be and smacked his side instead. Close enough. "Good Lord! You can't just... just... oh, Christ." She sat up, pulling away from him, because lying down was making her brain jumbled.

He sat up beside her. "Are you okay?"

"Am I okay?" She could hear herself shrieking, just a little bit. "Are you seriously telling me *I* took your virginity? On the fucking floor?!"

His tone wry, he said, "Didn't you tell me virginity was an outdated and patriarchal concept?"

"Piss off," she snorted. "Oh, my goodness. I feel terrible!"

"Why?"

Never mind why. "How the hell were you still a virgin at nineteen?"

She could hear the smirk in his voice. "I suppose I never got around to having sex."

"Until I... until I stole your innocence!"

"Yes," he said dryly, "that's exactly what happened."

"Could you not be sarcastic while I'm having an ethical crisis?"

His hands came to rest on her shoulders, pushing her back onto the bed. She let him, because it was easier than arguing while her mind shifted everything she'd ever thought, then shifted it *back* because this didn't necessarily change anything— or did it? She wasn't sure. Time for another shift.

"Relax," he said, his thumb grazing her lower lip. She couldn't tell, in the darkness, if he'd done it on purpose. "It's not that serious."

She took a deep breath and told herself that, since it was his virginity, he could decide if it was serious. "Are you sure?"

"Very sure."

"So you haven't been carrying a traumatising resentment that's secretly burned at the heart of our friendship or anything?"

There was a pause. Then he said, "I am definitely not traumatised, and I could never resent you."

She'd been half-joking, now that her initial shock had worn off. But he didn't sound like he was laughing anymore; he sounded deadly serious.

"Okay," she said slowly. "Well, that's... that's good."

"I only told you because I didn't want you to be embarrassed alone." He drew her in close again, the way they slept, all tangled up together in a way that shouldn't work but made her feel impossibly safe.

"So you're embarrassed about it?" she asked, her voice muffled against his chest.

"Embarrassed about my performance. But since I've had the opportunity to prove myself since..."

She laughed. "Yeah. I suppose you have. But you were fine then, anyway."

"Fine? Charming." He huffed out a little laugh, then said, "Go to sleep, love."

Love. She called him—everyone—that all the time, a habit picked up from her dad. But *he* didn't.

He probably picked it up from you. And he's tired. And you're tired.

"Okay," she mumbled, her lids already heavy. But her heart was light. Light, and still worryingly content.

She was secretly and unreasonably happy to hear that she had been Rahul's first. And she was absolutely elated to hear the word 'love' on his lips.

As soon as she realised that, her pleasure cooled and congealed.

This could not end well.

Chapter 19

Ten Months Ago

S he could see Rahul shattering.

    She didn't even know if he felt it. He was closest to the front, closest to the coffin that held his father. Everything about him was rigid, as it had been since the death. Harsh and hard as bone. Brittle. Soon he would break.

Jasmine hovered at the back of the room as Muslim guests recited Salat al-Janazah. She had an arm around Rahul's mother, since all of Deepika Khan's children were praying. The smaller woman wept, as she had almost incessantly since her husband's death, and Jasmine wondered which of the world's many gods could ever be so cruel as to fracture a family like this. How was it that a couple like Rahul's parents, who loved each other desperately, could be torn apart forever, while others— others like her mother—

But Jasmine couldn't bring herself to finish a thought like that in a place of worship.

She rubbed a soothing hand over Deepika's shaking back. Tears streamed down the woman's face, tracing her laugh lines in mocking, silver tracks.

Jasmine wished she could bring herself to believe in an afterlife. The thought of nothingness made her feel sick.

But more than that, the knowledge that Rahul was being ripped apart, that his silently swallowed grief was eating him from the inside out, made something close to acid burn her throat. There were so many things she wanted to say to him, things that would *fix* him—would bring him back to life, would force blood into the mannequin he'd become these past days— and she was absolutely bursting to say them, only...

She didn't quite know what they were.

Jasmine had never been good at talking. She was a doer.

So she'd done what she could, and she kept on doing. After the funeral, she filled in the family's stiff silences, thanking guests although it wasn't her place. Then she convinced an unyielding Rahul that he'd done more than enough, that his oldest sister and brother-in-law could take his mother home, that she and Rahul should go back to his flat.

She needed him to sleep. He hadn't slept at all since the death, bar snatches of unconsciousness gained by accident and tossed away with a self-disgust he thought she couldn't see.

When they reached his flat, she pushed him gently aside and unlocked the door. His hands had been shaking, shaking, shaking, no matter how hard he tried to still them. Perhaps, in the chaos and the devastation, no-one else had noticed.

She had noticed.

While he'd looked after his family—while he'd comforted his nieces and nephews, and made the arrangements, and shrouded his own father's body—she had watched him, and she had noticed. Not just the shaking hands, not just the lack of sleep, not just the fact he hadn't eaten. There was something dark and devastating haunting him, and she'd do anything to fix it, only she didn't know how.

But she'd start with getting him to sleep. Putting him to bed. That would work, and if it didn't, something else would.

A sensible and quiet voice in the back of Jasmine's mind told her to just wait it out, to leave it, to let time heal Rahul's wounds the way it was supposed to.

She'd never been good at listening to that voice.

———

"Lie down," Jasmine was saying. "You need to rest."

Rahul couldn't exactly remember coming home, or even entering his bedroom, but now here he was.

And here was Jas, speaking in low, soothing tones as if he were some wild creature. Guiding him onto the bed.

Rahul was following where she led. The minute he realised that, he resisted.

She gave him a wary look. "Come on. Just sleep for a while."

Everything about him rebelled at the thought. "Can't sleep."

"Rahul, please. I'm worried about you."

"Can't sleep." Why? He couldn't remember. Felt wrong. Felt like a very bad idea.

"You don't need to worry." She hesitated, then reached for him. Put her hand on his shoulder, her dark eyes meeting his. "I'll stay with you, if you want."

"I..." *I what?* He didn't know. He felt as if something inside him had been burned away, destroyed until only numb remains were left. There could be shards of glass scratching at his soul, and he'd barely feel it. The knowledge of the disconnect was worse than the disconnect itself. Nausea shook him.

Maybe she could tell, because her hand moved to his face. "Rahul—"

"Don't," he gritted out, catching her wrist. Today of all days, he couldn't take an ounce of that casual tenderness. Couldn't behave as though it meant less than it did. Couldn't pretend she was just Jasmine to him when she was everything to him. Not today.

The flash of devastation across her face lasted less than a second, but it was imprinted on his brain like the ghost of lightning across a dark sky. The sight angered him. The fact that she schooled her expression so quickly angered him too. How dare she care so fucking much when he was the one doomed to hunger and thirst for her without end? And why the fuck did she always have to hide?

Shit. He wanted to be angry, and he knew it, and she didn't deserve it, so he released her and turned his back.

"I need to be alone," he managed, his voice hoarse. He stared at the view from his bedroom window, the way cheerful, out-of-season sunlight poured through the glass, and tried to feel something other than his crumbling heart.

Didn't work. The sunlight faded, and he saw his father's face.

"Alright," Jasmine said, her voice calm. Steady. Utterly devoid of the reaction he'd secretly wanted. He wished she'd give him a reason to scream at her, or a way to scream at the gods, or a brick fucking wall to act as a substitute. He wished she'd give him something because right now he had nothing.

She left on quiet footsteps, and he pulled off his glasses and moved closer to the window. Now the sunlight was just molten honey, and the city below was living colour. He still saw his father's face, clear as day. Rahul stared, traced the familiar contours and wrinkles and shadows in his mind with a dangerous sort of love. The sort that belonged more to an adoring child than a grown man, and the sort that might destroy him because now it was lost. He realised all at once that he was crying.

He allowed it.

It did not make him feel any better. It only made time slow and sticky, made his head ache and his mouth dry. It only made him wish that his mother and his sisters were standing in front of him, so that he could examine each one as if testing a jewel and declare them 100% real. Alive. Safe. Still a part of the world with him.

He hadn't been ready for this. No-one had ever died before.

As soon as the thought crossed his mind, Rahul realised how nonsensical it was. But he couldn't shake it.

No-one has ever died before.

When his thirst became unbearable and his head pounded and his body shook, Rahul dragged himself off to the kitchen. He needed to move anyway. He needed to punish his idle muscles, to tear them all apart until they matched the state of his mind—but first he needed water.

When he saw Jasmine, she was just a moving shape in shades of earth and night. He hadn't picked up his glasses. He knew her anyway.

"You're still here." His voice sounded as dead as the autumn leaves outside. As dead as his father.

The sound of a running tap was cut. Her movements stilled. Then she said, "Of course I am. I was just giving you space."

"I told you to leave." *I want you to stay.*

"I can't leave you alone," she said, but her voice was shaking. "You're... you shouldn't be left alone."

He'd forgotten, only now he remembered, that Jasmine didn't take rejection well. In fact, she didn't take it at all. She should have stormed from the flat when he'd asked her to and never returned. She should've abandoned him and time should've passed and his heart should've stopped beating and he should have turned to stone.

Fuck. He shouldn't feel like this. People died every day.

As if in punishment for the thought, his legs gave out

without warning. Rahul slumped against the wall. His father did not die every day. He hadn't even died today. He'd died three days ago, at the breakfast table, with no warning at all, and Rahul had been just fine. He'd held his mother and comforted his sisters while Jasmine handled details that his mind, for some reason, hadn't been able to focus on.

Now he found himself sliding to the floor, and Jasmine—Jasmine was holding him. The kitchen tiles were hard beneath him and her arms were tight around him, keeping him together. She settled in his lap where she belonged and held his head to her chest, and he was crying again but his cheeks were dry. He must've run out of tears.

"Oh, my love," she murmured. "I'm sorry. I'm so sorry."

He looked up at her with eyes even blurrier than usual, dry and burning. He tried to think in a straight line and failed. He wanted to kiss her but if it wasn't fucking perfect he might just die himself.

He felt his own hands pushing up her skirt, clumsy and insistent, yet he didn't really feel it at all. She let him, her hands cupping his cheeks, her gaze steady on his face, simple and assessing. Even when he fumbled with his own trousers. Even when he freed the erection he didn't understand, because he wasn't aroused at all—he simply wanted more of her, all of her, touching him—she didn't say a word.

He pushed her back onto the floor. She'd pushed him onto the floor, once.

When he settled over her, she was soft beneath him. Her arms tightened around him, and he reached between their bodies and pushed at her underwear—

And she whispered, "Are you sure?"

Sure. *Sure.* He was sure of very few things in life, and one of them was gone. And one of them was Jasmine Allen.

She hadn't left. Would she ever?

Talia Hibbert

All of a sudden, he actually saw her. She wasn't wearing any makeup and her hair was pulled back tight in just the way she hated. Because she'd covered it for his father's funeral. She was biting her lip and watching him with wide and worried eyes, and his cock rested against the soft folds of her sex.

He squeezed his eyes shut, opened them again. "You'd give me this?"

"I will give you anything you need," she said, "because your heart is breaking, and I want to fix you. Is this how I fix you, love?"

He shook his head. Suddenly and sickeningly did not know himself. "I..." He sat up, pulled back. Looked down at his bare cock with dawning horror and then shoved it back into his underwear. "Fuck. I'm sorry, Jasmine. I'm sorry. Oh, shit. What the fuck am I—?"

"Don't make a fuss," she said.

Her tone was firm enough to cut through the clamour of his thoughts. She pushed her skirt back into place, and then she gently moved his shaking hands away from his own fly and took over. Zipped and buttoned him up until he was quite respectable again.

She stood and held out a hand. "Let's have some tea."

As if in a trance, he took her hand and rose. She led him to the kitchen table. She made the tea. He drank it scalding hot and it burned all the way down. She smiled at him with gentle approval, as if he hadn't just tried to fuck her on the cold floor.

He tried to smile back, and he tried not to love her.

He failed so fucking badly.

Chapter 20

Now

"So," Tilly whispered. "Are you guys, like... together?"

Jasmine almost choked on her tea.

Thank Christ Rahul was in her bedroom. Not her bedroom at his flat, the place she'd decorated after their trip to IKEA weeks ago—the place that felt like home. No; he was in her bedroom here at Tilly's, casting a skeptical eye over every fucking inch of the furniture, the paint job, the flooring. Not to mention taking a close look at the light fitting. Jasmine had gotten bored and left him to it.

She was starting to regret that decision. Because now Tilly was leaning against the kitchen counter, her artfully filthy fingers wrapped around a Wedgwood teacup as if it were a Greggs coffee, her eyes boring into Jasmine's.

"Um... no. We're not together." *We've just been* doing *everything together.*

Tilly looked almost comically disappointed. "But he's so hot. I thought if you stayed with him..." She trailed off hopefully. "You really haven't fucked?"

Oh, Lord, had they fucked. Everywhere. In every way. Over

and over again. Only, under Tilly's eager gaze, she was starting to feel uneasy about that fact.

"No," she lied smoothly. "You know I don't fuck my friends."

The rule existed for good reason. Several reasons. Relationships of any kind were hard enough, stressful enough, without complicating categories. She had to keep the many sides of herself separate, distinct, because being everything all at once was a little too close to being herself.

And being herself was dangerous, because when things ended or people left—and they always did—she'd start to feel like she was to blame. Like they'd left because she wasn't enough, or because she was somehow repellent.

And if that happened, she'd have to waste valuable time writing therapeutic diary entries and giving herself pep talks in the mirror and drinking entire bottles of gin just to feel human again.

Tilly took a dainty sip of tea and shot Jasmine a surprisingly direct look. "Fucking your friends isn't the same as having a boyfriend, though."

"Good thing I don't have a boyfriend."

The sound of Rahul's steps down the hall had Tilly's mouth snapping shut. She straightened up and smiled as Rahul entered the kitchen, her gaze going from direct to flirtatious in seconds. Jasmine was arrested by the disturbing urge to throw her tea in Tilly's face.

Rahul paused in the doorway, looking slightly unsettled to find both women staring at him. "Hi," he said finally, moving into the room. "Everything looks good in there."

"Of course it is!" Tilly giggled. Did she always giggle? Jasmine couldn't remember. A large part of her brainpower was currently being taken up by the little triangle of soft, golden skin at the base of Rahul's throat. Maybe she'd kiss it later.

In the week since their trip to Lucky's and their odd night-time confessions, not much had changed. Which was good, because changing perfect would always be a downgrade.

But the date she was due to leave had loomed large, like a deadline neither of them could acknowledge. And now it was here. Tomorrow, she'd be packing her shit and returning... home. Home, which wasn't Rahul's flat, no matter how much her heart seemed to disagree.

Suddenly she was sick of her tea. She looked down into the cup and found the mellow, brown liquid more disgusting than enticing. Vodka would be good right now, but she didn't want to ask for it.

Setting her cup down with a sharp click, she said, "Rahul and I have to go."

Tilly blinked. "You do?"

"Yes. We lost track of time. We have a very important professional engagement." With that utter nonsense, Jasmine stalked across the room.

Her confusion clear, Tilly called, "I thought he was an accountant?"

"Yes!" Jasmine said brightly. "He's my accountant! Got to dash." She grabbed Rahul's arm and flashed him a glare that she hoped said, *Get that look off of your face and go along with it.*

Maybe he picked up on the silent message, or maybe he was just used to her nonsense. Either way, he gave Tilly a confident smile and a little wave. "So sorry to rush off. We'll see you tomorrow!"

That just made Jasmine pull him harder. Because they'd see Tilly tomorrow when they brought all of Jasmine's things so she could move back here.

She really, *really* didn't want to move back here. And that knowledge lodged in her throat because the feeling was so fucking intense, and she couldn't possibly mistake the reason why.

She didn't want to leave Rahul.

Which was ridiculous. She wasn't leaving him. They'd never lived together before and it had never felt like a problem, and nothing had changed—

Liar. Everything's changed.

Nothing had changed. She yanked him through the front door and into the poorly-lit corridor, towards the stairwell. The lifts in this place always smelled like piss. She latched onto that fact, tried to convince herself that she'd miss Rahul's half-decent building instead of his constant presence, but that wasn't true at all, was it?

All of a sudden, all she could see was his smile, and his face when he came, and the way he looked when they played poker and he tried—and failed—to bluff, and—

"Jasmine." He'd been following along as she dragged him, but when they reached one of the platforms in the stairwell he pulled her to a halt. She whipped around to face him, and Christ, he was so...

She was doomed.

"What's wrong?" he asked softly, his hands taking hers. He pulled her close, and she should have resisted but she couldn't.

Oh, dear.

"I..." What the hell was she supposed to say? *I think I'm unreasonably attached to you? I should've known you'd have a magical dick?*

She wasn't even sure his dick was the problem. And anyway, she was overthinking, panicking about nothing. They'd never said it had to end when she moved out. They'd never said it had to end at all. So she'd go home, and he'd be a quick, Friday-night-fuck like everyone else she'd ever been with, and it would be fine.

Except it wouldn't, because he wasn't like everyone else. He belonged to her. When it was over, she couldn't just forget she'd ever known him.

Over.

"Are we done?" she asked, the words rushed.

He frowned down at her. "Done?"

"You and me. I mean—this. Whatever we've been doing together, are we—"

His hands tightened around hers. "No. And if that's what you want, you'll have to say it. Because I'm not giving you an excuse."

"That's not what I meant," she blurted out. "That's not what I want."

She had no idea how she felt about anything else, or what she *did* want, but her mind was being very fucking clear about this. She didn't want to give up Rahul. Ever.

He seemed to relax, as if he'd been holding his breath. "Okay. So what's upsetting you? Because if you think that's what *I* want, you're way off."

She chewed on her lower lip. "I am?"

"You are." He raised a hand to her face, his touch as gentle as his eyes. The harsh fluorescent light glinted off his glasses.

She wanted to take them off, but that felt too intimate for an already painfully intimate moment. The odd, creeping embarrassment was here again, the hot, prickling feeling she could never quite get a handle on.

"Listen," he said softly. "I know you live here for a reason. And I know we've talked about this before, but... Well, I suppose I'm coming from a different angle now. Jasmine... I don't want you to move out."

Her pulse thrummed loudly in her ears. "What do you mean?"

"I mean I like living with you. And I don't like you living

here." He gave the grimy stairwell a dark look. "But you know that anyway. You can live with me, and pay rent if you really want to, and stay in your own room." He smiled at her, sexy as always. "But you're welcome in mine, if you want. It's up to you."

She nodded slowly. Trying to process over the beating of her heart.

But his eyes lit up, and he said, "You want to stay?"

What? No. She shook her head frantically, then realised she'd spoken aloud when his face fell. Wanted to fix it, only she'd never been good at fixing things. "I mean—I'm just thinking. How would that work? What would that mean?"

He watched her carefully. "Mean?"

"If we kept doing... this." She didn't know what to call it. Every word that came to mind seemed either horribly wrong, or absolutely terrifying.

He didn't look horrified or terrified. His smile was slower this time, but he spoke with confidence. "You're asking me what it means if we sleep together, hang out together, live together—"

Well, when he put it like that.

Her throat tightened. It sounded painfully obvious, and also completely impossible, because she was Jasmine Allen. She'd never had a boyfriend or girlfriend or theyfriend, not in her entire life. Not even when she was just a silly kid and all the other girls in her class were playing those kinds of games. She'd known what she was cut out for, and this wasn't it.

"Most people would probably call that dating," Rahul said.

She dropped his hand and stepped away. "I don't do that."

"I know." His tone, his words, his gaze—they were all calm. Too calm, as if he were hoping to soothe her. Well, fuck that.

"You *know* I don't do that," she said, "and you know why."

"No," he said quietly. "I don't."

"You *do*. I'll fuck it up. I'm fucking it up right now."

"No, you're not."

"Yes, I *am*." Her voice came out louder than she'd intended. She'd been backing away from him, she realised, as if he were a threat. Her head bumped into the cold, dirty wall of the stairwell. That summed it up perfectly, really; she'd press herself against filth to escape the perfect man.

"Jasmine. Come here." He held out his hand. "We don't have to talk about this now. You don't have to think about this now. I shouldn't have—"

"Why?" she blurted out. As soon as the word left her lips it grew, swelling between them, its presence oppressive.

"Why what?" he asked, slow and careful.

"Why would you want me to..." She broke off with a sharp shake of her head. "You know what I'm like. You know better than anyone what I'm like."

"Exactly."

A single word, three syllables, as if it were really that simple. He knew her, and that was why he wanted her in a way she couldn't live up to. Well, she was glad things were so clear to him. She felt like she'd been hit over the head.

Because she had never deserved that kind of certainty. She hadn't done a single thing to earn it. And she was too intelligent to convince herself that the power of love, or some such bullshit, could fix all the gaping holes inside her.

Only *she* could fix them, and she was working on it, God damn it. But she'd been working on it forever, and she still wasn't better. She wasn't fixed. She wasn't *safe*, and he shouldn't be looking at her like that, or asking her for this, or treating her so gently when she could tear his heart out.

"I'm not good with relationships," she said. Understatement of the fucking year. "Any relationship. It's a miracle we're still friends."

He shook his head. "It's not a miracle, Jas. You're a good person."

"Stop it," she snapped. "You don't have to tell me that. Just like you don't have to tell me that I have intimacy issues and I drink my feelings and I corrupt everything around me. I don't want to wake up one day and realise I fucked up my best friend. I don't want to hurt you—"

"So don't." He made it sound so easy, so reasonable. "Just come home with me, and when you're ready, we'll talk. Doesn't matter how long it takes. Doesn't matter if you say yes or no. Don't freak out, Jas."

He looked so earnest, and so sad, and her heart was kind of breaking at the sight of his beautiful fucking face, and how little he asked of her, and how much he seemed to care, and the pressure was enough to turn coal into diamonds. But not enough to turn her into someone else.

She wished she could get herself under control and tell him —tell him that she adored him, that every time she saw him, something another woman might call *love* threatened to burst free. But she couldn't say any of that, because what was the point of mentioning love when she wasn't capable of doing it correctly?

Sour panic coalesced with biting anger, not at Rahul but at the fact that she was here, cornered and spitting like a cat, all because the guy she'd been seeing—*call it what it fucking is—* wanted to, what? Keep seeing her? Use words that suited adults instead of a scared teenager?

Why did she have to be like this? Why did her chest have to tighten, and her heart have to pound, and her gut have to swirl, and her skin have to burn? Why couldn't she just be okay?

She stepped towards him, but he didn't look relieved. Because he knew her, and he knew the look on her face.

"Jas," he said. "Don't say something you're going to regret."

"I won't regret this," she lied. Didn't matter that it already tasted like ash on her tongue, and she hadn't even said it yet. Truth was truth. She looked him in the eye and forced herself to say, "What happens when I leave?"

"Jasmine."

"You know I will. I'll have to. I'll have to leave you while it's still perfect, so it can always be perfect, and if we're just friends who are fucking, maybe that will be okay, but if we're anything else—anything more—"

He caught her hand. "I wouldn't be saying any of this if I wasn't serious about you."

She laughed, the sound bitter. "*Serious?* About me? Sweetheart. You're too smart for this."

"Don't," he gritted out.

"Don't what? Don't be a bitch? Don't push you away? Don't protect myself?"

"Don't treat me like I'm someone else."

She sucked in a breath. The words were sharp, deliberate, and they cut deep because they were true. She wasn't treating him like Rahul. She was treating him like her greatest fear. But she couldn't make herself stop.

"It has nothing to do with who you are," she whispered. "Nothing alive can last forever, and nothing dead is worth feeling. Whatever it is you need from me, one day the need will fade. When it does, I will react badly. I'm not ready for that. Not with you. I don't think I ever will be."

His hands closed around her biceps as if he wanted to shake her, but of course he didn't. He just pulled her closer, as if proximity could make his reality hers. "Listen to me," he said, his voice low, his eyes burning. "I am not going to leave you. Ever."

Her laughter sounded like a sob. "This is what I mean. We're not even together, and you feel like you have to say shit like that. What, do I need marriage before I can feel safe on a fucking date?"

"I would marry you tomorrow," he said, and he sounded disturbingly serious. "I would marry you, and then I'd take you on a date. I will do whatever you want, whatever you need, as long as I can be with you. And I will never leave."

"Rahul—"

"Do you know how long I've been in love with you?"

She felt like she'd been punched in the gut. The breath she tried to drag in choked her, as if a fist had really sunk into her stomach. "You're not in love with me," she said, her voice ragged, the world around her tilting slightly.

"Yes, I fucking am." His expression was ferocious and quietly certain all at once. There was that furrow between his brows, the one she'd always wanted to kiss—the one she *had* kissed. She squeezed her eyes shut and felt a tear leak down her cheek, which was really just the cherry on top of this absolute fucking nightmare.

He brushed a thumb over the tear. "Seven years, Jas. Always. I have always loved you. You're my best friend, and I need you, and I will never leave. No matter what. Even if you want to forget this ever happened and go back to being friends, I won't leave."

She jerked back. "You can't—you can't just—seven years?"

He gave a helpless shrug. "I tried to stop. I really, really did. But I couldn't. So if you ever doubt me, just remember, even when I did my absolute best not to love you, I couldn't manage it. It certainly isn't going to happen by accident."

She saw the truth of his words written over his face and felt like she might be sick. All this time. All this time, she'd tried not to want him, tried to be his friend, and he'd been... what?

She pushed him away. Hard. And he clearly hadn't been expecting it, because he stumbled back against the wall. "Jas—"

"So you were just... hanging around all this time hoping you'd get a chance to fuck me again?"

He set his jaw. "If that's what I wanted, we never would've been friends at all."

"Right." She nodded woodenly. "But you decided to play the long game. That's smart. You're smart."

"You don't really believe that."

"Don't I?" She had no idea. Her head was swarming with angry suspicions, and each one had a sting in its tail. She could hardly hear herself over the buzzing in her skull.

"No, you don't. You know our friendship is real. You know I wouldn't use you. You know I had no idea that this would happen." He was achingly still, everything about him rigid, and she knew what that meant. She knew he was in pain, that he didn't know what to do, that she was hurting him.

Already, she was hurting him. What a fucking surprise.

Almost as quickly as the accusation had formed, she realised how ridiculous it was. Whether he thought he loved her or not, he'd spent seven years being everything she needed. He hadn't started this.

She'd started this. And look how badly it had fucked everything up. Now her best friend had convinced himself the bond between them was love, which it fucking couldn't be, because only one person in the world loved her, and he was morally obligated and biologically motivated.

"Rahul," she said finally, when she could work words past the fear lodged in her throat. "I'm sorry."

"Don't say that," he gritted out. "You have nothing to be sorry for."

She shook her head, because she wasn't about to argue. "I'm going home." It took him a moment to realise what she meant. Or maybe he only realised when she skirted around him and started climbing the stairs again.

"Jasmine," he called, low and warning. "Stop."

"No. My room's ready. I'll pick my stuff up tomorrow." Or the next day. Or fucking never.

"Then let me walk back with you."

It was painful, but she forced herself to turn around and look at him. It was the only way he'd take her next words seriously. "I need you to leave me alone. As of right now. Please."

If saying it was hard, the look on his face was... Well. She only saw that flash of agony for a split second before he schooled his features into something neutral again. Every syllable painfully clear, he said, "Understood."

She left him there.

When Tilly answered the door, she frowned. "Did you forget something, darling?"

"No," Jasmine said shortly as she pushed her way into the flat.

Yes. I forgot myself.

An hour later, as she sat in the bedroom she barely recognised—the room Rahul had checked so thoroughly—it hit her.

Really hit her. The pain was a physical force, a blow that ripped a gasping sob from her, one that shook her whole body. Another sob followed. And another. Her chest felt dead and empty as scorched earth, her gut churned, and her heart was hopeless. Jasmine screwed her eyes shut and clenched her teeth against the sudden, suffocating fear, but a strangled wail tore her jaw open.

She pressed a hand to her chest as if that would stop her from breaking in two. It didn't.

"Shit," she whispered to the empty room. "Shit. Shit. *Shit.*"

She'd fucked up, hadn't she? She'd really fucked up. And this was the point where she lay down and died in the dirt.

Jasmine curled up on her bed and held her knees to her chest, but the pain wouldn't stop. It was a physical thing, and it had her by the throat, and its name was regret. All she could see was the look of utter devastation on the face of the man she loved, and all she could think was that *she'd* put it there—

Jasmine's thoughts stuttered. Stopped. Shock forced her eyes open, and she felt hot tears slide down her cheeks.

She loved him. She loved him. She loved him.

She was still for a moment, absorbing that fact. Taking it in. She *loved* him. She *could* love him. She *did* love him.

It took a long time for her mind to move past those truths and start thinking sensibly.

Does it matter? Does it matter now, after you hurt him like that? Would he even believe you if you told him?

She had a sudden vision of today's argument in reverse. Of Rahul rejecting her love, spitting on it the way she'd spit on his, denying her, taking a blade and twisting it deep in her guts.

Her stomach churned

Is this how you treat those you love? Is this what your love is worth?

Yes.

But she didn't want it to be. And suddenly, that distinction seemed to matter.

Maybe she was fucked up. Maybe she was cruel. Maybe she was a fucking mess. But she didn't *want* to be. That should count for something.

Not for everything, though.

Jasmine searched for the phone with frantic hands. Dialling felt like a nightmare in itself. Waiting as the phone rang was a torture worthy of the Spanish Inquisition.

But eventually, Asmita answered. "Hello, darling. How are you?"

Jasmine burst into tears.

Chapter 21

Now

I t was over.

He'd known it instantly, seen it as clearly as the horror in Jasmine's eyes when he told her—

Fuck. When he told her the truth.

He hadn't slept all night, remembering the way her lips had trembled before they'd hardened. The way she'd leaned into him before she'd pushed him away.

There'd been people like him in her life, over the years— usually men, occasionally others. People who thought they could change her. People who thought they could chain sunlight or cage a hurricane. He'd watched them fail and thought they were fools. But the truth was, Rahul was worse than they'd ever been.

He skipped the gym the next morning, because for once, staying still seemed like the only chance he had of keeping himself together. Of maintaining whatever scraps of control he had left, holding them tightly to his chest with both hands.

So when the doorbell rang, he was sitting on the sofa where they'd first kissed, trying not to think about the way she looked at him when she forgot to hide her feelings away. It took his tired, sluggish brain a moment to register what the ringing bell signified, but when it did, he leapt to his feet. She was here.

She was not.

Asmita stood in the doorway beside a woman he'd never seen before—but he thought it might be her girlfriend, someone Jasmine had mentioned a few times. He remembered her laughing about it with him one night. *I do believe Asmita has fallen in love. I'd be horrified if the girl wasn't so brilliant.*

"Hey," Asmita said. "This is Pinal."

That was it; that was the girlfriend's name. Pinal. He nodded at the smaller woman and tried to smile. She looked alarmed at whatever expression passed over his face. He stopped.

"You look like crap," Asmita said, pushing her way past him. Pinal hesitated, flicking a wary look in his direction, then followed.

Jesus. How bad could he look after less than a day of wallowing?

"What's going on?" he asked, shutting the door and following Asmita. She'd only been to his flat a few times, with Jasmine, but she steamed down the hallway as if she knew the place like the back of her hand. Then again, it wasn't exactly huge; she probably remembered it just fine.

"We're here to get Jasmine's things."

That stopped him in his tracks.

Of course they were. Of course she wouldn't come here, wouldn't be alone with him, after everything that had happened. And he shouldn't feel like he'd been slapped because of it.

He was starting to realise how fucked up he was over Jasmine. Not just after yesterday. In general.

Asmita paused between the two bedroom doors and turned

to look at him, flicking her hair like it was some kind of weapon. "Which one's her room?"

He took a breath and pointed. "That one."

So she and Pinal went in there, and he went into his own room to gather up her clothes, and the scarf she wore to bed, and the book she'd been reading. When he emerged with the armful, he found Pinal leaning against Jasmine's doorframe with her arms crossed. She looked down at the things he was carrying, then back up at him.

"Hmm," she said.

From inside the bedroom, Asmita called, "What, babe?"

"Nothing," she called back. "One sec." Then she pushed off from the doorframe and said to him, her voice low, "Walk with me."

He walked.

They wandered down the hall and into the living room in silence. He followed her to the wide window that looked down on the city, and they stood for a moment.

"I don't know Jasmine that well," she said. Her voice was kind of raw, kind of rusty. It was a nice voice. "I mean, I've heard a lot about her. And I've met her. And I spoke to her this morning."

His heart leapt. "You did?"

"Yeah. Because she and Mita spent all night at hers while she cried over you, and then I brought the car around for this little trip."

Rahul swallowed. "She... she *cried?*"

Pinal shrugged. "Don't ask me for details; I don't know them. Anyway; I've heard about you, too."

He watched the cars trace the streets below, rapid and shiny like legions of beetles. Tried to get the idea of Jasmine crying out of his head. Tried to stifle the need to find her and fix whatever the problem was, because honestly, he couldn't even *compre-*

hend the problem. Why would she be crying? Because of him? It couldn't be because of him.

He set the thought aside and said, "Yeah?"

"Yeah. I heard you've been in love with Jasmine forever."

Rahul's gaze snapped from the streets to the quiet woman beside him. She gazed out of the window as if she might find a secret message in the skyline. He waited, heart pounding, for her to continue.

"Asmita told me," she said. "She told me you've loved Jas as long as she's known the two of you, and Jasmine doesn't even know it. She told me you're best friends, and she doesn't know how you do it. I told her I know exactly how, because I've done it too."

He swallowed as those words sank in. Hope chose that moment to rise in his chest like a wave. "You have?"

"Yeah."

But she didn't say anything more. His fingers gripped the windowsill as he took a deep, calming breath. He didn't want to sound demanding, but he had to know. "What did you do?"

Pinal shrugged. "I lost her. It was the worst thing that ever happened to me. I'm fine now, though." Her dark gaze flitted towards the door. Towards Asmita. "I'm better than fine. Better than I ever was, back when I loved her."

Disappointment was so cold it burned. Slid along his spine like blue fire. "Oh."

"Yeah. I was a lot younger then. And I didn't realise it at the time, but I know now that I lost her because... I let needing her consume me." She leant against the window slightly, shifting her weight. She never seemed to stand up quite straight, never seemed to remain unsupported. He looked down, but her long, blue skirt grazed the floor.

Rahul considered those words. "You mean you—you wanted her too much?"

"I mean I had nothing left to want with. I didn't give her anything to want. It got to the point where I only existed to pull when she pushed." Pinal shrugged. "You can't love or be loved when you've turned yourself into a tool." She looked at him again, then down at the bundle of Jasmine's things under his arm. "Anyway. I should go and help Mita."

"Right," he said, his voice hoarse, his mind racing.

She held out her arms. "Want to give me that?"

It took him a minute to understand. He looked at the collection of clothes and personal items he was carrying, the things that had slowly littered his room over the past weeks as he'd allowed himself to sink deeper under Jasmine's wave. Then, his heart lodged in his throat, he handed them over. "Yeah. Thanks."

When it was over and they had left, he stood in the room that had been Jasmine's. It was bare now, the fairy-lights she'd strung up over the bed gone, the little decorations she'd placed on every spare surface absent. All was plain and sleek and cool again, blue and chrome and empty.

He went into his own room and found it alive with memories.

So he returned to the room that had been, but was no longer, hers. He sprawled across the bed, and finally fell asleep.

———

It was like a riddle. *How quickly can eternity end? Is inaction as real as action?*

Had he already given everything he had to Jasmine Allen?

For a few days, it felt that way. As if he was drained, more of a ghost than a man. He lay on the bed with his hand on his phone, as if she might call, as if *he* might call—only he couldn't. Because she'd told him to leave her alone.

Pinal's words settled in his mind, too big and heavy for his skull, and he tiptoed around them and stared at the ceiling and let his phone die.

Seeking her out was a habit he broke by seeking out nothing. As long as he didn't get up for more than the bathroom and a bite to eat, he couldn't do anything he'd regret. As long as he didn't leave the flat, he couldn't find himself at her door. He'd discovered an odd sort of determination, somewhere in the empty space she'd left behind; a determination not to go after her. Not to pour any more water onto concrete.

Not because he didn't want to. But first, he had to figure out how to make it matter.

When the knock came at his door, he didn't think for a second that it was Jasmine. So his heart didn't drop when he opened it to find Mitch glowering like a ginger demon.

"Jesus Christ," spat the shorter man, his amber eyes sharp. "What the fuck's happened to you?"

Rahul sighed and stepped back. "Come in."

"You know your mother thinks you're fuckin' dead?"

"No, she doesn't."

"You're right, she doesn't. Because she called Jasmine yesterday to see where the fuck you were, and Jasmine told her you were snowed under with work, right—so she calls *me*, and the first thing she says is, *Mitchell, why is Jasmine lying to me?* And what the fuck was I supposed to say to *that*? Eh?" He'd followed Rahul into the living room as he spoke, and now he slumped down onto the sofa with a glare.

Rahul took the armchair and tried to gather the explosion of emotions firing off in his chest. It wasn't a good sort of explosion. It was the kind that burned and decimated and choked with foul smoke.

"Tell me," Mitch said. "What would *you* say with someone's mam on the phone doing that *bloody* voice they do—"

Rahul looked up. "Well, what did you say?"

"I told her I'd come round and see for myself and report back. Which I wouldn't have had to do if you'd been answering your phone, you shit. Where the fuck have you been? I haven't seen hide nor fucking hair of you for weeks, but at least you'd been *texting*."

Rahul released a heavy breath. "I'm sorry about that. I was... distracted."

He'd been with Jasmine. He'd been drunk on a fantasy and desperate to make it real. Then again, he was starting to think he had been for a while.

Mitch stopped snapping for a minute and stared at Rahul, frowning hard. The deep lines on his forehead cut into the freckles that blanketed his skin. Then he said, "Ay up, she dropped you, then?"

Rahul ground his back teeth. "Who?"

"Our Jas."

It was exhausting to realise that everyone in the world knew he was an absolute fool for Jasmine Allen. He straightened his spine and ran a hand through his hair, suddenly realising that he must look a state—must look as out of control as he felt. And that wouldn't do.

He pulled off his glasses and began cleaning them on the edge of his pyjamas. Mitch became a milk and ginger blur. Rahul cleared his throat and was relieved to hear familiar iron in his voice when he said, "I don't want to talk about Jasmine."

Mitch snorted. "That's a fucking first."

"Mitchell." Rahul put on his glasses and tried to convey exactly how fucked up his head was with a single look. "I do not. Want to talk. About Jasmine." Just saying her bloody name felt like swallowing razor blades.

Apparently, he'd succeeded with the look. Mitch nodded

slowly, his face as somber as it ever got, and said, "Fair enough. Just know that... if you do, at any point, you can call me."

Rahul took a breath. "Okay. I appreciate that."

Their eyes met over the coffee table. Then Mitch slapped his thighs and said, "Alright, you miserable fuck. *Match of the Day?*"

And that was that.

Rahul went to work the next day and did a decent job of pretending he'd never stopped showing up. When his line manager demanded to know why the hell he hadn't called in, he managed a half-decent excuse that she was apparently prepared to swallow. Probably because he was good at his job, and it hadn't happened before. Definitely not because he was at all believable.

Work helped. It always did, so he should have known, but he felt like he was relearning everything. He felt like he'd been dropped into an alien reality, a parallel universe where he was forced to attempt to exist without her.

Which was how he knew Pinal had been right. It shouldn't feel this hard to function.

———

He texted the bartender, eventually. Ben. They talked a bit. Went for a run together, because Ben lived in some idyllic little town that had paths winding through tall, leafy trees. When they met up, Ben asked about Jasmine.

Something about the look on Rahul's face must have told him all he needed to know. Ben changed the subject and didn't bring her up again.

They'd met in the morning, and the newborn sun peeked through the trees that surrounded them. The summer heat was cooling off, a sharp breeze wicking the sweat from Rahul's skin as he ran. By the time they finished, he felt as new and as ancient as the pale sun. He and Ben agreed to run together once a week.

Maybe it was something about that decision that made him ready to face his mother. Or maybe it was just a coincidence. But the next day he went over to the house he'd grown up in, the house he'd been avoiding in the last year. Ever since his father died.

Turned out he was afraid of ghosts.

Mum was alone, which wasn't unusual for a Sunday morning. His youngest sisters would be upstairs in bed, his older sisters at their own homes dealing with their own families. So there was only Mum in the quiet of the kitchen, her sleeves rolled up and her long hair trailing down her back in that familiar, dark ribbon. A dark ribbon streaked with silver now.

He didn't bother announcing himself because she knew each of her children and grandchildren by their footsteps. He just walked into the kitchen and sat down at the vast wooden table at its centre, and watched as she kneaded chapati dough on the counter. She stared out of the kitchen window. Probably watching the birds.

"You finally come to see your mother," she said after a while, her tone even.

He rubbed a tired hand over his face. "I'm sorry."

"Get over here and help me. Lazy boy."

He shrugged off his jacket and rolled up his sleeves, moving to stand at the counter. He towered over her. He took after his father. Her profile was sharp and achingly familiar. She was almost too bright to look at, too warm, and he felt like hissing and backing into the shadows because he knew that if he didn't, she might make everything better.

He was rather attached to his pain.

The sideways look she gave him was as cutting as only a

mother's could be. But she softened it with a slight smile as he scooped up some dough and got to work.

They fell into a silent and familiar rhythm, working together on food that would feed his family later in the week. His heart rate, always too fast and thundering lately, slowed. He almost forgot to feel like he was missing something, like part of him had suddenly disappeared.

"So," she said after a while. "How is Jasmine?"

His throat tightened. Still, he forced out the words, "She's fine."

Mum turned to look at him fully for one, long moment. Then she said grimly, "As I thought."

He knew exactly what she meant by that and wished to God he didn't.

But then, misunderstanding wouldn't have saved him from her next words. "Your father always told me you'd marry that girl."

Rahul kept his eyes on the pale dough before him, on the patches of flour dusting the marbled countertop. It didn't stop his father's face from appearing in his mind's eye. Just what he needed; the memory of one of the people he missed most in the world, while he was trying not to think about the other.

"I agreed with him," Mum said mildly. "Not at first. She was much too flighty, and you are such a grave boy. But eventually, I realised, that is a sort of balance. So I agreed with him, in the end. I usually did."

Rahul managed a grunt.

"You have nothing to say?"

He sighed. "I love her." It was a relief to say the words. To say them aloud without seeing Jas's eyes widen in horror, the way he'd always known they would. One thing about he and Jas; she surprised everyone else constantly, but she rarely surprised him.

"I know that," Mum said. "But there is a difference between the feeling and the action."

"Yeah," he said. "There is."

"You talked to her, then?"

I pushed every dream I ever had onto her in a filthy stairwell and wondered why she ran away.

"Yeah. I talked to her. But right now I'm taking a break from... from needing her." Not from loving her. He'd already tried that. It hadn't gone so well.

"Hmm," Mum said. Then, after a moment: "Perhaps that's wise. And what about everything else?"

"Everything else?"

She stopped working the dough. "The way you've been tearing yourself apart. Worrying about all of us. Working too hard. Trying to be your father."

Every word was like a blow. Rahul swallowed, his jaw tightening. He tried to say something, but his mind was raw and messy, and his words weren't fucking working.

She seemed to understand that, because she turned back to the dough. The steady motion of her hands was soothing, hypnotic. "I love you very much. I know you are a big boy now, but you are my child, and you always will be. The only adult in this family is me. You understand?"

That, at least, dragged a smile out of him. The muscles in his cheeks felt rusty. "I don't know about that, Mum."

She swatted his arm with a flour-dusted hand. "Don't you argue with your mother. Get back to work."

Chapter 22

Now

Jasmine held it together for nearly two weeks. Ten days, to be precise. She was almost proud of herself.

On the ninth day, Dad and Marianne returned from their cruise. On the tenth day, Dad picked her up for dinner, pulling up in front of her flat and barrelling out of the car with his arms wide and his grin wider.

When she saw him, her heart caught in her throat. The edge of her razor-sharp anxiety, of the pain that clung to her like a parasite, faded for a breath. She ran at him like a child and threw her arms around him. Breathed in the fabric softener he'd used since she was a kid. Heard his familiar rumbling laugh. Felt something that might have been happiness. It was rusty and heavy and awkward to bear, but it still warmed her up like a soft blanket in winter.

She took a deep breath and shut her eyes and squeezed him so tight, she was surprised he could breathe.

"Bloody hell, Jazzy," he laughed, pushing her back slightly. "Let me have a look at you."

He always did this. Whenever they spent any time apart,

229

he'd squint down at her as if she'd transformed and say, "*Let me have a look at you.*"

"Hmmm," he muttered, his expression dramatically wary, as if they were in a pantomime. "You look right mature. Sensible, like." He flicked the collar of her starched up shirt.

"I've been at work, Dad," she smiled.

"Work." He wrinkled his nose. "Don't know why you can't be a good girl and eat bonbons all day."

"If I did that, I wouldn't be your daughter, now, would I?" Smiling felt strange. Uncomfortable. Not because she hadn't been doing it—she had. She'd smiled manically at everyone she saw, every day since that night she'd fallen to pieces. She'd sparkled brighter and laughed harder and charmed more people than ever before, but it had been as uncomfortable as scraping at candle wax.

Now she *meant* her smile, and she'd almost forgotten what that felt like. The realisation sobered her.

She felt her happiness fade, and then she wanted to slap herself. Was that the best she could do? Three minutes of contentment without him?

Deliberately, she calmed. There was no point getting angry over things she couldn't control. She only had time for useful emotions now.

"You alright, Jazzy?" Dad's dark eyes were shadowed, concerned as he studied her, and serious this time. A frown creased his brow, turning his rough features into something most people would find terrifying. But she could never be afraid of the father who loved her so dearly.

"I'm not alright," she said slowly. Cautiously, even though she'd thought about these words often, practiced them with Asmita. "I'm safe, and I'm well, but I don't think I'm alright, and I'd like to talk with you about it."

He blinked. Worry cloaked his expression. She could almost

see his urge to take down whatever dragon she was facing, but he reined himself in and said, "Alright, then. Let's get in the car, shall we?"

"Okay."

"You still want to eat?"

She shot him a grin. How much easier it felt, now that he was home. "What do you think?"

———

"So," Dad said, leaning back in his seat. The waiter had been dispatched with annoyingly specific menu choices. Their drinks —beer for Dad, lemonade for Jasmine—were served. The restaurant was quiet, the soft hum of voices rising around them. He tapped his tattooed fingers against the table. "What's going on, my darlin'?"

She took a deep breath. She'd practiced this part too, or rather, thought about it so much and run over it so often that she knew it by heart. "Something happened while you were gone. And it made me realise some things."

He looked at her for a moment, his face unreadable. He could do that, sometimes, turn blank and hard, and it unsettled even her. Finally, he said, "Something bad?"

"Not exactly. It was perfect, at first. Then I made it bad."

He frowned. "You shouldn't blame yourself."

"You don't even know what happened."

"But I know you shouldn't blame yourself!" He sat upright, his expression fierce.

She sighed. "Sometimes I should. When it's my fault, I should. But that's a discussion for another day, I think. Today I want to talk to you about... about Mum."

She'd expected his expression to shutter immediately, to close up again. It always had, ever since that one Sunday. The first Sunday Mum hadn't come, or called, or answered the phone. The first Sunday she'd ceased to exist.

He didn't pull away, though, or shut her out, or change the subject with a sharpness that dragged over her skin. Instead, he sighed, and sank back in his seat and said, "I see."

It had been years since she'd brought this up. She'd learned not to, eventually, though it had taken a while. A while before she'd swallowed down her questions, before she'd stopped sitting at the bottom of the stairs on Sundays, before she'd started crying where he couldn't see, because he'd be sad if he caught her. And she couldn't risk making Dad sad when she didn't even have a mother, now, could she?

She'd started to think of her life as a patchwork quilt. If she sat and traced the stitching, she could pull apart every piece in her mind and see where the hole had begun.

Her fingers felt weak and bloodless when she reached for her lemonade. She was *trying* not to drink alcohol anymore, which was a motherfucker. Trying to stick with water, actually, but that could get pretty fucking boring, and this conversation warranted the extra sugar. She had to get her energy from somewhere, because recently she felt like she had none. Or rather, like she had only the smallest, meanest amount, and she had to ration it out carefully, or she'd power down halfway through the day like a robot.

She sipped the lemonade, feeling better already. Placebo effect, he'd say, and laugh at her with gentle eyes.

Don't think of him.

No, she could think of him. She could. Choking her own thoughts, she had decided, was a bad move.

"Alright, princess," Dad said, sounding more resigned than anything else. "What do you want to know?"

"Know?" Jasmine shook her head. "I know everything I need to know. She left for reasons that she thought were valid

232

and that I will never understand, because I'm supremely biased. She's never coming back, and if she did, I'd tell her to piss off anyway. There's nothing I need to know. I just want to talk."

So that's what they did. The words were slow and stilted, at first, like a smattering of pebbles knocked loose and rolling down a cliff's edge. But they gained weight and momentum, until they were tumbling free, one thought rushing into the next and knocking over the third, Dad's words blurring with hers.

"I thought you didn't want me to talk about it—"

"I didn't. I wanted you to forget it ever happened. I wished you were littler so you wouldn't remember. I thought that was best—"

"But I didn't understand, and I had so many questions and all I could think was that she didn't want me because there was something wrong with me—who doesn't have a mum? That's how I thought about it at the time, you know. And the older I got the more I realised that it was fucking me up, but I didn't know what to do about it—"

"I'm sorry, love. I'm so sorry. I thought you were okay—"

"You think I'm perfect. You taught me I was perfect. It helped me sometimes, but I still had this *thing* inside me, telling me the opposite was true. I was so close to perfect, in the places people could see, but there was something rotten at the core. I felt like goblin fruit. I felt like two people, or three, or five—"

"No-one on earth is just one person, Jazzy."

For the first time ever, they didn't eat much. But when he dropped her off at home later that evening, she felt better than she had in a long time.

The feeling wouldn't last, of course. But recently, she'd had this idea that if she was kind to herself—if she took all the steps she'd been so afraid of taking—maybe she could learn how to hold on to happiness.

And she was determined to try.

Chapter 23

Autumn

"So how do you know Pinal?"

Jasmine took a sip of her lemonade. "Technically, I know Asmita."

"Yeah?" The guy—Tom, his name might be—leant back against the leather seats of the booth. She let her gaze settle on him for a moment before looking away, focusing on the slightly sticky tabletop.

He looked kind of like Rahul.

Not a lot. It was the nose, and the glasses, and he had a nice smile. His eyebrows were very disappointing, though.

Not disappointing. He doesn't exist to please you.

Right. Yes. Autonomous beings abound, and all that.

"I *do* know Pinal," she added. "Just, we only met through Asmita. And I've known Mita forever."

"Oh, I see." He nodded.

It wasn't his fault he reminded her of Rahul. She'd already been thinking about him tonight.

There was rarely a time when she didn't think about him, actually. But it had gotten worse as summer ripened into autumn, because soon it would be the anniversary of his father's death. And she couldn't reach out to him then, not for the first time since... since everything.

But she couldn't leave him alone, either.

So she had to talk to him. Soon. Except she was afraid.

Acknowledging your thoughts and fears is good. Doctor Madison's voice ran through her head, low and soothing. *Once you acknowledge them, you can understand them, and understand yourself.*

This fear wasn't hard to understand. She was terrified of reappearing in his life, after almost two months, and having him slam the door in her face. Not because of who she was, not because of some intrinsic flaw he saw in her. But because of what she'd done.

Would he care that she was trying? Maybe, because he was a sweetheart and he cared about her. But that didn't mean he'd be waiting patiently to offer her everything she'd rejected.

And God, did she want what she'd rejected.

It was hard for an awkward silence to fall in a bar with lively music and chatting patrons, but Jasmine managed to bring one down on she and poor Tom anyway. Still, he gave it his best shot. He leant across the table, a hand clutching his beer, and nodded towards Pinal and Asmita. "They're cute," he said.

They stood at the bar, on the other side of the dance floor where most partygoers laughed and sang along to 'Does Your Mother Know?'. Pinal, the birthday girl, leaned against the polished wood, wearing the shiny, pointed hat Asmita had forced on her. Pinal's arm wrapped around Asmita's waist, and their faces were close, their foreheads and noses touching. Creating a world of shadows between them, a world where all that existed was the two of them.

Jasmine stared, feeling almost voyeuristic. Voyeuristic and so fucking hungry. Starving. Her breaths came heavier, as if the air were too thick.

She tore her gaze away and looked over at Tom. "I'm in love."

He blinked. "You... are?"

"Yes. I want to say that I've been in love for a long time, for years—but I don't think I *can* say that, because love is kind and open and free and all these wonderful things that I... haven't been. And loving is like a superpower, and I don't want to claim a power that I didn't have. But I have it now." She nodded firmly. Found the familiar warmth in her heart, that warmth that was there purely because Rahul existed somewhere on earth, even if it felt like he was existing miles away from her. "Yes. I definitely have it."

Tom's brows were arched in that way brows arched when a lot of information was being processed by their owner. "I... see?" He said. He didn't sound like he saw at all. But then his brows sort of... settled. And he said, "So who do you love?"

"My best friend. I haven't seen him in weeks."

"Why not?"

"He told me he loved me, and I couldn't believe him. And I suppose I was scared that I couldn't love him back. And he deserves to be loved back. A lot."

Tom nodded slowly. "Right. Big bust-up, was there?"

"You know, you'd think there would've been." She took a meditative sip of her lemonade and wished it were gin. "We argued, yes. Once. But the whole thing was more like... when you make the tiniest pin-prick in a balloon, and the air eases out, and sometimes you think you can hear it, but you look at the balloon and it seems okay—so you think it's fine.

"But then, every so often, you look back, and the balloon is a little bit smaller. And by the time you realise it's dying, there's this hissing noise as the last of the air escapes, and then you don't have a balloon anymore. You have a thing that used to be a balloon, and you wonder how it disappeared without a bang."

"Huh." He sat back slightly. "You're pretty good with words."

"I'm having cognitive behavioural therapy," she said, because she was practicing telling people and not feeling ashamed, since it wasn't shameful. "There's a lot of... word-age. I'm learning to express myself."

"Oh. Right." Tom nodded again. He looked slightly shell-shocked. He took a swig of his beer. Jasmine barely even *liked* beer, but she had to shove down the impulse to snatch it from his hand and take a gulp.

"I'm going to go," she said, "because I appreciate me for not sabotaging myself tonight, and I don't want to push it."

He blinked. "Um... alright."

And now he reminded her of Rahul again. Taking life's weirdness like a champ.

As she stood, Tom seemed to jerk back to life. "Hang on," he said, raising his beer. "Just so you know—I reckon if you said all that to him, this guy you're in love with... it might be alright."

She smiled slightly. "Maybe. But I need it to be better than alright. If it was just alright, it would be like the balloon again. And if it wasn't alright..." She grimaced.

He seemed to think about that for a moment. Then he said, "If you say so. But I bet you'd win him over." He downed his beer.

Jasmine stood as if frozen. She stared at him for a beat too long, then forced herself to turn away, because if she didn't, she'd just keep staring. Her gaze focused on the flashing, multi-coloured panels of the dance floor, flicking from white to red to blue, as her mind replayed the words, "*I bet you'd win him over.*"

She'd never turned down a bet in her life.

"It wasn't a bet," she mumbled under her breath, unable to hear herself over the music. "And even if it was, your inability to turn it down is not something to encourage. You need to take responsibility for your desires and decisions. You need to find your own courage."

She repeated various combinations of those words and concepts to herself as she paced beside the dance floor like a deranged Roomba. It wasn't long before she felt a hand on her shoulder. She turned to find Asmita looking at her with clear concern.

"Jas. You okay?"

"Fine, poppet." She made herself smile. Gave a thumbs up for good measure.

Asmita looked gravely alarmed.

Jasmine sighed, her shoulders slumping. "Sorry. I don't want to take your attention from the party—"

"There are, like, fifty people here. They can carry the party for five minutes while I make sure you're not having a meltdown."

Asmita had done that often over these past weeks—kept meltdowns at bay. But not so very often, recently, which Jasmine was secretly proud of.

She patted her friend on the shoulder and said, "You are such a dedicated baby-sitter. I should make you muffins. But I'm not having a meltdown; I'm just..."

What *was* she doing?

Telling herself not to sprint across the city in platform heels in the middle of the night to bang down Rahul's door and tell him she loved him.

Why was she telling herself that, again?

"I'm thinking about Rahul," Jasmine said.

Asmita nodded slowly. "Okay... Are you going to talk to him?"

"Yes."

Asmita's eyes lit up. "That's great, sweetie! That's fantastic!"

"Right now."

"Um... what?"

"You don't mind if I leave early, do you?"

"Of course not. It's not early, anyway. But, Jas, have you... thought this through?"

"Not remotely. But it occurs to me that I am currently filled with the motivation to bite the bullet—to *actually* talk to him—and if I don't, the feeling might pass. And if it does, I might not find it again."

Although, she wasn't so sure that the feeling would pass at all. Tom's casual words had sparked something in her chest that burned brighter with every passing second. Something that felt a lot like possibility, like putting an end to misery one way or another and getting shit done.

She'd always liked getting shit done.

Asmita's slight frown faded. "Well. I suppose that does sound... reasonable."

"Reasonable?"

"Yeah, not reasonable at all. Kind of bonkers, actually. But, you know." She flashed a smile and nudged Jasmine's arm. "I support you."

"Thank you, love." Jasmine enveloped Asmita in a hug, burying her face against the other woman's silky hair.

She took the time to hunt down Pinal, too, and wish her happy birthday again, and give her a hug goodbye, even though nervous anticipation had her bursting at the seams. As soon as the farewells were over with—she saved a smile for Tom—Jasmine was gone.

She stepped out of the bar and onto the wet street, the concrete gleaming under the street lights, the air fresh with rain and slightly smog-tainted. It was cold. Her dress was tiny as ever and her shoes fucking hurt. The bar was in the centre of the city, surrounded by other bars, pubs and clubs, and it was fairly busy for a Thursday night. Rahul's flat was twenty minutes away on foot, her phone didn't have enough battery for an Uber, and she refused to pay green cab fare.

She started walking.

———

Walking had been a good decision and a fucking terrible one. On the one hand, she had plenty of time to think, to polish the apologies she'd spent weeks imagining until they shone like gems.

On the other hand, *time to think* meant time to realise that she was being an arse.

Plus, her feet were torn to shreds. She hadn't been out in a long while, and her high-heel immunity appeared to have faded. She'd probably have blisters in the morning. Great.

By the time Jasmine reached Rahul's door, the last of her determination had evaporated like steam. She slumped beside his doorway, resting her head against the cool, white wall, and wondered what the hell she was doing.

Before... well, before everything, she'd had a habit of showing up at Rahul's in the middle of the night when she was wasted and couldn't get home, or didn't especially want to. He would drag himself out of bed and answer the door if she'd forgotten her key, which she usually did. And he'd put her to bed after pouring water down her throat, and she'd sometimes remember to thank him.

So often, she was hit by all the ways she'd taken him for granted.

But right now she was more focused on the fact that she'd accidentally repeated a negative pattern, coming here in the middle of the night and expecting him to open the door and listen to her shit.

She put a hand flat against the cool wood and realised that she had missed his doorway. She wasn't exactly surprised by that; since they'd parted, she'd found herself missing the way he buttered toast, the little nerd strap he used to keep his glasses on his head when he ran, the ferocious growl he only used when criticising the Chancellor of the Exchequer—

"Jasmine?"

She stiffened. Her eyes closed. The sound of his voice, warm and soft and so fucking perfect, warmed her from the inside out. Her cheeks flushed a little and her stomach tightened nervously, because fuck, she'd *just* decided to leave, and she was stroking his front door like a fucking weirdo, and now, of course, here he was.

Behind her.

Waiting for her to turn around, probably.

She should definitely turn around.

She took a deep breath and faced him. He was exactly as beautiful as he'd always been, but it hit her harder than it ever had. Her eyes devoured him even as she tried, mentally, to preach temperance. *Don't take in too much at once; you'll get dizzy.* Only, she was already dizzy. It felt like she'd been trapped underground for months, and now she was finally seeing the sun.

He stood before her in dark jeans and a pale blue shirt, the kind of blue that she'd always said suited him best. His hair was soft and loose, curling gently over his forehead—and there was that furrow between his brows that made her hyper-aware of her own heartbeat, and that firm set to his mouth that told her he was worried about something.

Oh. Probably worried about the fact that she was staking out his flat after almost two months of silence.

He hadn't called her once. Of course, she'd told him to leave her alone.

So she had no idea if he was respecting her wishes or following his own.

"Hi," she said. She sounded only half as nervous as she felt, which was still really fucking nervous. He didn't say anything in response; just stood and stared.

She began to feel self-conscious, which wasn't exactly a familiar feeling. But she could identify it and call it what it was, even as her hand tugged at the hem of her dress and she fought the urge to touch her hair.

He took a deep breath, his broad shoulders rising and then falling as he exhaled. His frown wasn't letting up. Finally, he said, "Are you drunk?"

"No," she said quickly. "I'm not—I haven't—it was Pinal's birthday and I—" What? Had a trite moment of oversharing with some random at a bar and decided to come here on a whim? There didn't seem an easy way to explain a decision she barely understood herself. But she had to say something.

The truth seemed best. Expressing herself honestly, putting everything on the table; that seemed best.

"I've been wanting to come here for a while," she said, "to see you. But I was afraid. And then tonight I got the courage at an... inappropriate moment, and I suppose knowing I *could* come kind of eclipsed the fact that I shouldn't."

"Why shouldn't you?" he asked softly.

"It was inconsiderate," she said, clearing her throat. "It's late. I wasn't going to knock. I didn't realise you were..." She nodded at him, as if a nod would substitute for words like *out* or *busy* or *not needing me at all, just like I knew you wouldn't.*

"Well," he said, "I'm here now. So if you want, you can come in."

Fuck. She could hear her blood pumping in her ears, like the insistent rush of a waterfall. "Okay," she croaked out. "Thanks."

He gave her a strange sort of look. Then he stepped towards the door, and she forced herself to turn away from him because, all of a sudden, he was so close. She wanted to study every hair on his forearm as he slotted the key into the lock. She wanted to touch him like she always had, casually, as if she deserved it. She wanted that in the way she wanted water when she woke up thirsty in the middle of the night.

Instead, she followed him inside and crouched down to take off her shoes.

"Don't worry," he said, "if you can't."

She looked up at him. "Sober, remember?"

His lips quirked, barely, but the twitch shot through her heart like lightning. "Right. I forgot."

In that moment it sunk in that she was actually here, with him, *finally*. The urge to grin was natural and terrifying all at once. He might not smile back.

She stifled a sigh of relief as she stepped out of the high heels, her sore feet pressing against the cool floor. He must've caught the sound, because he gave her another of those unreadable looks as he led her into the living room.

She paused for a moment as she entered. After everything that had happened—all the things that had twisted, broken, transformed—this space should look different. Should feel different. It didn't. Instead, the familiarity of it all wrapped around her like a blanket. She hobbled over to the sofa, ignoring the pain in her feet, and sat.

He joined her, putting more than a body's space between them, turning to face her. Jasmine resisted the instinct to curl up on the soft leather like she always had. She was just a guest now, and not an important one. She looked down at her knees for a moment, collecting her thoughts.

When she looked up again, she was snared by the dark intensity of his gaze. For a moment, all she could do was stare as memories flooded her. Memories of all the times she'd been foolish. All the times she'd been happy. All the times she hadn't even known she needed him.

Then she turned her head away sharply, snapping the connection. Pulled herself together. Cleared her throat and started with, "I'm sorry."

Chapter 24

Autumn

Rahul felt like he'd walked out of reality and into... what? A dream? Not quite. In his dreams, Jasmine showed up and threw herself in his arms, babbling some soap opera shit about always adoring him. The kind of crap he wouldn't believe for a second if it came out of her mouth—would take as proof that she'd been abducted by aliens, in fact. But in his dreams, he swallowed it like water.

Right now, he was struggling to process the word 'Sorry'.

So he watched her instead, allowing himself to sink into her details. The way her curls vibrated slightly, even when she seemed still; the fine lines beneath her eyes, like creases in silk; the strip of dark, shining skin on her forearm. He wondered if the cut on her ankle had scarred like that. He wondered what it was about her that seemed subtly changed, like returning to a familiar place at a different time of day.

He looked her in the eyes and said, "What are you sorry for?"

"A lot of things." Her gaze was steady. "I don't think I've always treated you that well."

His heart caught in his chest, but it didn't shudder to a stop.

It kept on beating, even if it felt like it was shrinking. He didn't know why she was here, but he did know that fairytales weren't real and fantasies were easily corrupted.

"You've been a great friend to me," she said, her voice quiet. That voice still sent a surge of power through him, as if his instincts had learned over the years—*this is the sound of impossibility made possible.*

That was the thing about Jasmine: she brought magic to life. But she was only human, and humans were too fragile to bear the weight of every dream.

"I didn't always deserve you," she said, "and that's the first thing I wanted to say. But also..."

He watched as she gathered her thoughts. He could almost see her doing it. It would be easier for her, he knew, if she could just say everything that came into her head until the right words tumbled from her lips, no matter how many wrong ones came first. But she seemed like she was trying to be careful.

He didn't want her to be careful.

Then again, what he *really* wanted was to touch her. To close the space between them and drag her close, and tell her not to pull this shit ever again, and kiss her like he owned her, and show her that she owned him.

His desires, frankly, weren't to be trusted.

Rahul held himself carefully still, his muscles tight with the effort it took not to reach for her. He'd turned the lamp on, rather than the main light, but he shouldn't have. Because now everything about the room seemed gentle and intimate, and the bare skin of her shoulders glowed, and he wanted to run his hands over every inch of her, just to know that she was there. But he didn't know if she *was*, exactly. Because if she intended to leave again, she wasn't really there at all.

"I said some things to you," she finally managed. "Things that weren't true. Accusations that I'm sure were upsetting. So I'm sorry for that. I'm sorry for pushing you away. I'm sorry for losing my temper and... and trying to hurt you."

Trying. Jasmine succeeded in everything she did, and she knew it. *Try* was inadequate when it came to describing any of her actions. Everything about her was devastating, and living without her was, too.

But he'd done it, for a while. Maybe he'd do it forever. He knew he could.

He'd rather fucking not, though.

"Jas. Tell me why you came."

Her eyes widened slightly, then skittered away from his. She hesitated.

He took a deep breath. "You're always going to be my friend. But I can't do whatever you want, or be whoever you need, at the drop of a hat. I just can't. It's not your fault that I feel the way I do, and it's not your fault that you couldn't feel it too. But if I'm going to get over this—"

"I don't want you to," she blurted out. "I don't want you to get over this. I don't want you to get over... me."

Rahul stared. She was biting her lip so hard, her lipstick cracked. There was something desperate in her eyes that he recognised, something he felt in his gut, and even though he shouldn't be getting his hopes up—

Fuck it. He moved closer and took her hand. Just her hand. The contact shouldn't flood him with this searing, soaring, flawless heat, shouldn't feel like the path of a shooting star burning through the night sky. But it did.

He squeezed, and when she squeezed back, contentment filled him. Against all reason, it did. God, he'd missed her.

"Tell me why you came," he said again, his voice hoarse.

There was no way of knowing if the touch affected her the way it did him, but it seemed to steady her. To earth the tension crackling through her like electricity. She met his eyes again and said, "I came because I love you."

He let go of her hand. He couldn't help it. It wasn't a conscious decision so much as a sudden release of everything about him, a slackening. All the ability he had was put towards comprehending that statement. *"I came because I love you."* Said so simply, peacefully. If he'd ever dared to imagine Jasmine Allen saying she loved him, the words would've been sharp with regret, or edged in resentment, or too light and teasing for belief.

"I'm sorry," she said abruptly. "I didn't mean to just—come out with that. I was going to tell you about the things I've been doing. Like, I'm not drinking. At first I wanted to cut down, but then I got tremors, and... you know, withdrawal symptoms. So I thought, holy shit, I might be an alcoholic. Or something. So I don't do that anymore." She licked her lips nervously. "And I've been talking to my dad about, you know, things. Well, about my mum. And I, um, I got a therapist. So I'm very responsible or whatever. And I don't feel so... I don't feel so detached from myself all the time and I can say what I mean now and..."

She broke off, shrugging. As if all of that was incidental. Everything about her was so vital, she seemed like her own source of light in the room. Looking at her, and hearing her, and trying to understand exactly what all of this meant, might just fry his brain.

"I came because I love you."

"Oh, Christ," she muttered. "This whole conversation was supposed to be much more elegant. Or at least vaguely coherent. But things don't always have to be perfect, do they?" She looked at him as if she was really asking.

Hers was the most perfect imperfection he had ever known.

"What I'm trying to say is, I realised, the day we... the day I left. I realised straight away that I fucked up. I knew even while it was happening, but I didn't know how to stop it. And the more I thought about feeling helpless in my own head, seeing something I wanted so badly and not being able to take it—" She snorted. "Fuck that shit."

He felt his lips quirk. Then that quirk turned into a full-blown grin, one that made his cheeks ache, but wasn't wide enough to represent the emotions swirling in his chest.

A tentative smile appeared on her face. "You look kind of happy."

Finally, he managed to speak. "Maybe I am."

"Right. Well, I decided to, um... I always used to tell myself that I was dealing with things. Like, I saw all the little problems inside my own head and I patched them up with shitty duct tape and said, *I'm working on that.* But I wasn't. So I decided to actually try. Because when you said—when you told me—" Her stream of speech came to a jagged end, something achingly sad passing over her face.

"When I said I loved you," he murmured.

She looked at him, gratitude in her eyes, along with something else. "Yeah. You said you loved me. And all I wanted was to be the kind of person who could take that. But I wasn't. Only, the more I thought about it, the more I realised that I was close. It was, you know, do-able. To be the kind of person who could... who could accept love. And even more than that, I wanted to be able to say that I love you too. And I suppose, well, mission accomplished!" She laughed nervously. "Anyway. If you could talk or something, that would be great. I think my palms are sweating."

He caught her hand again. "Your palms aren't sweating."

"They aren't? They feel like they are." She used her free arm to lift up the thick weight of her hair. "I feel so hot. Is it hot in here?"

"No. Come here." He pulled her closer, and she shuffled towards him with a look of wary hope. She was wearing her favourite red lipstick and the kind of eye makeup she only bothered with for important events. What had she said? That it was Pinal's birthday?

Even with the makeup, and the barely-there dress, all he could see was the way she used to smile first thing in the morning, her face bare and her gaze vulnerable and her body cocooned in a burrow of blankets, even when it was warm. He released her hand, grabbed her waist, and pulled her into his lap.

Her hands settled on his shoulders, her face close to his. He pulled off his glasses and thrust them in the direction of the side table, but he couldn't stop staring at her.

He liked seeing and not-seeing all at once. He loved it with Jasmine. It reminded him of slow mornings and moonlit nights. It reminded him of making her swim and of running through the rain.

He cupped her face with his hands, then slid them into her hair. Rested his forehead against hers and let himself breathe. Felt her every exhalation. Felt her lashes flutter against his as they both closed their eyes. He drank her in as his pounding heart slowed, as this new reality settled into his bones.

She was here, and she was loving him.

"Jasmine," he whispered.

"Rahul. I love you. I love you. I love you."

His heart swelled, joy turning molten in his chest. "I shouldn't have tried to change you. I don't want you to change."

"I should have trusted you. And I—I haven't changed. I don't think I ever will. But I've grown. I'm growing."

He kissed her. When his lips slanted over hers, something inside him cracked open. It was raw and new and natural, and it felt like a cosmic event. Everywhere he touched her, every point at which their bodies connected, became a site of transformation. He was scorched into something new, as if a layer of him had burned away and he was cleaner now.

He broke the kiss and whispered, "I love you. More than anything, I love you."

She sobbed, and he tried to pull back, tried to look at her, but she dragged him closer. Her hands tangled in his hair. "I don't know why I'm crying," she said. "Ignore me."

"I can't ignore you." He brushed his lips over the tears tracking her cheeks. Tasted salt.

"We probably can't just... go back to how we were," she said. "You probably want to take things slow. If you want to take things anywhere at all."

"Is that what you want? Slow?" He kissed her before she could answer. Her touch held the kind of brilliance that memory couldn't trap. He'd been utterly without this for so long and now, finally, here she was. He felt almost dizzy.

"I don't want slow," she murmured against his lips. "I feel like we've been slow for a thousand years."

"Seven. Seven years."

"Please allow me to be dramatic."

He laughed and kissed her again. And again. And again.

The kisses weren't supposed to turn hot and desperate, but they did, and really, he shouldn't be surprised. It was always like this with her. A touch was all it took for him to combust. When she shifted on his lap so that she was straddling him, Rahul's hands slid to her thighs. Her dress rode up, and he trailed his fingers over her skin, anywhere and everywhere, relearning perfection. The sounds she made, soft little mewls of pleasure against his lips, tightened the need in his gut.

When she pulled away from him and stood, he didn't reach for her. He didn't need to. She held his gaze as she pushed down her dress, and he was torn between alarm that it could come off so easily and gratitude that it wasn't more complicated.

She held out her hand. He took it and stood, his eyes drinking in every inch of her bare skin, every sweeping curve and vulnerable crease and achingly human line of her body. Her underwear, black and plain and tiny, cut a sharp line across her hips and cupped her pussy tight.

He slid his hands over her sides, her shoulders, down the length of her arms, and drank her in.

She smiled. "I like this."

"You like me touching you?" He trailed his fingers down her spine, palmed the swell of her arse.

She gasped lightly and twisted her fingers in his shirt, pulling him closer. "Yes. Anywhere. As long as you touch me, I'm happy."

Rahul hooked a finger under the tight fabric of her underwear. He pulled gently, and she reached down to shove them off. Then she looked up at him, her lips parted, her eyes glazed.

He pressed a gentle kiss to her lips. "I don't want to go slow. But if you think we should, I will."

She took a breath. "What do you want?"

"I want to call you mine." He picked her up, and her legs wrapped around his waist. Not for the first time, he found himself carrying her through the house while he could barely see.

"I'd like that," she whispered, her fingers tracing paths of fire and ice over his scalp. He sighed as the touch spread through him, liquid relaxation loosening his muscles even as his cock became iron-hard.

When they reached his bed and he set her down, she looked around in surprise. "It's different in here."

"I don't sleep here anymore." But the condoms were here. He reached over to the bedside drawer and pulled out the box.

"Why not?"

"I missed you too much."

She swallowed, turning her face towards the pillow. "Can you turn the light off?"

"Why?"

"I keep..." She turned back to face him, rolling her eyes with a rueful smile. "I keep feeling like I'm going to cry. And if I do, it'll be a thousand times less awkward if you can't see."

He sat on the bed and pulled her up into his lap. "Jas. I want to see you. I don't care if you cry." Which was true, and undoubtedly a good thing, because she squeezed her eyes shut and a tear leaked out. He kissed it away.

"I didn't think this would happen," she whispered. "I didn't think this would happen at all. I thought you wouldn't want..."

"It's okay." He wrapped his arms around her and held her to his chest. "It's okay." He pulled back the sheets and murmured, "Go and lie down, alright?"

She gave him a damp sort of smile. "I don't know when I got so dramatic," she said, crawling into the bed. Another thing he'd missed: how confident she was in her own skin, the way she moved when she was naked, as if she'd never been meant to wear clothes. All she did was get into bed, but every movement seemed like poetry.

"You've always been dramatic. But you're not being dramatic right now. You're just feeling things." He stood and stripped off his own clothes. His shirt smelled like Mitch's cigarettes and beer he hadn't drunk. To his unfocused eyes, Jasmine's hair rippled like a dark sea across the white pillow. He undressed faster. Then he slid into bed with her, pressed his naked skin to hers, and pulled the sheets over their heads.

Under the covers the world was hazy, like sunlight through clouds. He kissed her, because every time, it felt like something healed inside of him. She hitched one thigh over his hip, and he ran a hand over her heated skin. "Is this okay?"

She nodded. "This is perfect."

Chapter 25

Autumn

Beneath the sheets, the air felt thick and hot. Jasmine liked the way it dragged through her lungs, because it matched the heavy warmth in her chest, and the molten desire in her belly, and the sparks that trailed in the wake of Rahul's roaming hands.

His eyes creased at the corners as he smiled, and just the sight of him broke her heart and put it back together again. She felt like she was floating. She felt like she'd stumbled into Wonderland, and everything was upside down and back to front, because there was no way that she could be here, with him, just like that.

But she was. He pulled her leg tighter around his hip, and she shivered as the movement parted the folds of her pussy. Then she felt his fingertips graze her inner thighs, and the shiver turned into a slow, winding roll of her hips that she couldn't quite control. "Rahul."

"I love you," he whispered. Every time he said that, it felt like the sweetest opportunity. Like a chance. One she was determined to deserve.

"I love you too." Saying it aloud was a blessing.

His fingers trailed higher, closer to the aching heat of her pussy. She tried to hold her breath and failed; it came in rapid pants, her hips straining towards him. He ignored the unspoken invitation, his eyes holding hers, his touch teasing and barely-there.

"Please," she managed.

"What, love?" His tongue slid over her lips, dipping inside, sending a spark of pleasure through her core.

"Touch me," she whispered. "Please, touch me."

His hand moved higher, his fingers following the crease where her thigh met her mound. "Here?"

Sweet tension swelled within her. She felt so exposed, spread open for him, his hair-roughened chest pressed against her sensitive nipples, and he watched her with a gaze that tore her apart. She jerked her hips, her clit desperate for pressure. He just smiled.

"I want to come," she told him, the words strained and panting.

"I know," he soothed. "You will." His fingertips teased her labia. "You're so hot, Jas. I can feel you burning up."

She clutched his shoulders, her nails digging into him. "Please. Fuck, *please*."

"Be patient, love. Let me play with you." She could feel the insistent press of his cock against her stomach. All she wanted was that, between her thighs where it belonged, fucking her open the way she'd missed so badly.

Instead, he stroked the other side of her pussy, avoiding her slick, inner flesh or the tight, desperate nub of her clit. And every time she jerked her hips and gasped and begged, he smiled. Her stomach was tight, her nipples stiff and tingling and sensitive, her pussy spasming, needing to be filled. Her head felt light, her breathing heavy.

"You're so beautiful, Jasmine." He kissed her cheek. "I love you so much." He kissed her jaw. "I want you so badly." He kissed her mouth. And yet he caressed her slowly, gently, as if he had all the time in the world. Still, she let the words fill her up, let them settle inside her heart and warm her soul. He loved her, and she believed him. He wanted her, and she wasn't afraid.

When his finger finally slid over her slit, she had to choke back a scream. Her spine bowed, tension almost at the breaking point, as the crest of her arousal built impossibly higher. He dipped into her cunt, his finger easing inside her, just a little. She felt herself clench around him, the urge uncontrollable. He kissed her hard, and then just as suddenly he pulled back.

"Is that what you wanted?"

"More," she gasped, her hips moving without permission, beyond her control.

"Not yet, love. Show me what you need." He caught her lower lip between his teeth, bit down, released her. "Fuck yourself on my hand, Jas."

She didn't even hesitate. She needed too much, wanted too badly, felt on the verge of shrugging off her body and floating up to heaven. She worked her hips, pressure building inside her. He gave her another finger, and she moaned as she worked them deeper, as she rode the digits as if they were his cock.

Then his thumb found her clit, circling it slowly. Their gazes caught and held as he massaged the swollen bud, moving steadily despite her jerking hips. She squeezed her eyes shut as the pleasure of it all overwhelmed her. Then he growled, his voice almost unrecognisable, "Look at me."

She opened her eyes and felt like something in her was shattering. "Fuck. God, I love you."

His lips found hers, his control evaporating. She felt it in the frantic press of his lush mouth, the thrust of his tongue—and then his fingers moved inside her, deeper than she'd managed to take them, echoing the rhythm of his kiss. The thumb circling her clit moved faster, and everything inside her tightened unbearably, and then all at once—

He swallowed her cries hungrily, held her close as she shook and writhed against him, as the world tilted and rearranged itself around her. When her orgasm washed gently away and her body turned limp, she felt his lips press against her forehead. Then the warmth of his presence faded for a moment as he moved away, but before she could worry, he was back. She heard the slick, sharp tear of foil, and then he settled over her.

In the white and golden world beneath the sheets, she gazed up at him and ran wondering fingers across his face. The sharp line of his nose, his jaw, his cheekbones. He closed his eyes as she explored, that furrow forming between his brows, exquisite pain and pleasure on his face.

Then he looked down at her, and the love she saw in him stole her breath.

He slid a hand under her head, his fingers twining through her hair, until his palm cupped her skull. His other hand grasped her hip, his body pushing her thighs apart. "Put me inside you, Jasmine."

She reached between them and found the searing heat of his cock, the condom slick and tight over his skin. She stroked him gently, and he groaned, his hips twisting.

"Now," he gritted out. He wasn't smiling anymore, wasn't teasing. She didn't care.

With her other hand she cupped his balls, squeezing slightly. His cock twitched as he moaned. A smile tugging at her lips, she finally guided him to her entrance.

He pushed inside and she gasped as the sweet stretch began, as he spread her wider, opened her up and filled her. The thick intrusion curled her toes, had her arching up against him, begging for more until low moans stole her words.

As he thrust, his grip on her hip tightened, forcing her onto his cock. His hold caged her, surrounded her, cradled her. She grabbed his arse with both hands, her nails digging into the taut muscle.

"More," she gritted out, the electric beginnings of another orgasm curling inside her. "Fuck me. Please, Rahul, please, please—"

"Yes. God, yes." He kissed her hard and gave her exactly what she'd asked for. His thrusts were powerful, almost violent, their bodies smacking together as he pounded into her. He held her tight and fucked her deep, and their mouths never parted, her gasps merging with his low groans.

Jasmine raised her hips, shifting to meet him until every stroke of his cock rubbed at something electric inside her. His hand trailed over her body to grab a greedy handful of her arse—and then he slid his fingers over her tightest hole and pushed gently, not enough to penetrate, but enough to send sparks of dizzying pleasure dancing up her spine.

She ground against him, her movements frantic and clumsy and desperate, bringing perfection ever closer, until it was *there*. She came hard, so fucking hard. For a moment she barely remembered where she was—*who* she was—as pure pleasure overtook her.

Then she felt his thrusts stutter and speed up, heard him rasp out her name on a breath, so soft in comparison to the power of his body over hers. His cock jerked inside her as he collapsed, letting her take his weight. He knew she loved that. Knew she lived for the feeling of him anchoring her after they'd floated so high.

After a few moments of heavy breathing and senselessness, he ran a gentle hand over her hair. "Stay here tonight," he murmured.

For reasons she couldn't quite explain, she felt her cheeks heat. "I don't really have a way of getting home, anyway."

"I'll take you," he said. "I'll drive you, if you want. Stay here."

She took a steadying breath. Then she kissed his cheek. "Okay."

"Good." He held her close and kissed her senseless. She waited for familiar panic to claw at her.

All she felt was happiness.

While Rahul went to deal with the condom, Jasmine lay back against the pillows and threw the covers off. She didn't need them. Even her body temperature was onboard with the whole 'perfect' vibe. She wasn't even worried about the fact that she'd just rubbed her hair all over cotton sheets, probably turning it into a mess.

She had Rahul. *Rahul.* He was... hers? She nodded firmly. *Yes.* Definitely hers. "Definitely."

"Who are you talking to?"

She looked over at the doorway and found him leaning against the wall, arms folded, a smile on his face.

"Oh, you know," she grinned. "Just having a little chat with myself."

"Of course." He came over to the bed, and she watched the way his muscles flexed beneath his skin as he moved. Graceful, powerful. As if he were prowling towards her rather than walking.

When he lay beside her, Jasmine wrapped her arms around him automatically. Not holding on to him felt irresponsible.

He ran a thumb over her lips. "Your makeup put up a good fight, but..."

She could see faded, red stains smeared faintly across his lips, over his jaw. "Whatever." She kissed the tip of his thumb.

His lips twitched. "Mmm. We should talk."

Her heart fell, of course. But she told it very sternly to behave itself and stop expecting the worst. Then she schooled her features into what she hoped was pleasant acceptance and said, "Okay."

His hand cupped her jaw. "I'm not going to ask you to move in with me, or marry me, or carry multiple babies right now."

"But in future," she murmured, "you expect at least a hundred babies, I assume."

"Fifty is the bare minimum," he replied solemnly. "But what I'm trying to say is that... I don't want to overwhelm you. I don't want to steam in with ideas about where we should be, because I've been in this place a lot longer than you have. I want you to take the lead."

Ah. She nodded slowly. "That sounds... good."

"Yeah?"

"Yes. Except I didn't really think this far ahead, because I— well, I wasn't expecting this to happen. I didn't expect you to forgive me."

He frowned slightly. "Jasmine. It's not about forgiveness. I already understood why you reacted the way you did. And I know what you said earlier, but you *have* been good to me. Always. I don't know where I'd be without you." He kissed her softly, and she wondered how he always knew when to do that. Every time she found herself missing the touch of his lips, he was there. "We just... You needed to work through some stuff. I needed to work through some stuff."

She spluttered, her brows flying up. "*You?*"

"Yeah, me." He grinned, and, as always, the sight did terrible things to her. But this smile was slightly, sweetly self-conscious, as well as sexy. He ran a hand through his hair, rising up on one elbow to look at her. "I mean, you *do* realise how weird it is that I was secretly in love with you for almost a decade?"

"Oh, we're rounding up now?"

He huffed out a laugh. "For emphasis, yes."

She smiled up at him, her fingers moving to play with his chest hair. "I don't know. I've been thinking about how we were. When I met you, it felt like... like meeting someone I'd already known my whole life. And I always felt so close to you. Remember when you moved to London?"

He sighed. "Don't remind me. That was a fucking disaster."

She frowned at the look on his face. "I thought you enjoyed that?"

He shook his head. "I did, sometimes. Parts of it. All of it, except the fact that you weren't there, which kind of ruined everything. I only applied because I thought... I thought staying away from you would help. I thought I could fall out of love with you." He shrugged ruefully. "Obviously, that didn't work."

She bit her lip. It was still so surreal to reinterpret everything she'd ever thought about him—about *them*. To realise that every time she'd found herself watching him too closely, needing him too sharply, telling him things she shouldn't and seeking him out whenever her heart ached, he'd been wanting her. If she'd been a different person, she might've realised how he felt a long time ago. It had become apparent, in the past couple of months, that everyone else had.

"I'm glad it didn't work," she said finally. "But I don't like thinking of... of all the ways I must have hurt you."

"Hurt me? Because you didn't want to be with me? No, Jas." He drew her against his chest. "If I thought like that, I'd be an entitled prick. Love doesn't need anything in return." He paused. "But, to be clear, I am very much enjoying getting something in return."

She snorted. "I bet."

"Behave." He pressed a kiss to her head. "We should sleep."

"I'm not tired." Even though she'd been out half the night,

and even though she had work tomorrow, she couldn't just... go to sleep. Energy hummed through her veins. She'd never been so wide awake.

He trailed a hand over the length of her body, his palm following the curve of her hip, her thigh. "I'll have to wear you out then."

She snorted.

Rahul grinned. "You don't think I can?"

"Under normal circumstances, maybe." She tried to keep her voice steady, but it was hard when he kept stroking her. Heat followed his touch. "I haven't had sex in months. I'm impossible to wear out right now."

He laughed, even as he rolled on top of her, pressing her into the mattress. Then, a wicked gleam in his dark eyes, he murmured, "Wanna bet?"

Epilogue

Seven Years Later

Jasmine smoothed back her son's wild hair and slid his unicorn headband into place. Then she picked him up by his squishy little middle and turned him to look in the mirror.

Amit's eyes widened in delight. He patted the glittery horn popping up from his head with both chubby hands. "Oh, shiny, Mama! Look!"

"Yes, my love." She pressed a kiss to his impossibly soft cheek, then set him down on the floor. "Off you go, then."

At her words, he suddenly remembered the fact that he didn't want to be here at all. His cousins were in the playroom building some sort of mammoth Lego tower, and Jasmine had plucked him from their midst to get all that hair out of his eyes.

He bolted out into the hall and she tried not to be anxious about his speed. Rahul was always telling her that no matter how fragile their three-year-old might seem, he was actually quite sturdy, and needed to 'explore the world' or some such rubbish. She listened, because Rahul *did* have countless nieces and nephews, after all.

She followed her son from the bathroom at a much more

sedate pace, watching his chubby legs disappear around a corner at the end of the hall. She almost didn't notice her husband leaning right by the bathroom door—until he reached out and caught her hand as she passed.

"Oh!" She pressed her other hand to her chest, her heart pounding. And not just because he'd surprised her.

Jasmine's husband was despicably gorgeous.

"Afternoon, wife." He pushed her back into the bathroom, lips tilted, eyes warm as melting chocolate. "I see the little mischief is enjoying himself."

"You know he loves visiting his cousins. What are you doing up here?"

"I came to check on my boy, actually, but you beat me to it." He followed her in and shut the door behind them. She heard the click of the lock, and then he gave her that rakish smile and her blood heated.

"Is... is the cricket done, then?" she asked.

"No. But I want you."

Jasmine grinned like a fool. Not on purpose, exactly; more because hearing him say that, even after all this time, started a burst of happiness in her chest that spilled over uncontrollably.

He dragged her towards him and turned, pressing her against the door. His hands caught hers, their fingers twining together as he raised her arms over her head. She swallowed and studied the familiar lines and curves of his face, the sharp brows and the soft lips, the gentle curls of his hair. He always wore it like that now, ever since the day little Amit had patted Rahul's head and said, *"Daddy like me!"*

"Will my sisters miss you for five minutes?" he murmured, his lips gliding over her jaw.

She shivered. "No. Not if it really is five minutes."

"I'll do my best." He caged her wrists with one big hand and brought the other to her hip, squeezing through her skirt. "Let's start with this, shall we?" And then, as he dragged up the fabric, he kissed her.

Rahul kissed Jasmine constantly. She kissed him just as often. For two sensible adults, they spent far too much time connected at the mouth like a pair of teenagers. So it should've felt mundane by this point in their lives.

And yet, every time, it felt like flying.

She arched into him as his tongue glided over hers, as his familiar scent and comforting warmth surrounded her, as her need spiked.

He pulled back slightly, slid off his glasses, rasped, "Jas—"

And then someone banged at the door.

"Quick!" shouted a high, whining voice. "I need a wee! I need a wee!"

She couldn't help herself. She burst out laughing.

While Jasmine tried to get her giggles under control and her skirt back into place, Rahul cursed and put his glasses on. He rubbed at his temples with a tired expression, but a little smile curved his lips.

She tapped his nose. "Maybe next time, huh?"

"Quick!" *Bang, bang, bang.*

Shaking his head, Rahul reached past her to open the door.

Their six-year-old niece, Zahra, stood in the doorway, hopping from foot to foot. When she saw her aunt and uncle staring back, she paused. Frowned. "Why are you both in the bathroom."

Jasmine patted her cheek and smiled. "We were just having a chat, Zahra. A chat about bathrooms."

"An argument."

"No," Rahul said, tugging the end of his niece's braid. "Not an argument. Now, I thought you were desperate?"

"Oh! Yes! Yes yes yes." Zahra barged past them both into

the bathroom, already yanking down her leggings. Rahul rolled his eyes, stepped out, and shut the door behind them.

Jasmine gave him a rueful smile. "Back to cricket for you, I think."

"Ugh. Why can't I have dosa and tea with all of you?"

"Because your sisters don't want to have girl time with their grumpy brother in the room. Go away." She smiled as she moved past him, down the hall. But he caught her wrist.

His eyes held hers as he kissed her palm. "Later, then," he said.

Her breath hitched at the desire in his gaze, raw and sweet all at once. Because she felt it so keenly and so suddenly, she had to say, "I love you."

He smiled, squeezing her hand. She could *see* the happiness in him every time she said those words. "And I love you."

She breathed the words in. Basked in their sunlit glow. Felt them with everything she was, and knew they would always be true.

————

Thank you so much for reading Jas and Rahul's story. If you want more of these two, join my VIP newsletter for their steamy bonus epilogue.

taliahibbert.com/viplist

And if you fancy another obsessed hero pining after his reckless heroine, read on for a sneak peek at *The Fake Boyfriend Fiasco*, which features a tattooed goth, a himbo sports star, a fake relationship, and a steamy Spanish holiday...

The Fake Boyfriend Fiasco

"Aren't you a *vision*," Keynes drawled. "Skulking in the shadows, admiring your handiwork."

Aria narrowed her eyes as the best man wandered off the dance floor toward her. His suit jacket was nowhere to be seen, his bow-tie hung loose around his neck, and his shirt sleeves were rolled up to reveal caramel skin dusted with tawny hair. He was grinning, and gorgeous enough to make a (vain) girl jealous.

"Fuck off," she said.

He came to lean against the cool marble pillar beside her. The party swept on without them. "You first. Got a light?"

"Nope."

"Doesn't matter; I have. Got a cig?" The slang sounded preposterous in his private-schoolboy accent, but she'd gotten used to Keynes over the months since they'd first met. In fact, if this were primary school, he'd be her second-best friend by now.

Still, she glowered at him. "You're interrupting my brooding."

"That's the idea, love. Got a cig, or not?"

"You know I have."

"Yep." He produced a lighter from his pocket—a sickeningly slick little thing, silver and gold. No common-or-garden plastic Bic for Mr. Olusegun-Keynes.

With a sigh, Aria hiked up the gauzy skirt of her sunshine-yellow gown.

Keynes averted his eyes with all the drama of a stage dame. "Behave yourself, madam. You know I'm immune to your wiles."

"More's the pity," she muttered, snatching a cigarette from her garter. "I've only got one. We'll have to share."

"One, because?"

"Because your sister scared me into almost-quitting, and I'm trying to be good."

"Don't listen to her." Keynes lit the cigarette as Aria held it to her lips. "She's all talk. Once she's had a few drinks—"

"Stop enabling. I should quit, and so should you."

He plucked the cigarette from her fingers and took a drag. Then he said, smoke trailing from his full lips like dragon's breath, "I *have* quit, love. But enough about me. What are you doing over here?"

Excellent question. Aria was usually the life and soul of any party—and this wasn't just a party. It was her best friend's luxurious wedding at a fancy Greek hotel. A wedding Aria had organised, with Keynes's dedicated assistance, which made it the greatest celebration of all time because, you know, taste.

But it was all over now, and the prospect of long, uneventful months without a reason to force herself into Jen and Theo's happy life was... unappealing, to say the least. Not that she'd ever admit that. No-one needed to know how pathetic she'd become.

So instead, she offered a secondary truth. "Scouting for boys."

"Me too. But the pickings are slim."

"They are not," Aria snorted. She nodded toward a table of young men at the edge of the terrace, where the marble floor turned into La Christou's glorious patio. They were clearly appreciating the atmosphere, lounging around with casual grace, drinks in hand. Part of Theo's family; cousins, she thought. They shared his razor-sharp bone structure, and some of them were almost as handsome as he was. "They're gorgeous," she said. "Tell me they're not."

Keynes scoffed. "I've known those boys for too many years to take one to bed. I vaguely remember sharing a bath with the eldest."

Right; because Keynes and Theo's families were tight like that. Although it might be more accurate to say that Theo's family offered Keynes and his sister a respite from their nightmarish home life. Tomato, tomato.

"But," Keynes said, "any of them might do well for you, no?"

Once upon a time, she'd have thought the same. But that was before she'd learned the hard way just how dangerous her brand of 'romance' could easily become. "No-one here is doing it for me."

"Rubbish," he said. "You're just thinking about it too hard. You're not even drunk, are you?"

Stone cold sober—all the better to protect herself from her own desires. "Whatever," she replied, rolling her eyes. "You know, since I'm the maid of honour, I *should* be sleeping with the best man."

Keynes grinned, full lips parting to display American-white teeth. Honestly, the man had no right to look the way he did. If they were actors in a teen movie, he'd be the bad guy. He was too beautiful to be anything else. "Oh, love," he said. "If I were so inclined..."

"Blah, blah, blah. Stop trying to charm me. I'm not even

close to your type." Gender aside, Aria knew for a fact that Keynes preferred his partners... clean-cut.

Aria was as far from clean-cut as a country singer's mullet.

"Listen," he said. "You're moping, and we both know it. But look at all this." He swept a hand through the air, indicating the beauty around them—and the figures of Jenny and Theo, intertwined on the dance floor, swaying to every song as if it were a waltz. "Frankly, that slapped-arse expression is bringing down the mood. Want to take a break?"

The tip of Aria's tongue worried the silver ring bisecting her lower lip. "A break?"

"Yeah. Let's wander off. Go on an adventure. It'll be very Enid Blyton."

"Only Greek," she added, pushing off of the wall.

"Only Greek," he agreed, already leading the way.

"You know where you're going?"

"I know that you're following."

Well, she thought. *Fair enough.*

———

Nikolas Christou had a problem.

He wasn't really used to problems—which might be why he was handling this one so poorly. That was the downside to a charmed life, he reflected, as he jogged through his family's flagship hotel: a chronic inability to handle one's own shit.

Eventually, he'd have to learn. Maturity yawned out ahead of him, tapping its metaphorical foot, reminding him that his glory days were officially over. He'd have to grow up, now, wouldn't he?

But Christ, not tonight.

Nik had just retired—prematurely, to some, but not to his bank account—from pro football. The beautiful game had done something to his left knee that was, unfortunately, rather ugly. He'd come home to annoy his mother, harass his little sister, and decide what to do with the rest of his life, since he had no useful skills. He had not expected to bump into Melissa fucking Bright while licking his wounds.

Although, *bump into* seemed too generous a phrase. It was more accurate to say she'd hunted him down like a gazelle.

He could hear her voice now, echoing off the marble walls behind him. "Nik! Where are you? Did you see him, Perrie?" There was a pause, and then she practically shrieked, "NIK!"

His name on her lips had sounded so much better in bed. Strange, really.

He took a sharp right and hurried along the corridor. He certainly wasn't going to *run*—he did have some pride—but he couldn't be fucking bothered with this woman. Honestly, of all the questionable people he'd ever made the mistake of sleeping with, she was the absolute worst. Bloody exhausting, bless her. Though really, a part of him admired her tenacity.

But dealing with that tenacity usually gave him a migraine and made her, after she was done screaming, burst into tears. Nik hated to make a lady cry, even if that lady was a grasping, manipulative dingbat who couldn't take no for an answer. The thought of upsetting a woman made him imagine his tutting mother and scowling sister saying *God, Nik, you're so insensitive! Now look what you've done!*

He took a left, then a right, then another right, until he was tied up in knots. It was horrifying to realise how little he remembered of the hotel he'd grown up visiting; clearly, he'd been living and playing in England for too long. Melissa's voice chased him no matter which way he turned, growing closer and closer until she might as well be on top of him.

By the time he came across the deep, shadowed alcove bracketed by classical statuary, he was practically frantic. And by the time he noticed the two people *standing* in that alcove, staring at him as if he were a headless chicken, he was literally desperate.

He almost fell over in shock when he realised that one of the people was Keynes. Or rather, Olumide Olusegun-Keynes, man of the world, mystery, and excellent practical jokes.

Keynes's lips twitched as he took in Nik's panicked expression. "You alright, mate?"

"No," Nik said. He had never been one to prevaricate. "I am being ruthlessly corralled by a trio of lionesses."

Keynes gave in and allowed himself a full-blown smirk. At any other time, Nik might pause to admire the lips involved in that smirk.

The man as a whole was worthy of admiration, actually; he looked like a model, or maybe a wet dream. But that didn't matter, because Nik was—tragically—putting his days of carefree sluttery behind him.

"That's rough," Keynes said. Then he looked over at his companion, so of course, Nik did too. Which is when his jaw almost, very nearly, dropped.

Because the woman standing in the shadowed alcove was unlike anyone he'd ever seen.

He'd heard of people being called *striking*, and he certainly felt like he'd been struck. Her dress, long and buttercup-yellow, was pretty, but it was the rest of her that affected him most. Everything about her commanded attention, from the contrast between her platinum blonde hair and dark skin, to the tattoos that covered every visible inch of her. A silver ring glinted down the centre of her glossy lower lip, accompanied by little studs on either side of her nose and what looked like a thousand tiny gemstones decorating the curves of her ears.

She watched him with eyes rimmed in pitch-black makeup and glinting with amusement. There was a sardonic tilt to her lush mouth that made him think she was laughing *at* him, rather than with him. Then he heard Melissa's strident tones echoing from somewhere way-too-close, and the woman's slight smile turned into a full-blown, wicked grin.

That grin was giving him ideas. But, worse than that, *something* about her was giving him fucking heart palpitations. He couldn't even describe the feeling that overtook him at the sight of her. It was like... like running onto a pitch and sprinting through icy drizzle, eyes narrowed, feet fast, the earth soft beneath his studs, knowing absolutely nothing could stop him.

Weird.

"In trouble?" she asked. And Jesus Christ, her low, teasing voice alone did more for Nik than porn ever had.

"You could say that," he managed, his eyes flitting from the smirk on her lips to the arch of her brow. She was tall, but the way she stood made her seem taller—or maybe it was the energy that surrounded her, strong enough to suffocate the weak.

Nik wasn't weak. But he wouldn't mind giving up his oxygen for her.

Which was possibly the strangest fucking thought he'd ever had.

"If you're a friend of Keynes's," she said, "then whatever's happening here must be your fault. He only likes disreputable people."

Nik heard, as if through a tunnel, the sound of Keynes snorting out a sarcastic response. He barely registered the words. He didn't register a damned thing except her, bright like sunshine, burning him alive in the most beautiful way. "If you're his friend, too," Nik said, "doesn't that make you disreputable?"

"Of course," she smiled. It was a real smile, so brilliant it set him off balance. Her brows arched as she grinned, one slightly higher than the other, and her eyes tilted up at the corners.

Nik didn't know if he'd just felt the earth shake or if he was actually losing his mind. Phantom or real, *something* jarred his bones and his brain all at once, until everything felt fundamentally... different.

He blinked slowly, readjusting to this slight shift in his world. Something inside him unfurled; it was the urgency that took over on the pitch, its demands a low growl. But for once, it wasn't telling him to win.

Her. Take her.

Wait, what?

The Fake Boyfriend Fiasco is available now wherever books are sold.

Author's Note

The Roommate Risk is probably the most angst-ridden, emotional story I've ever written. When I read my first draft back, that fact gave me pause. I'm not an angsty sort of person, and frankly, I don't know how I ended up writing this book.

I thought about changing the story up, shifting the characters, making things lighter. But in the end, I just didn't want to. Sometimes, people go through stuff. They find love anyway, even if they have to take the long way round. That's life, and it's lovely, in the end.

In this book, Jasmine drinks a lot. I mean, a *lot*. When she decides to stop drinking, she's not yet at the point that would be considered alcoholism, but she is in the 'danger zone'.

If you're worried about your own drinking, you can call Drinkline in the UK on 0800 917 8282. It's a free advice helpline for anyone with alcohol problems, or anyone who's concerned about their alcohol use.

And if you want to stop drinking, you can call Alcoholics Anonymous UK on 0845 769 7555.

Remember: substance misuse isn't always dramatic or traumatising or immediately life-derailing. Don't feel like things have to get bad before you ask for help.

Talia x

About the Author

Talia Hibbert is a *New York Times* bestselling and award-winning author who lives in a bedroom full of books. Supposedly, there is a world beyond that room, but she has yet to drum up enough interest to investigate.

Talia writes sexy, diverse romance because marginalised people deserve joyous representation, and also because she very much enjoys it. Follow her social media to connect, or email her directly at hello@taliahibbert.com.